Praise for Previous Works:

"I liked being transported to a different location, then a different historical time both with authenticity and charm." -GVWM, *Amazon*

"If you like Wilkie Collins' Armadale and The Woman in White, you would love this one." - *Larry H., Amazon*

"A compellingly written novel" -Gail Coombs, *Amazon*

"Memory's Hostage will delight lovers of historical fiction and mystery." -Chad Novacek, *Amazon*

"Tight, well-researched, and well-plotted" - *Shanna, Amazon*

Also by Margaret Pinard:

Memory's Hostage

Dulci's Legacy

Therese,
Hope you'll do
no 'Keening'
in 2016

THE KEENING

Margaret Pinard

Margaret Pinard

Chapter 1

It was bitterly cold before dawn, even on this late May morning. Neil rose from his bed of wool and straw and went out of the blackhouse. As he splashed some water from the trough onto his face, he heard Sheila roust his sister Muirne. She came out soon after, and they stood in the shadow of the croft house and ate their first meal of the day, cakes of dried oatmeal from the day before and a chunk of their mother's cheese. It would last them until noon.

They bundled up in layers of wool and thriftily patched linen, ready to be shed as the morning sun and the heat of work warmed their bodies. Neil, older by a year, led the way up the hill. The high, flat ground above their house looked westward to the Atlantic and the Carnaburg isles. The western horizon showed a dark blue above the slate grey sea.

The deep pit was full of dried kelp stems, arranged carefully so that they would burn cleanly together. Neil could see that Muirne was worried by the way she kept glancing toward the large cover over the hole, imagining rocks that had fallen in or an empty pocket that would slow down the fire. Muirne had done most of the ferrying of the kelp from the cliffs below where it dried up to the rough kiln. There were weeks' worth of work tied up in this pit: the gathering, the laying out to dry, and the transporting of the kelp to the pit to be laid in, layer by layer. And this every time there was a winter storm that threw up more of the weeds from the sea.

It had been a cold winter, but not a meager one, since their family had had the comforts of a salted side of pork, and their walled vegetable garden, as well as the fishing not five minutes' walk from their home. The blackhouse had stood for three generations, its two rooms and thatched roof welcoming many a neighbor and protecting the MacLeans from many an ill wind. And there seemed to be a lot of those in recent years. The high rents they had paid the year before, made possible by the high price paid for the kelp ash, had stood them in good stead with the Laird of Torloisk, and he had allowed them free access to the turf-cutting beds for their winter supply of peat.

Neil was hoping for some of that extra money to go for a tutor from up the island, who could further his education. At sixteen, he was more than finished with the parish school's curriculum, but they hadn't had enough money two years ago to send him out for more. *Maybe this year*, he thought.

He looked over at Muirne as they arrived and bent to remove the cover that protected the kiln. She was done with the village school as well, even earlier than Neil. She was needed to work with the wool, and cook the meals, and tend the garden, and all those other homely tasks. *Well*, he thought, *and that will put her in a good way to being a wife.*

Me, I'm happy to do a bit of everything here on the Laird's land: fish, farm, hunt—even though it's strictly forbidden. But it might be better if I had a bit more education, to see all the mechanical improvements that are happening put to good use.

Just as Muirne had stamped down the last of the kelp, and the first light had shone off the hilltops of the mainland, their stepfather arrived from fishing around the Carnaburgs. He was the one to bring the fire starter and long paddles. They waited for him as he scaled the hill, his limp barely slowing him down.

"How was the fishing, Father?" Neil asked.

"Tol'able good, Neil. I've packed it away already in the smokehouse, so it'll keep this day while we do the burning."

"That's good," replied Neil, as he glanced at his sister who, as he expected, looked relieved not to have to pack the day's catch in salt.

She took the flint from Gillan and braced the steel against the ground. "Ready?" she asked.

"Ready," they replied, and she started striking while they waited with paddles raised. As the sparks floated onto the tufts of gathered dry grass, she tossed one down, half-lit. Small embers glowed in the half-light of dawn, and Neil and Gillan stayed alert, watching for the first curl of fire strong enough to encourage with the paddles.

"There," said Gillan, and one side of the pile was crackling to life. Muirne moved around the circle and struck again until the next section had caught. She did this four more times. The little bits of explosive fires reached out toward one another in communion.

Her arms hung from her shoulders without strength, and she rested as the men dragged the paddles over the kelp stems, prodding and rustling to get the fires higher. Another few minutes and Gillan was sure they had it going, so he sent her back to the house. Next year's rents would depend on this day's work.

* * *

Sheila watched Muirne's return to the house. She stood in the vegetable garden at the back of the house to check on the dairy cow still sheltered on one side of the house. It would soon be put out to pasture to graze, but she liked having the cow close to home, warming the smoky air. She ducked back into the house, letting her eyes adjust back to the darkness. By the time Muirne came in, she was squatting next to the pot on the fire, stirring with one hand and reaching into the sack of potatoes with the other.

"Good morning, *Mathair*," said Muirne softly. Her two younger siblings were still asleep. Her mother didn't look up from the pot but nodded.

"How did it start?"

"It looked well by the time I left."

"Aye, that's good."

"You're cooking their dinner?"

"Yes, love. They'll need more than bread and cheese after six hours," chided Sheila.

A yawn cracked through the quiet moment they shared. Muirne looked over at the corner bed and saw Alisdair turn over and continue sleeping. At six years old, she might allow her stepbrother that, but Sheena was also asleep, and eleven. Past being the baby of the family.

Muirne shook her shoulder, trying to avoid moving Alisdair. "Sheena, you should be up and helping by now. It's burning day and there's more weeding to be done."

A groan escaped before Sheena shook her head awake and nodded. "Aye," she whispered.

Muirne went back to her regular tasks: milking the cow, feeding the cow and hens, cleaning the spare pot, taking in more peats from their stack outside. Sheena soon went out bundled in her own layers, and set to work in the garden rows to clear out the weeds around the potatoes.

Sheila tried to tamp down the worry she always felt on

burning day. So much depended on her son and her husband, up there all day and into the evening, stabbing and stirring the kelp until it was all burnt to ash. Not too hot, not too cold, they had to work poised like miners to keep it going. True, everyone else in the village had the same little drama unfolding. There were those that didn't have enough menfolk to perform the task, so the mother had to be up there too.

Thank the Lord I've no cause for that, Sheila thought. *Bad enough when I was five years without a husband while Alec worked on the canal, and we had the never-ending war with the French.* She shivered, thinking of those long, lean, and lonely years. Three children on practically no income, just what food she could eke out of the garden and what Alec's family or the church members came by with.

Now she had the four, and they all seemed healthy, so there was an end to her worries over that. *Well, Sheena's never been strong*, she amended. *Not after her first years spent practically starving.* She sighed. Gillan would help her with them now. Perhaps this year she would even be able to see one of her children tutored in Tobermory, maybe even attend a university on the mainland. Sheila experienced a little thrill as she thought of it. Here she was in her kitchen, scouring potatoes and stirring soup, but her son Neil might become an educated lad, catch the Laird's eye, and make something of himself. It all depended on the ash—and the buyers, too, of course.

She'd listened to her neighbors who'd done the kelp before, and relayed it to Neil and Gillan that first time, in the winter of '17: make sure to have good quality ash, no stones, make sure to let it cool sufficiently before trenching, be careful loading the heavy bricks of ash onto the cart, and make sure to be on good terms with the man doing the weighing. They'd had several years of it now, and thank the Lord, as their rents had gone up just as fast as they were able to make money from the kelp-ash.

The final phase was the easiest for her husband Gillan. From what her neighbors had told her of the weighing process, it was bargaining like at any county fair. You told them it was a prize cow; they told you it looked like a starving beast. You told them you'd used best sea salt in the curing; they told you the color looked off. That was nothing to be afraid of, no—just country bargaining and shinning at its best. Gillan could bargain anybody out of his hat, she'd always said.

True, it depended on who you were bargaining with. Can't never trust those English. They didn't know the game, or else they refused to play it. The week before her marriage to Alec in 1803, her memory was burned by the treatment she'd received at a lace shop on the mainland, run by an utterly disdainful English-woman, who'd made her feel like dirt before she consented to sell her a dear piece of lace for her dress. Her mother had been right, she should have just used her own skills, but the new machine-made lace was so white, so regular, so perfect-looking.

Ta for that, she reminded herself. Look where those machines have landed England. Riots, Combination Laws, chaos. *Serves 'em right*, thought Sheila, *after all they took from us*. At the thought of what they'd taken from her family, she felt the familiar constriction in her chest at Alec's absence, and tried to breathe deeply to calm herself. Several others from Mull had lost family to the conscription for the Caledonian Canal, and many more had lost men to the wars against Napoleon. Most seemed to have moved on fine.

Old news, Sheila thought. *Not worth the crying.*

Chapter 2

The next day, Sunday, it was the menfolk who stayed abed into the morning, and the little ones who were up and about, tamping down the mud near the door, cleaning the spoons, prodding the kitchen fire. Sheila directed them when they finished a task and didn't know the next one. They'd done well with the burning, and now the dusty blue mass was cooling. The cover was back over the pit in case the clouds threatening rain actually delivered any, but they were on about different business today: going to kirk.

Neil pulled himself out of his dreams of the future to rub his eyes at the smoke coming from the hearth. He noticed Muirne looked tired, and with good reason: she'd had a spell at the paddles while first Gillan, then Neil, had taken a break to eat and sleep. It wasn't merely the physical weight of the stirring that wore her out, but the weight laid on the success of the whole venture. Neil knew she was terrified of parts of the kiln getting too hot or too cold, the kelp drying unevenly and making the whole batch look like a lower quality ash to the buyer-man. The last few years they'd gotten one of the highest prices of the surrounding villages, and she was nervous about letting down her family. He rose to get more peat for the fire.

Yesterday, he'd gone back to the kiln after an hour's rest to hear Gillan say, "That's enough, lass, your brother can come back on now till the end. Go on home." *Scarcity of compliments, scarcity of land, scarcity of everything here was the norm*, thought Neil as he heard his stepfather. He whispered to his sister, "Fairly done, Muirne, we're almost there," as she left, and was rewarded with a lightening of her features, an easing of her shoulders, and a quick glance of gratitude.

Neil saw her flex her still-stiff shoulders and winked at her, making her smile again. They washed up quickly and each donned their best shirts and skirts or trews. Sheila knelt before Alisdair to wipe his face and hands.

By the time the sun had risen fully above the horizon, they had to wake Gillan, who was still exhausted from the full day spent up the hill, after his pre-dawn fishing. He washed and dressed quickly, eyeing the low fire and simmering pot of porridge briefly but not dwelling on it. Sunday was the day for fasting. The stew from last night would have to last them a while yet, for they walked a mile down the coast to hear the Presbyterian minister each Sunday. And the Reverend Lachlan McManus liked his sermons long.

* * *

There was generally no talking on the walk to kirk, but the children often exchanged glances to make each other smile and the walk go by quickly. This morning was very pleasant however, and there was no need to hunch against a stiff wind, or hold the wool blanket close to keep from catching cold. Sheena and Muirne held hands, and Alisdair skipped alongside Neil, as their mother and father led the way. The companionable silence spoke of hope and contentment.

Neil's thoughts turned to his empty stomach. He suspected his mother would try to make their supper extra hearty to account for the extra hard work they'd done. He knew she was offering prayers of thanks as she walked, because her hands were clasped in front of her, gnarled fingers twining under and around the edges of her arisaid.

Maybe she's also asking the Lord to send kindly buyers this year. The Laird had arranged for the buyers to come to the Isle of Mull in the last years of the war, and it had taken the edge off hunger for those who could take advantage; they in turn shared with their neighbors who could not. With several years of burning, as well as the fishing and small croft crops, the MacLeans had a chance of doing better for themselves, if they could just stay ahead of the rent increases. Neil offered up a prayer of his own.

All still in their own thoughts, they arrived at the kirk in Kilninian and saw the Reverend Mr. McManus outside the door, greeting attendants as they entered as usual. As they got closer though, Neil saw that something about him looked different. His expression was restrained, very nearly compassionate, when usually it was stern and disapproving, especially to the younger children.

"Good morning, MacLean, Mrs. MacLean, children. Neil," he said separately, acknowledging his stepping into the yoke of adulthood.

"Good morning, sir. Quite a fine morning it is," Gillan said.

The pinched expression became more severe, and McManus just nodded slightly. To Neil that did not seem like a good omen. Mr. McManus must think it was not a fine morning. They were bound to find out during the sermon that some thieving had taken place or some girl had got with child before marriage. *Ah well*, thought Neil. *God has allowed it and a great many other things*. He knew his stepfather would clout him for such thoughts, and his mother pierce him with an accusatory gaze, but that was his attitude toward the good and bad in the world: *God wrought it all, there must be a reason*.

The family sat down in their habitual pew, taking up the book that Gillan had carried along to read the first verses posted on the wall. The kirk was almost full and they waited only a few minutes before the doors were closed and the precentor raised his arm to signal them to start the verse. The minister walked up the aisle, his head down in thought instead of his usual proud stare forward. *Something must really be wrong*, Neil thought.

However, the service went forward as usual, the sitting, the standing, the repeating, the blessings. The time came for the sermon, and everyone seemed to feel the tension as the Reverend Mr. McManus held off, looking at the cover of his book for several moments.

Finally, he shook himself slightly and regarded the congregation.

"It is very painful, the news I am charged with delivering today, so I will introduce it with a story from the Bible." He told them the story of the tribes of Israel being cast out of the Promised Land by the Egyptians for many years, the trials and tribulations to God's chosen people, endured by them because they had their faith and eventually a leader in the person of Moses. He hammered on the fact that although they had to leave everything behind, God took care of them in their new home, the desert, and welcomed to his bosom those who were not strong enough to survive the years of servitude.

Neil wondered if this was not a reminder to help those returned from the war in worse shape than his stepfather had, with the limp and one shoulder that would not set straight anymore. It sometimes made him grit his teeth and exhale loudly, but he never complained. He did the jobs he could do, and they got by fine. He knew there were local boys younger than he who'd had legs sawn off and hands shot off. He reminded himself to ask his mother about saving some food to distribute to their nearest war-wounded neighbors this week.

Mr. McManus was winding down now, his voice dropping to a defeated-sounding murmur. "So stay together as God's flock, His Chosen People, and keep the faith He gave ye, and ye will have your reward in Heaven."

"Amen," replied the congregation.

"Now," he started, then stopped. Cleared his throat. "I have been charged with delivering the following message from the Laird MacLean." He unrolled a scroll of paper to read aloud:

> "To all crofters who hold lands under me, be advised that from today the Crown will be importing barilla-powder from Spain, as it did cheaply before the wars. This year then, and from this day forward, your kelp-ash will not fetch nearly the price it did formerly, and thus there will be no way to make the rents needed to keep such large families as you all have on the pieces of land that you are on. I am therefore forced to evict a large number of families on the worst land, in hopes that you will find better elsewhere to sustain yourselves. Those families who must leave will receive a notice at their home and must vacate their land by the end of this month to make room for more efficient and profitable uses of the land.
>
> Executed by writ of Sir Hector MacLean, Laird of Torloisk"

There was complete silence among the congregation as the minister finished—all crofters and fishers perched on a precarious edge.

Then, a gasp from one of the women on the right side of the nave, who stretched out her hand to the pew to keep her balance. It was the Widow McKinstry, whom everyone knew had a very poor plot, too close to the ocean's salty breezes and hardly big enough to furnish the grass for her milk cow to graze on. A murmur swept through the crowd, as wives turned to husbands, fathers looked at sons, and they all thought the same thing: *Will it be us?*

The Reverend Lachlan McManus, his unsavory task over with, blessed them all and walked out, as slow and erect as ever. He remained at the door to wish his parishioners well on their walk home. Some wanted to know how serious the Laird was, whether it would be like the evictions in other parts of Scotland, the ones they'd heard horror stories about.

"Nay, nay, I'm sure the Laird knows better than to treat his own people like chattel. It is simply a matter of economy. Some of this flock shall have to be the strong ones to go seek new places for the Glory of God. Would ye turn from such an honor, Matthew Dirnley?" he said.

"No," mumbled the fifteen-year-old Dirnley.

Similar conversations were held as they all filed out, about seventy people in all.

"And what of the Independents? And the Seceders?" Neil heard one old man ask. "If it is a matter of economy, it'll touch them too."

"Aye," replied McManus. "It will." But that was all the answer he gave. Either he knew and did not want to say, or had not been told. Either way, Neil wouldn't hear the answer there. He decided to pay a visit to his friend-of-sorts Willy, whose family were one of the few Seceders and lived over the vale further inland. He would discover if they had heard the same distressing news this day.

When the family returned home, the sun was past its zenith and its June heat warmed their backs, but there was little enough room to spare for thoughts of gratitude for the day's weather. They fell to eating quickly. The stew of kail and cabbage and pork broth was fragrant and warm but stuck in their throats as they meditated on the morning's news.

At length, Gillan said, "At least there is no note left on our doorstep."

Sheila looked up from her bowl, but held her tongue.

"And yet, we may get such a notice at any time, like the minister said. So we had best make plans."

"What sort of plans, Father?" said Alisdair. Even his six-year-old mind grasped the seriousness of the situation, and moderated his tone.

"Well, if we must move quickly, we should decide who could take us in. And I may have to go away to find work that will put a new roof over our heads. Neil, too." Neil tried to keep his gaze steady, but felt as if a trio of walls was closing in on him, leaving only one way out. *No time for a tutor now.*

Sheila now spoke. "If it is at all possible, I would wish that we stay together, if we do get the note." Her voice was quiet but firm, making it sound more like a dictate than a request. They all felt the reason behind this dictate—her previous husband's long absence—but said nothing. She treated the silence as confirmation.

It was a somber meal. When everyone had done, Neil asked if he could walk over the vale to Willy's for a visit.

"Aye," said Gillan. "'Twould be good to see how others are faring, whether—" but he did not finish his thought.

"Can I go, too, Father?" Muirne asked.

Gillan frowned at her, "Do you know anyone in the house?"

"Yes, Ellen from the village school."

"A'right. Ye may go."

It was silent again, as the two eldest put on their outer layers again, and Sheena helped her mother wash the dishes.

* * *

Neil and Muirne set out, and both now welcomed the sun's warmth, after the frigid conversation at the dinner meal. Neil picked the path forward over the blooming bracken beside the little burn that trickled down to the loch.

Neil asked, "Did you have anything to say to Ellen in particular?"

"No, but I like to listen to you and Willy talk. I know you'll hear different things, and I wanted to be out today."

"Mmm," Neil said thoughtfully.

"Don't be telling tales, Neil MacLean. I'm not looking to be married off quite yet, and anyway, they're Seceders. Father wouldn't hear of it."

"Maybe that's true and maybe it's not."

"Don't be silly. Anyway, perhaps I should be asking if *you* have anything to say to Ellen in particular," Muirne said.

"Don't be daft, girl," he said brusquely. "I can have no thoughts of marriage until we find a more secure way to win our bread. Can't go getting extra mouths to feed, now can I?"

Muirne nodded. "Who do you think would take us in, if the Laird does go through with an eviction?"

"Mother's cousins over in Morvern. Or Father's—our father's—in Glen Etive. Don't worry about it too much, Muirne. Family will always be there."

They were quiet a moment, and Neil could see his sister's

forehead, with the one vertical crease of worry that always cropped up.

"But what if it's like the evictions in the North and the East, Neil? The ones that Kitty told us of, back last winter."

Neil remembered, and his hard sense pressed him to take it as accurate, as a possibility for his own family, but he couldn't manage to see the heritor at Torloisk, a minor head of the Clan MacLean, doing what was said to have been done by the Earls and other big landowners over in the eastern highlands: burning of roofs, dragging out old women in the snow, dogs set on crofters, ears deaf to the cries of decency.

Surely that was part of the old troubles—a political or clan battle simmering for a long time until one side got the upper hand and used it. That would not happen here. The Laird knew what his tenants could bear, would be fair. People went to different churches but knew each other to be decent, law-abiding, God-fearing. No, it would not come to that here, surely.

Muirne reminded him of a detail he'd managed to forget. "Kitty said her distant cousins had come knocking in the middle of the night, nothing but the clothes on their back and a few handfuls of bread. What would make a family do that, if not the horrors she described? And only last year. It could well come here this year, Neil." Although it was June and hard to think of being thrown out into the snow, Neil felt a shiver of cold run up his arms.

Muirne shivered too, and Neil put his hand on her back, soothing her as they walked. They dreaded a little what they would hear at the Currans' home.

The last few minutes along the coast, brother and sister watched the clouds move slowly across a brilliant blue sky. As they turned with the inlet of water, the cottages surrounding a small freshwater loch came into view. The Currans' house was the one on the far right. No one was outside, but that was normal on the Sabbath for the Seceders. They would be inside, reading or praying together as a family.

"Let us hope they still accept visitors," Neil said.

"Aye."

They stopped a few paces from the door. Muirne hesitated, then said, "It seems extra quiet, Neil."

"Hallo, the house!" Neil called.

But no one opened. He knocked, called out again.

No one answered. He went around the side of the house, where the line for washing was usually extended to a stake in the yard, but there was no line. Muirne met him in the back, shaking.

"All the cabbages and potatoes have been torn up, Neil. That means they'll not be here for the winter. It means—"

"Hold up, hold on, let's go back and try again."

They went back to the front door and knocked. When there was still no answer, Neil lifted the iron latch, which clicked easily down as he pushed it inward.

It was dark inside, after the bright sun, but they stepped in cautiously. When their eyes adjusted, they stared in shock.

Not a scrap of furniture was left. It had all been taken away. The rocks of the firepit and the cupboard for the bed, attached to the wall, were all that was left as evidence that the small house had been lived in. Everything else, which Neil knew included linens, crockery, their loom, more than a case of books, their larder, which had always been well-stocked, and a framed painting on the wall next to the door—it was all gone.

Muirne looked in shock around her, her eyes going to where those things had stood. She teared up, though whether it was for her friend Ellen, any hopes for Willy, or the proof of their Laird's cruelty, Neil could not tell. His eye caught on the rocks in the center of the room. He advanced and saw that a paper had been pinned down among them.

He eased it out carefully. It had been left to be found by friends. He read it mutely then handed it to his sister. Muirne's eyes ran over the notice, its official appearance communicating far more of fear than Kitty's stories had. It was *here. Now.*

Muirne's hand cupped over her mouth in fear.

"Wait," said Neil, as he took it back from her, looking at the back. "They've written on the back of the notice: 'Gone to Glasgow, South Side, Wisham Close, The MacPhersons.' So at least they had somewhere to go…"

He debated whether they should take the paper with them. Who knew what would happen to the Currans' little village now? Perhaps it would be best if they held their new address for others who might ask. Yes. He put it in his pocket, and opened his arms to his sister. She put her arms round him and they stood, looking down from this precipice of their young lives.

Chapter 3

Six days later was Sheena's birthday, and Sheila tried to make it a merry occasion. Gillan would not be swayed; he stayed aloof and would not be drawn into any desperate effort to be cheerful. It had turned out as the Laird had said in his letter: the blue ash cakes had been cut well and showed very high quality work, but the buyer had barely stayed at the crossroads for an hour that Friday inspecting the carts, weighing the lots, before leaving. Gillan had had to agree to a paltry sum for all their efforts of the winter, and felt very bitter about it.

Gillan sent letters written by Sheila to the neighbors and friends that had left, asking what reception they had had in their new communities. For as it turned out, much of the inner island had already been notified. Friends had not had time to visit them before leaving the island, but left their plans with the minister instead.

After one evening spent visiting a different kirk up-island, Gillan returned late to say that his youngest sister's family had carted everything off to Glasgow. Sheila's brother's family had the bigger news however, as their minister told him they'd gone off to America.

"No!" Sheila scolded. "Surely Kenneth would have told me before leaving the country altogether! Impossible." She was tired, and fearful, and irritable, after spending extra hours the whole week hurriedly planting extra turnip and potato seeds given by departing neighbors: she hoped that they would still be here to harvest them in the winter.

"I tell ye, woman, the minister said that's where they went. Took 'em five days, he said, and they left behind the name of the person who was taking charge of their passage across, as a reference."

Facing this evidence, Sheila's mouth fell open in shock. She and Kenneth had always been very close, and she struggled to imagine leaving so quickly that she wouldn't have had time to bid her own brother goodbye. Not succeeding, she shook her head and turned back to her youngest daughter.

"Now, Sheena, I know you like your pudding, so this year I made two. There's the flapjack, your favorite, and I thought we all might like some cranachan. I got the raspberries from over Tom's field, they're just lovely."

Sheena beamed her pleasure at the extra treat and took her place to serve each person before herself. She did not seem to sense the struggle it was for her parents and older siblings to muster the good cheer to celebrate her day. She and Alisdair plowed through their sweets, oblivious, smiling and giggling.

The rest of the family savored theirs more soberly, enjoying the summery treats. Muirne eyed her mother and stepfather sitting by the door. Sheila was writing in the last light as he dictated, her fist clamped on the pencil in concentration. If they were writing to Aunt Jenny, she would be able to tell them if there were good working conditions for a family at her new Glasgow address.

"Who are you writing to, Mother?"

"Mr. Spigham," said Gillan. This was the name Sheila's brother Kenneth had left with his minister, as they had heard earlier.

A look passed between Muirne and Neil, and their mother glanced over at them, sensing their trepidation. Muirne nervously spoke.

"Father?"

"We are writing. You mun wait."

Muirne turned to Neil, and in a tortured whisper, asked, "What if they turn us out like they did in Sutherland? What if we're burned in our beds? Hadn't we better leave now?"

But Gillan overheard and looked up. "There'll be no talk of what may or may not have gone on elsewhere in the country. There's no telling what other people will do or say was done to them, to avoid—" He was interrupted by Muirne.

"But what if it's true? Kitty Lee heard it from her cousins, who were *there*—"

"I said there'll be no talk of it," said Gillan gruffly. "Now, I will finish this letter in peace, and we will have some sound sense of what to do when we hear how it is in the city, and perhaps even in America. Nae fear, girl." His gaze bored into Muirne, and she coughed a few times to hide the lump in her throat that threatened tears. She slowed her breathing, picked up her spoon. Life would have to wait until Gillan allowed it.

* * *

The next day the family rose early for kirk, setting out together as the sun rose. There was still tension around the matter of leaving, and it seemed the wiser course not to speak of it while Gillan was present. Hence, another silent walk.

They arrived and sat through the service, variously listening to the minister and their own inner thoughts. After their shock of seeing Willy and Ellen's house empty, Neil and Muirne half expected to see their Presbyterian flock cut down as well, but most of the islanders from the coastal crofts were here.

The sermon this week was about fortitude through adversity: not Moses in the desert, but Job and his desperate pleas for help. If this was meant to strengthen the resolve of the parishioners to survive, it did not have the desired effect, as Muirne saw the woman seated in front of her start shaking, unable to control her body's response. It was Nancy, Angus's fair young bride only two months past. Angus, a full head taller even seated beside her, put his arm around her and pulled her in to him, whispering something Muirne could not hear. It sounded like, "Dinna be afraid. We'll stay together."

Afterwards, Mr. McManus stood outside the door as usual, bidding his charges goodbye, speaking a few private words with this one or that one. When the MacLeans came out, he motioned for Gillan to step aside with him.

Neil moved to hear their conversation, while Sheila kept the younger children a foot or two away, not wanting to upset the men by seeming to intrude. Alisdair waited by his mother, a serious expression on his face as he watched his father and the minister conversing. They, and the rest of the congregation filing out, could hear every word.

"MacLean. Ye may have heard that some on the island are leaving on ships for the Americas. Your wife's brother, I believe?"

Gillan nodded curtly. He did not like others knowing his family's business before he did, even their minister.

"Well, I've been told there is more opportunity for the same. I don't know how you feel on the subject, but I've told a few of the families here, the ones that have younger children or those who live on the least land, you know, in case they wanted to consider it." He looked at Gillan, waiting for some sort of acknowledgement or response.

"Thank you, Mr. McManus, for your pains. I am in fact writing to some family relations to see how it fares with them, but I had hoped Glasgow might be a good choice as well. I am not yet ready to move my family, not until I have heard back."

"Aye, that's prudent. Perhaps I will send you the ship dates when I hear them, and any news of the new settlements that comes back to my ears. I think some are fair civilized, successful even, but that's for you to decide."

"Yes, sir. Thank you, that would be a help."

They shook hands and Gillan returned to his family, escorting them down the steps and out of the churchyard as the clergyman returned to his position outside the door to bless the last few families. Gillan looked over at Sheila before they moved toward home, and she understood the brief moment of pleading she saw there in his face. His request for peace for the moment granted, the subject that Mr. McManus had brought up was dropped. They trooped home, in much the same state of agitation and uncertainty as before.

Chapter 4

Tense weeks went by, but the daily chores continued: fish smoked or salted, butter and cheese churned and set, more potatoes sown and barley tended. The situation in the house was not eased by Gillan's continued enforcement of silence on the subject of eviction or moving. It created new habits in the household: silence at meals, whispered conversations in corners, and the beginning of resentful stares.

During summer it was always the custom to be out of doors when possible, so Muirne made sure to engage different girlfriends so that she was out almost every evening after supper, walking by the loch or sitting on the hill overlooking the sea. Neil did the same, and they discussed their gathered intelligence after dark outside their house. Other households were not stopped from talking about the evictions, and they both hungered for news of what was happening elsewhere on Mull, on the mainland, on the other islands.

Neil usually had more information, as boys had a better chance to be part of the adult conversations. But he had not heard much yet about the people who'd left the area around Torloisk. They would have to wait for replies to Gillan's letters. As for what was happening elsewhere in Scotland, Neil listened when the gossip was flying, but relayed no stories. Muirne guessed that he held back, which only made her more afraid of what she didn't know.

Neil kept a watch on his siblings as the days went by. Alisdair continued unaffected, but Sheena started to show strain: she spoke less and glanced around the table more, very cautious. His mother was in no state to notice these things about her children, as she was trying her hardest to shore up any resources they might have, in case all was ripped away from them. This blackhouse had been her family's for three generations, and it was to here she had returned, when Neil's father had disappeared on the Canal.

She would fight for it. She would show the Laird that their little plot of land was more than enough to support her family, and they didn't need the money from the kelp-ash after all. She wouldn't be able to pay the rent on the land with the produce she was planting, but when the store of coins from the ash and the savings for Neil's school were combined, it would be nearly enough.

To make the difference, she would sell some of her new weavings at Tobermory at the summer festival. It would have to be in secret, since Gillan didn't approve of many of the festival-goers, but when she returned with those extra shillings, how happy he would be that they would not have to leave!

That is what Sheila was thinking of when a knock interrupted the stillness of their house. Gillan rose from the table where they were sitting for tea to open it. Framed in their doorway was Alex Eglund, whose son had been at school with Neil. Their family were the only other Seceders on the Treshnish headland, and they kept to themselves in the plain, austere style compliant with the doctrines of that kirk.

"Good day, Eglund. Welcome to the house, will you come in? Have you had news?"

"Good day, MacLean. Aye, I will come in. I've summat to speak to you about."

His eyes flicked around the house, taking in the well-made table and chairs, the neat pile of blankets by the two beds, the stacks of peat turves at the wall. His gaze settled first on Sheila, who looked tired and strained. His eyes then flicked to Muirne, a picture of blooming womanhood, with her curving figure, fine head of golden hair, dimpled cheeks, and unlined forehead.

"Will you have some tea, sir?" said Sheila, already picking up the hot pitcher and a clay mug.

"Obliged, missus," he replied.

They waited for the news while Sheila poured, but Eglund waited for her to finish before he said anything, and then it was only a polite comment about the fine weather they were having.

Muirne, seated by the fire, felt the tension at the table. *Lord, what is the man on about?* she wondered. *It's not as if we're familiar enough to take tea together for no reason.*

Finally there was a direct question, and its abruptness made the room spark with anticipation.

"MacLean, my minister tells me these are hard times. Have you made any plans concerning your family, their safety? Any decisions on your course of action should it come down to it?"

The baldness of the question, from a near stranger, almost made Muirne gasp, but she clenched her ribs, producing a painful hiccup instead. It went unremarked-upon, thankfully. *What will Father say?*

"Have you come to offer advice, or aid? I am waiting to hear from certain friends and relatives who have moved, to see how they fare. Why, have you decided to go on?"

This was very unlikely, as the Eglunds had many branches of family in the area and on the mainland just across; unless all of them decided to go, they would not emigrate.

"No," Eglund said quickly. Muirne thought there was some dismissiveness in his tone. But weren't his family all Seceders, well acquainted with misery and scorn and destitution for decades? He must have some independent income or wealth.

"No," he said again. "But my Robbie is ready to leave home and start his own."

"Congratulations," said Gillan, an annoyed note creeping into his voice. Muirne glanced at Neil across the hearth; he'd heard it, too. *For Eglund to speak of his good fortune right after the question of moving—was he trying to embarrass them?*

"Well, he is *hoping* to start his own home, which is why I've come to talk to you. He'd be here himself, but he's away in Greenock fetching some special tools for the new method of threshing, you know?" When Gillan did not jump in to confirm his knowledge of the new method, Eglund dismissed the idea.

"Any road, Robbie did not want to delay, in case you were already set to leave."

"Ye mean..." Gillan glanced at Muirne. She opened her mouth, understanding now the purpose of the visit. *Surely my father won't make that decision for me without asking me my preference?*

"Yes," Alex said. His self-satisfaction oozed from the single word. "Robbie has an eye out for your Muirne, and wanted that I should speak for her, before you made any hasty decisions. We will be staying, and able to provide for her."

"Well, I thank you for the visit most sincerely, Eglund. Would it be all right if I call on you tomorrow? There are some things we must discuss as a family before making sure of our answer."

"Well, yes, that should be fine," he replied in a voice that expected agreement. "Good day to you then, MacLean, Mrs. MacLean."

* * *

The sound of the door being pulled to, and the feet whispering away in the lush summer grass, were all that was heard for several moments after Alex Eglund left. Finally, Gillan turned and walked back to the table, sat down. All eyes were on him, and he felt it.

Neil and Muirne were both remembering how sure they'd been the week before that Gillan would reject any offer from a Seceder, and wondering if he had changed so much in this turmoil that he would consider it. Muirne prayed quickly that he had not. She thought of Robbie but could barely call to mind a round white face and long lashes, since she had been young when he and Neil had gone around together. She knew they hadn't been close friends, but Neil had been kind, as usual. Perhaps this Robbie was touched in the head, and that was why his father came outside their community to ask them. *Ohhh.* She moaned inwardly as she flew through the last verse of the Tenth Psalm:

> *O Lord, of those that humble are*
> *thou the desire didst hear;*
> *Thou wilt prepare their heart, and thou*
> *to hear wilt bend thine ear;*
> *To judge the fatherless, and those*
> *that are oppressed sore;*
> *That man, that is but sprung of earth,*
> *may them oppress no more.*

At long last, Gillan looked up at his stepdaughter. "Muirne, ye are fifteen, and it may be ye've not had thoughts of marrying yet, but you will nae doubt have offers in the next year—pretty, able thing that ye are." He smiled, but Muirne had no room for levity in her face, as she pressed her fear of the proposal down into her lungs. Her mother made a movement with her hand, as if to support her daughter, but stood still by Gillan and waited for him to speak.

"Do you have any wish to accept Robbie at this time?"

"No, Father. I do not."

"Well, then," he said gustily, "we've nothing to worry about. You don't want him, I don't want him. What about you Neil, anything to be said for this young Robbie?"

The air rushed out of her lungs with Muirne's relief that Gillan's stubbornness and unwillingness to think about the evictions had, for this decision, paid off. He would not abandon the principles of his kirk so easily. And she would not have to march off to the Eglund household now, when her family needed to be together.

"Not much, Father. He was quick enough at school, nothing wrong with his head or his hands. A good worker, for all I know. We went out on the water a couple of times, but he didna have much to say. He's got all those brothers, so you'd think he'd be able to tell stories or a bit o' craic, but he's a silent one."

"Hmph," said Sheila. "He's the oldest, is he, Neil?"

"Aye, a year older than me, and with four younger ones after him, I think."

"I bet I know why he's so silent. Feels for that mother o' his, dying early from all the work. That Alex don't lift a finger. Why, I wouldn't send—"

But Gillan interrupted his wife with a look, and said they

were not to worry, he would talk to the man and tell him their plans meant they could not accept the proposal at this time, honorable as it was.

"I only hope I can choose words that will soften the blow to the man's pride. We don't need to be making any enemies right now."

Muirne came over to him, bent and kissed his cheek. "Thank you, Father," she said quietly.

"You don't suppose you could get the Laird's son to come over and offer for ye, do ye, Muirne? That would solve all our problems, then, wouldn't it dear?" he said, laughter in his eyes as he looked at his wife.

"Tush, don't make it her responsibility, Gillan. We will find out the best course, and we will take it, as a family, when needs must."

It sounded like the final word; Gillan just nodded. Muirne saw her eleven-year-old sister's eyes on her, filled with an innocent longing. With a wave of chagrin, she realized that her own time of youthful dreaming was past, and that now she must look out for a situation for herself. Her stepfather might well laugh about the Laird's son, but she knew the kernel of truth held in the joke: she could be a help and a credit to her family, if only she could marry well.

Chapter 5

Another week of patchy, warm, and wet July weather passed. Sheila was dedicating hours to her loom weaving, making ready for the festival in Tobermory on the first of August. She'd passed the tasks of hoeing and weeding to Sheena, while Muirne did the daily mending and cooking for the house.

Gillan had managed to have the talk with Alex and came back thinking it had come up well, with no bad feeling. He spent his long evenings repairing nets, while his days were spent checking the lines of small oats and barley and the furrows of potatoes on their ten acres. He talked with other men about the Laird's announcement and the effect it had so far had. For, aside from Neil and Muirne's discovery that Willy and Ellen's family had fled, it did not seem to add up to much. Further up the island, yes, some of their family had already cleared out, but then they finally received word from Gillan's sister in Glasgow.

They had moved so quickly because there was a job held for her husband at a cotton mill just south of Glasgow. Unwilling to let such a chance go, they had moved with their two children to the site immediately. She invited them to come visit if Gillan was thinking of moving, but he only replied that he was glad to know they were safe and comfortably set up. No promises.

To Sheila, Gillan seemed more anxious about the reply from her family in the Carolinas. Finally, at the end of a hard week, just before a storm was about to come up the island's west side, a messenger arrived with a letter from across the ocean. The wind whistled outside and the sky darkened as Gillan took the letter and the rider rode away on his horse, seeking shelter further from the shore.

Gillan tossed the envelope on the table and went round to close the shutters and stop up the sill-holes with old rags. It was sounding like a proper setting-up out there.

Sheila glanced at the table and saw Kenneth's hand on the thick envelope. She kept her expression guarded and continued ladling out the leek soup for supper, but she felt a hard bubble press up under her ribs. How fervently she hoped for good news for her brother's family, yet more still she hoped for Gillan to come round to sharing his mind with her. Sheena took the baps out of the fire with tongs and placed them in a basket for everyone on the table. Alisdair fetched the butter in its ceramic crock from the floor and pushed it to the center of the table as well. His eyes caught on the envelope.

"Mama, can I open it?"

"After supper, child, wait till after supper, then we'll all hear it."

Appreciative murmurs went round the table as they tasted the soup.

"It's extra sweet, what did you add, Mama?" Muirne asked.

"Yon teacher of Neil's, his wife that lives by the roadside, on the way to Loch Coruisk, she dropped off a load of early parsnips, said they're good for thickening, and sweet, too.

Turns out she was right. I think she was thanking us for the help last winter."

"Well, it's very good," pronounced Gillan. "Do we not have parsnips planted in the garden?"

"Maybe it's a different variety. Ours aren't ready until September," Sheila replied. "I think she got the seeds at the market in Salen. She knows a good seed-seller up there, fair prices, even with—" but she didn't finish her thought. The meal lapsed into silence again.

After everyone helped themselves to seconds on rolls and soup, Sheena cleared the dishes into the bucket for washing at the well, and everyone's attention turned to the letter.

"I am surprised that there's a reply so quick, since I thought it took four weeks at the least for a ship crossing," Sheila said.

"Aye, but there are those new clipper ships that can make it in twelve days now, Mama," Neil said. "The tea clippers, made for the war, you remember? I learned about them from Master Wilson at school. They might use those for the post as well."

"Well, any road, it's come. Alisdair, you may have the honor. Be careful now," Sheila said.

The little fingers gingerly slid under the flap, lifted it without tearing, since the glue had been cheap. "Well done," said his mother, and Alisdair beamed. He stood at the corner of the table between his mother and father, waiting to hear the news.

Neil read it aloud for the family, slowly and clearly.

Dear Sheila,

I am much grieved that I could not stay to say goodbye to you. You will have learned by now of my leaving with the family, and if you've been dismayed by the silence, I am heartily sorry of it.

We received the notice from the heritor at Duart in early May, and debated what to do. No one else had received such a demand that we knew, but it ordered that we move by the end of the month. Mary and I talked and talked, and finally decided to take up the offer of Mr. Brown, an acquaintance from Fort William, who was arranging voyages to the Americas. It was made on a Monday and we sailed on the Wednesday, so there was hardly time to take our things down to harbor, let alone visit you with the news or send a proper word.

The journey was longer than I expected, four weeks total, which I'm told is normal. All the children survived, although little Nina has been ill since just before we arrived with a sort of chest congestion. We are living in the hills above Wilmington, North Carolina, in a house about the size of our blackhouse back home, but on someone else's land. I have worked out a deal with the owner, a man named Tom Willis, to work under him for five years and earn a bit of land beside his. It will work for now, although there are many ships of immigrants from the north of Scotland already claiming the forest all around us. I cannot think but that we may have to earn the land only to sell it back and try to buy a plot less crowded, probably further inland, or even further West into the Plains. But there, there is the danger of Indians, and so we must see if there are other possibilities.

I write to you at Dalcriadh in the hope that you have not been forced into a similar situation and will receive this letter. If you are thinking of coming to the Carolinas, I would say look elsewhere, since as I say it is crowded and competitive, and not as open as the dealer made it sound. However, we managed to find employment and some hope for a future *holding, so we can't complain.*

All my love to you and the children,
Kenneth

Sheila caught Gillan's eye. She waited. He did not speak.

She said, "There have been no more announcements or notices since the one at kirk. No officers or tacksmen down to see if we're out since the last of June. Is that what makes ye sure that—"

"No, no, I'm not sure of anything, and that's the trouble. Is it better to leave or to stay? To keep together or split up to find work? All we see are the people who completely vanish, so they aren't much help. The ones still here are in the same boat as we are."

Both Neil and Muirne looked restlessly at the floor: they had never heard their stepfather sound so frustrated and they were embarrassed for him. That he should hesitate, unable to decide, unsure what the best course was for his family—it was unmanly. They stayed silent, hoping that Sheila might have a solution.

"Well, Kenneth says no on the Carolinas, but Jenny says yes to Glasgow. There's a chance to take. Perhaps you and Neil should go there for a visit to see if there is good work, in case we do have to leave here."

All eyes turned to Gillan.

"Aye, perhaps. I'll think on't."

Muirne sighed with relief.

* * *

The next morning Gillan came in early from the fishing, annoyed that it had not been a good catch. He threw the half-dozen or so fish in the net on the table, and yelled at someone to take them to the smoke shed. They'd all been shivering, not wanting to get out from under blankets to stoke the fire again, but Sheena jumped out, wriggled into her long coat, and dashed outside with the line of fish, letting in a blast of pre-dawn air.

The sun was angling its rays above the mainland through a blue-grey mist, but had not yet broken the horizon. Sheila got up and patted the blankets down in the corner then went to the cooking fire to stoke it up. Neil rolled himself up from the floor where he slept by the fire and added his blankets to his mother's. Alisdair stayed asleep, and Muirne stayed in bed with him, eyeing all the action.

Gillan sat at table, clutching his hands together, leaning forward, watching Sheila bending over the fire. "Woman!" he finally said. "Sheila, come here to me, I've made a decision."

Sheila came and sat on the bench next to him, but with her back to the table so they looked into each other's faces. "Yes, Gillan? What'll we do?"

"I'll take Neil with me to see the situation in Glasgow with Jenny. We may as well leave today. You must write the letter for me, and it should arrive in enough time before us. I think it'll take us under a week, with the ferry and any luck."

"Today? But I've no extra food packed for ye, and the money—"

"We'll be fine, fine. The ferry's only a few shillings for us both, and that counts the return. Any road, you can always make it back with all that weaving you're doing. It's coming along fine, Sheila."

She opened her mouth and emitted a gasp full of anguish and shock, but covered it quickly, looking down and smoothing the folds of her dress. "So you'll go today," she said, glancing at the cloths near the loom, wrapped in muslin to keep them clean of the ash in the house.

"Aye." He gave her another glance, then turned his attention to Neil. "Neil, you ready for a journey?"

"Yes, Father." Neil finished tucking his shirt into his old trews and grabbed up his plaid. He rolled up and folded under the large square of cloth so it could fit under his elbow easily. He turned to his mother. "Anything you need before I go?"

"Coom here, son." She clutched him in a tight embrace.

Muirne stood up in her shift and wrapper, an old muslin cloth, and her eyes sought Neil's. He came over to embrace her as well, and she whispered, "*Hurry back.*"

Alisdair got his hair ruffled as he was waking, and then they pulled together the food and walking clothes they would need for the first few days at least: gaiters for their feet, Gillan's large plaid to sleep on, the sheepskin for the cold, dewy nights, all the oatcakes stored in the drawer of the baking table, all the cheese from their one cupboard.

Just as they'd rolled it all up into a haversack, Sheena came back in. She looked at the men, dressed to leave, and burst into tears. Her hands were icy and smelt of fish and salt, and she rubbed them against her eyes, making the tearing worse. "You're leaving us?"

Sheila's heart broke at the sight. Sheena could barely remember her father Alec, who'd left for the Canal when she was just starting to talk, and never returned.

"Aye, young miss," Gillan answered. "But we'll be back, nae worry. Neil and I are going to visit your Aunt Jenny in the city, and see whether it's all as good as one could wish there. Don't worry, there, we'll be back in a few weeks."

Her sobs subsided, but her mother had to go fetch a towel to wipe away the salt from her eyes and rub her hands back to warmth. Gillan stepped in, claiming a kiss from his wife, and then the men were gone.

Chapter 6

The two men headed up the hill to the road, then southeast to the ferry. A pleasant grey light had crept over the hills, and it was easy walking that warmed them with the effort. They tramped over dark purple heath and green sedge grass. They hopped over little chasms carved by winter streams. They passed neighbors' houses, members of their kirk, but most were not looking out the small high windows, and did not see them pass. People were breaking their fast and looking inward, not out.

Mid-afternoon, their path brought them to a high point from which they could see north to Skye. Gillan pointed to the black crags, visible from Mull as a shady crooked line with a deep v-notch. "The Cuillins, Neil. It's a different view from here, but they're the same."

Neil looked where he pointed but did not recognize the mountains. Dark shapes with crags at the top were shady and far-off, separated by water and the small isles in between. From Dalcriadh, their home, they could see Ben Mor, the largest mountain on the island. From this side of Mull, he saw Loch Ba for the first time, where their minister lived, and

Sgurr Dearg, the reddish hill marked by dangerous scree. The Cuillins across the water looked wild and foreign.

Starting down the green hills littered with wildflowers, Neil realized he hadn't seen much of his own island. He knew most of the Treshnish, but that was only the northwestern sea-end. He'd seen maps: there were great big mountains and high-up lochs he'd never explored.

He made a promise to himself that when he came back to the island, he would visit the four corners of it, so that it would truly be his.

His hands skimmed the rose bay willow herb as he jogged down after his stepfather, who kept his hands at his sides. Gillan was looking down to where the barge stood waiting. A few passengers were forming a queue, so it was to leave soon. "Hurry up, lad, we may just make it!"

With that, they scampered down, hoping the ship captain would see them and wait a few minutes. It took a quarter of an hour before they were standing at the ticket gate, panting a little, but proud of themselves. The ticket seller asked if they needed the return. They nodded yes. He took the few coins from Gillan, then handed them their tickets. They walked over the gangplank, and as soon as they reached the boat, a man hoisted it up after them.

"You see," Gillan said, "they waited for us to sail. It's a good sign."

Neil nodded, but kept his opinion to himself.

* * *

Another hour, and the barge was nearing the harbor of Oban. Neil and Gillan had stayed out on the deck the whole time, their packs on their back. Gillan had kept their return tickets for safekeeping. All in all, it was looking like an auspicious day.

They munched on a late breakfast of bread and cheese as the barge docked and let down the gangplank. Gillan hung back, and Neil was curious to see why. They watched as other passengers exited the covered portion of the ferry, Gillan with his eyes narrowed at each one. There were only perhaps two dozen others on the small boat with them, and when they had passed, Gillan muttered something, spat, and cocked his head at Neil to disembark.

What was that all about? thought Neil uneasily. *Who was he looking for?*

Whatever it was, he would have to hold his peace, for Gillan stepped through the main town of Oban in no time, and they were on the open road through more green hills again. Gillan whistled a few tunes, but Neil stayed mostly silent through the day. When the sun dipped past the horizon, Neil wondered when they would stop for supper, and where. He'd only seen a few cottages in the last hour of walking, and no smoke, a very strange sight. He wondered if anyone lived in them at all, or whether they had all been evicted as well.

Just as his stomach was beginning to rumble, a cottage came into view off the road, nestled up against a small rise in the land. Smoke wound out of a hole in the roof, and Neil's spirits lifted. Perhaps there would be a chance for some stories and exchange of news with the crofters.

"Could we not stop to ask for some supper here, Father? It is still the highlands." He looked hopefully over at him.

"Aye, I was thinking the same thing. I shall go and knock."

An answer came immediately, as apparently they had been sighted coming up along the road. A little woman opened the door to let them in. She was Mrs. Munro, a widow with four children all grown and left. She stayed here in case any came back, but would perhaps soon be leaving too. And what was their business?

"We are on our way to Glasgow to see my sister. She says they may have good work in a cotton mill there, and my family on Mull may have to be moving on," Gillan said, not sure whether he should broach the subject of evictions with their hostess.

"Oh, evicted, as sure as not, don't you know, everybody is getting theirs sooner or later. It's just terrible. As if the lairds had any better duty than protecting their people, now the King and Prince are gone."

"Mrs. Munro, I do not say we disagree, but who is the Laird in these parts? Has he been any kinder than the tales we hear of the Duke of Sutherland?"

"McDonnell it is, and no kinder than any other. Some out in the isles I heard were putting in improvements to let people stay, but if you're here, and on your way to the city, then I suppose that puts paid to that illusion."

"Aye, perhaps. But I didna see any people leaving on the ferry today from our island, the Lord be thankit."

The three of them toasted to that, and Neil had his answer to Gillan's scrutiny on the boat.

Mrs. Munro poured water from a jug by the door into a pot over the fire and invited them to stay for tea. They accepted gladly. With the foremost worry out and done with, they could pass on to other news and stories. Neil told of his schoolmaster's habit of falling asleep at the end of classes because he was staying up late a-courting. Gillan told of his discovery of the perfect cast to catch the silver trout off Dunawald. And Mrs. Munro told them of the time her husband had walked forty-nine miles, clear over to Inverness, to fetch her the flowers she wanted for her bridal bouquet. She still had the dried wreath in her wooden chest.

Time flew by, and several bannocks and cakes had been consumed before the men stood and said they should really be going, that they had many more miles to cover before sleep. The old widow smiled and blessed them, clasping each of their hands and waving them off before shutting her door. They set off on the road again. Neil glanced back to where the moon shone in the west, over his island. He turned, and walked on.

Chapter 7

Two more mornings passed on their journey before Neil and his stepfather came into view of a lively town. Broughton it was called, north of Dunbeg, and to the west they could see the works thrown up, belching forth smoke into the sky. At first Gillan was for skirting round the main road but thought that perhaps it would do Neil good to see a bit of the world.

He nodded toward it and Neil followed, hardly taking his eyes off the sight of so many houses together, the clouds seeming to gather over them and knit their brows fiercely. Neil did not know what the large mass of motion was off to the right, but it was making noise enough to be heard across the ten miles. Eagerly he kept his eyes trained on any movement in front of them.

When they reached the edges of town, Gillan told him to wrap his plaid around himself and his pack and to keep a close look-out.

"We don't know these folk, after all, and there may be troublemakers. Best be prepared," Gillan said.

Neil hitched his sack higher on his back, threw the plaid about himself, and held on to the tails of it as he walked. At the edges, the city still looked like his island home, with houses a bit closer together and not so shaped by the wind since there was cover from the sea. A few children ran by on errands here and there, only one giving them a curious once-over with his eyes.

As they continued, the gulley beside the road started to smell of rot and other wasting things. Neil glanced over and saw still, brown water, with odd bits of muck stuck underneath. More people were about now, crossing the road, but once again, not taking too much notice of the two traveling men. Gillan took this as a sign that there must have been many men traveling through here, and told Neil so.

"But not from Kilninian," Neil replied with a wry grin.

Gillan responded with a grunt that said *Yet*. This was a pessimistic mood, even for his stepfather. "I wonder if they've come for the works here, whatever they are. Can you tell, Father?"

"Right by the water like that? Probably a woolen mill or maybe mining something from the cliffs."

"Did you ever do any mining before?"

"Pshhh, no, there's none of that out on Mull. We're fishers and farmers, son."

The noises coming from the works on the right got progressively louder, a great hammering and whining and small pops of something falling. It was nearing the noon hour, and they had managed well on others' hospitality so far, stopping at crofts and being greeted with a meal and any news of the goings-on in this part of the country. However, as Neil looked around, none of these houses were of the kind that looked welcoming or hospitable.

Long, low buildings on the right of the road seemed to house workmen only, and some were used for secondary works such as blacksmithing. Taller buildings on the left of the road were connected, presenting an imposing front. The only windows were high up near the roof eaves, the field about was pocked with dig-marks and broken bits of wood, and no entrance could be seen. Neil pointed this out to Gillan.

"Where's the entrance there? Away out back?"

"Must be. But we're nae going in there, now."

More houses, these lower and leaning against each other, showed alleyways and angled dirt roads. Neil wished for the cleansing salty scent of the sea, as the black pall they'd seen from a distance seemed to close about them and stuff his nostrils with a foul, dry odor. He brought his plaid around to cover his nose and mouth, but it did little good.

Here and there they could spy the steeple of a kirk, and when they got to the center of the town, they saw how all the businesses radiated from the square: the tailor, the cobbler, the post office, a grand-looking bank, and several small groceries. Neil sensed that it was Gillan's wish to be rid of the town before stopping for a meal, and he couldn't have agreed more. It somehow got under his skin: this air, these people. As they crossed the square, with its large fountain and fine statue of some royal bust, Neil heard a snatch of conversation between a mother and her son.

"Don't you go being like yer father now, or it's to the slates with ye! I haven't worked sae hard..."

Slates—they must be mining slate! thought Neil. *What a terrible way to grow up: being threatened with your eventual employment.* He hoped the cotton mill near Glasgow would turn out better.

* * *

Three mornings and several slate towns later, they neared Glasgow. Neil did not hold out much hope that he would like the big city, especially if it was simply a bigger version of these mill and quarry towns. However, as they packed up and shook their clothes free of the leaves of Loch Lomond's forest, he was hungry to complete their quest and meet his aunt. He'd only met her once before, when she and her family came to Kilninian from the other side of the island for Gillan and Sheila's wedding.

After several days in the long glens with fine weather, Neil was disappointed when a sudden mist hid his view of the city as they approached. The noise escalated, the traffic of horse and cart and person multiplied, and before he knew it, they were standing on a street pavement, weaving in and out of the way of dozens of others. They had arrived in Glasgow at supper time midweek, when all the workers in the city's businesses—its trade houses and mercantiles, its shops and entertainment venues—were all closing shop and heading home at the hour of five.

Neil looked up. He saw far grander buildings than he'd ever imagined, six stories, bunted balconies, window dressing in stone, and grey, grey, everywhere. He tried to look through the crowds of people as well but saw no other highland travelers like themselves in the middle of the city. *I wonder where all those travelers Mrs. Munro spoke of have found their work then, if not here.*

After they passed through the center of the city, with its fancy buildings and richly dressed denizens, Neil saw once again the low, squalid buildings of the mill towns appear, at the ragged edge of the city. The stink once again asserted itself, and he guessed that everyone must immediately toss the contents of their chamber pots out the window upon returning home.

They kept to the pavement, Neil following Gillan, who seemed to know the general direction for his sister's address.

However, when they reached the first clump of houses south of the city proper, Gillan said, "We'll have to stop someone and ask for a direction, since I'm not familiar with the names Jenny gave."

Neil nodded; as he did so, his eye caught at a still figure in the doorway across the street. It was a man who stood there, shielded from the light rain, watching them. When his gaze met Neil's, Neil felt a shiver down his spine, though outwardly he kept still.

He had long silvery hair, a tad matted, and long sinewy legs, visible between his ragged and weathered kilt and his sturdy leather boots. "Hallo there," he said after a moment. He moved to stretch his back, puffing out his chest in his dirty linen shirt. He looked, thought Neil, as if he'd been out tramping the hills.

"Hallo there," replied Gillan, in a wary but polite tone. He called across, "Can we help you?"

"I think it is I that can help you," said the man with a curl of his lip, adjusting his stance yet again. "Do ye know where ye are going?"

"Aye, just not sure where it is," Gillan attempted to respond with humor. "Hurley Crescent, that mean anything to ye?"

"Hurley… I think that's a ways further south. Take that road behind ye, and ask at the next crossing, they should give you better from there."

"Thank you, sir, much obliged," said Gillan, inclining his head.

"Thank you, sir," Neil added before turning and hurrying after his stepfather, trying to shake off the chill that seemed to have wrapped a hand around his lower spine.

They asked directions a few more times, choosing more conventional passersby to approach, and soon found Hurley

Crescent. Jenny threw open the door to bid them come in and warm themselves by her fire. After several rounds of "My, how you've grown" and "What a fine man you are," names were exchanged all around, and Neil helped himself to some of the scones cooling beside the griddle.

Inside by the fireplace, a new-fashioned one at the side of the house instead of in the middle, Neil finally shook off the chill from the eerie encounter with the old highlander in the doorway. He pulled off his boots, feeling as weary as a grown man with responsibilities. He was very content to leave that weight with his stepfather for the moment. He listened as Jenny and Gillan exchanged old and new news, then accepted with gratitude the bowl of rich meaty broth as Jenny told them of her husband's experience with Garrigan's cotton mill.

Chapter 8

"Aye, clear hours posted, and Charlie doesn't work beyond them," Jenny was saying. "He's settled in good and proper in the last coupla weeks, and though there is no union—it's against the law of course—there is the Christian Men's Association in Bockham town, just one over from the mill, and they sort of take charge of when the men have any issues with the bosses. It's been very courteous and civilized so far."

"Well, and glad to hear it, for Charlie's sake, and for the family's. How did he hear of it, anyway? Was there someone recruiting up in the islands, so?"

"No, no, that wasn't the way of it. His cousin that lives in Glasgow knows the foreman, and they were looking for a machinist, so this cousin thinks of Charlie, his being so handy with repairing the pumps and building that oven there, and other such things." Jenny motioned to the oven, which had made the journey with them.

It sat lumpily in the center of the wall, with a drawer for coals and a door for the food, and the surface on top to be heated as well. Neil, who hadn't seen such a one before, was curious about it. The scones he nibbled had been done on the griddle above the fire, or so he thought, but perhaps the heating surface would do just as well.

"And the schools for the children, are they like at home? Paid through the church rates, and all?"

"Aye, same as home, and there are better parish schools around, so it may be they'll get a better chance," she said with a little note of wistfulness, as she glanced at her youngest, standing in the crib, watching them. Neil remembered their youngest was named Katie; at one and a half she was very quiet. He imagined her four older siblings did plenty to keep her occupied.

"And the minister at the kirk, he's a tolerable religious man?"

"Oh, well, he could do with a bit of cheer. The two times we've seen him, it was after a funeral, and he could barely talk to us. I don't know if that means he's very close to his parishioners or just a melancholy sort. I did not want to ask him, and the only gossip going round about him is why he's not married, young and handsome as one might call him."

"Hmph," said Gillan. "I'll not be worrying about that particular piece then," he said to tease his sister. "It would be nice to be closer to you, so, as I would not even recognize these children, so fast as they grow, and how little I've gotten to see 'em."

"Aye, well, they'd like well enough to have another uncle and cousins about. Charlie's brother and his wife are over in Preston, and met us when we arrived, but they've only the one child. I don't doubt that she's had some birthing problems; they've not been able to have any more," she finished in a low voice.

"It makes them a bit stern with the children. Their own Martin will be going to the university this year, just as soon as harvest is over. He's been accepted on scholarship, and they're quite pleased about it."

"With only the one, I'm sure young Martin has been pounded on well enough with his sums and Latin," Gillan said. Jenny nodded.

"There is a fair bit of family down here, you know. I'm not sure about your Sheila's folk, but Uncle Darren's two daughters are settled west of the city, and Pa's cousin Davey, his lot as well came to call last Sunday, although they do live a ways down. Seems we're all getting pulled into the lowlands," she said with a sigh.

The conversation petered off, as the two siblings reflected more on the past and their present difficulties, the door opening and closing with the arrival of each child, and finally ushering in Charlie. Jenny had dinner on the table the minute after he sat down. Neil and Gillan were peppered with questions. Further reminiscences were kept hidden for another occasion.

* * *

In Dalcriadh, Sheila and Muirne were sitting together at the table, hoping first that word had reached Jenny and then that Neil and Gillan had reached her as well. There'd been no word back yet, but they knew not to expect any for a few more days. However, in the week since the men had been gone, there had been another announcement at kirk, and the date of removal had been changed. The Laird of Torloisk had allowed that people could stay until they got their harvests in, but then those that had received notice must quit the land as soon as the crops were in. Inspections would begin in September.

This gave the remaining MacLeans in their blackhouse a little comfort, since they had still received no notice. Ever wary of trusting the gentry, Sheila was still resolved to go to the fair in Tobermory and see what she could get for her loom work. She'd shared her plan with Muirne, and they agreed she should go.

The day after next was the first of August, and with the men gone, Sheila had asked that their neighbor John, a fellow fisherman with Gillan, would share supper with her family in her absence. It was also to check that her children were safe, since the times now seemed so uncertain and chaotic. He'd agreed, and the next day, her worry assuaged but her conscience still needling her, she started her journey skirting the hills and lochs to reach Tobermory.

That night, she stayed with cousins on the east coast of Mull. They admired the high stack of woolens in her large creel, assuring her they'd fetch a fair price at the festival market.

"Everywhere, there's always someone willing to spend money on beautiful things, Sheila, don't you worry," one of them said.

But she did worry. About her children, managing three days without her. About her son and husband, gone off to seek employment in some industrial concern or other. About her family, and whether they would yet be torn from the land of her ancestors, and the dear small house where her mother and grandfather had been born. About her brother in the Carolinas, who seemed to be coping with the changes, but only just. She listened to the good-natured chatter around her, and after it died down, she turned her head to the wall on her pallet and prayed for all those she loved.

Chapter 9

Gillan and Neil went up with Charlie to the mill, stopping only to post a message home about their safe arrival. Charlie thought there would certainly be places for two able-bodied men, and his quick stop in the office of the foreman confirmed it. The boss came out to look them over, and seeing no immediate evidence of drunkenness or sullenness, gave the nod to Charlie to show them around.

Charlie demonstrated his job, at the end of a line of shuttling machine parts, where he checked the speed and lubrication for the moving arms of the looms. Neil's impression was of overwhelming noise, metal arms of perpetual motion, and shadowy figures darting amongst the clouds of white fuzz floating through the air.

Skylights high above the floor let in natural light, but it was badly obscured by the clouds of fluff floating about. To Neil, it sounded like the clanging of Hell's minions he'd always heard about from the Reverend Lachlan McManus.

"Yes, sirs, they tell me this is low speed, that the mill hasn't fully recovered from the war years, but that in the next months, now that duties are being repealed, we'll have a chance to get back to full capacity, and even expand," Charlie shouted over the din, grinning. "I expect that's why you're asked on so easy."

"That is good news," Gillan shouted back.

Charlie took them outside where they saw the factory yard with its wagons. Some were full of raw cotton to be unloaded, some were taking on the finished bales to cart away. Beyond the wagons was the river, tinged an unnatural greenish-blue. Gillan asked about it.

"That's from the bleaching. The cotton's got a lot of debris in it when it comes in, so the bits we can't remove in the tumbling get broken down and bleached so that they form part of the material anyway."

Neil felt sorry for the river. He looked past the place where the waste water splashed in. Several fish floated there, pinned to the side by the currents, their bellies to the sky. His nose started to run.

"Well, and what'll ye do?" Charlie asked. "Start now and send for your family, or head back and help them to move?"

"Haven't decided yet," said Gillan. "But I reckon we should do some more poking about the neighborhood, see where we might find a house and all that, to make sure we can afford it. What did you say the starting wage was here?"

"Nine shilling a day for a nine-hour day, and that's six days a week. The boss had it going on Sundays, twenty year ago before the war, but hasn't had it since then. Although, if it picks up like he says..." Charlie trailed off suggestively.

"All right, I see the way of it. Sounds very good for you, Charlie, I'm glad. Now Neil and I will be off and check around some today, if that's all right."

"Course, o'course," Charlie said. "Now I'm off to work, so ye'll find yer own way back," He grinned and waved them off as he headed back inside.

Neil's ears had still not stopped ringing from the time inside the mill, and Gillan had to repeat his question before Neil was able to answer.

"I said, what do you think, Neil?"

"Oh, it's quite loud in there," he said, shaking a finger in his ear.

"That's true," said Gillan, looking at him speculatively. "Let's walk."

They walked back home to Jenny, only asking directions twice when they turned down the wrong alley. Other than that, Gillan seemed quiet, considering something. Before they went in the door to Jenny's wee house, Gillan turned to face Neil.

"Neil, I'm thinking we should not take this step until we have to. There's the harvest to take in, the chance we'll make our rent another year, and it looks as though this place will have enough room to take in newcomers for quite a while yet. I say we shouldn't leave until we must. What do you think?"

Neil shifted his feet, stunned at being asked this question by his stepfather. "I think—" He paused, started again. "I think that while we have a chance to stay with our home, we should. It's what we're used to, and we have friends there. Perhaps Aunt Jenny did not like her home as much, and so could leave more easily, but we all like our place at Dalcriadh. Could the price of the kelp-ash change back again, do you think, Father?"

"Ach, no, put no more faith in that, boy. The politicians in London got the Laird into that fix, and then dropped him. Now the Laird's dropping us. Maybe. We shall wait and see." He smiled at Neil, another surprise, as Gillan was not generally of a sunny disposition.

"Right," replied Neil. They would stay another night to see more of the neighborhood so that they'd be familiar if they had to come back, but both men put their hopes in not having to do that. It was not the life for them.

* * *

The market day had been exhausting for Sheila, but she had made more money than she'd hoped. Enough for the rents, but not enough to replenish the fund for Neil's schooling. She hurried home with her earnings, taking the back roads and silent paths, even though she'd well hidden the money in the folds of the only blanket not to be sold, and no clinking could be heard as she walked.

As soon as she came into view of the house, Sheena ran out to meet her with the news that they had received the notice from Neil about their safe arrival. It did not say much else, only that they'd had no ill luck on their journey south, and were fair happy to see Jenny and would send word of any decisions just as soon as they could.

The letter had come in the post the day of the market, so Sheila considered it a doubly lucky day. She asked Muirne about how they'd gotten on with John, and Muirne blushed a bit in recollection. "We had a very pleasant supper with him, Mama."

Faced with this tight-lipped response, Sheila turned to Sheena. "And what did ye talk about then, ma wee hen?"

"We talked about the village festival, and the baking contest, and who might win. And Muirne made a pan of flapjack for us." Sheena turned to smile at Muirne at that, but then turned back to Sheila.

"We also talked of ways to get money for the rents. John was set on poaching from the loch back up by the pit, where he says there's fine trout to be had. He said he could sell it at the market where no one would ask a word."

"Oh? Well, that's sure to land him in trouble. Nothing else

then?"

"Oh, and John did happen to mention that some 'lucky young buck' would be asking for Muirne's hand soon."

Muirne glared at her younger sister and turned a few shades more scarlet. Little Alisdair looked up in confusion.

"Is Muirne going to move? Or are we?" he asked.

"Nobody is moving right now," Muirne said firmly.

Sheila allowed herself a small smile at her daughter's embarrassment. She must think of a proper match for the girl then, if people were starting to talk.

* * *

As the family was sitting down to enjoy Muirne's whelk stew, there was another knock on the door. Sheila left the children sitting in front of their steaming bowls as she went to open the door slightly. "Who is it?" she asked of the hazy figure in the late dusk.

"Lachlan McManus, ma'am. I'm sorry to disturb you at the dinner hour…"

Alisdair grinned at his use of the word dinner. Sheena shushed him with a look, not wanting to explain why some called dinner 'luncheon' and supper 'dinner.' She liked their minister with his old-fashioned puffy wig and fine clothes. She often wondered about the other side of life in the manse house. *But why would he come knocking now?*

"Only it's that I'm here already and did not want to make the journey down again," the clergyman started.

"Most welcome, sir." She ushered him in and bade him sit. "Did you need to stay the night? It's a fine evening for walking, but if you'd rather—"

"No, no, I'll be walking back, but I had a message for you." Sheila and Muirne exchanged glances: another message, after those he read out at kirk?

"The Laird was visiting again, and it seems something was got wrong. Many people who were supposed to get notices did not. More'n likely it was the mercy of one of his tacksmen, gone awry, for what good could it do when you'll still need to clear out? Any road, that is the sad news I have to deliver to several of the families hereabout." He waved a small piece of paper. "This area is reckoned to be a grand one for winter grazing, and so I'm to be sure to tell the families who got no notice, that they are indeed required to move out by the end of harvest."

Sheila was shocked. She'd been expecting good news, as the first two messages had been good, and everyone knew, good or bad, it came in threes.

"Even if we pay the rents same as before, sir, the Laird is set on us losing our land?"

The man tucked in his chin with a jerk. "Well, I'll no say that's a surprise if ye do have it, as I figured everyone around here got their siller from the ash, but then I don't know. You will have to take that up with the Laird himself. I won't ask how you come by the siller, only," and here he raised his eyebrows, "don't be breakin' the Sabbath, woman. No good will come o' that."

"No, sir. Only my husband and son have left to see about a job, so it may be they'll work it until the rents are due, then return home. I must write to them right away to suggest it."

"And who will stay then to bring in your harvest? You've only girls left, and this wee tyke, who'll be no good wavin' a scythe." He motioned toward Alisdair.

"We'll manage the field, I think," Sheila said, a determined note creeping into her obsequious tone.

"Well, but don't forget you need to ask the Laird if he'll even let you pay. It may be he needs the grazing for other reasons. It's happened that way in other places, and he may be no different. But I've done my duty," he finished, and stood, ignoring the still-steaming tea that Muirne had placed in front of him.

After the door closed behind him, mother and daughters looked at each other. Sheena sniffled back tears, and Alisdair seemed in danger of catching the impulse, so Sheila redirected their attention.

"We must trust to God, my pets. He has sent me silver through the woolen market," she said as she poured out the coins from her blanket sack. "And He must have had a good reason for doing so." Muirne had the sudden thought that they might be needing it for finding a new home, but she kept quiet. Sheila saw the thought cross her face.

"Whatever it is we need it for, we will know when the time comes," she said.

"Shall we write to Father and Neil then? What shall we say?" asked Muirne.

"Here, Sheena," said Sheila, handing her an old piece of paper. "Make the whitewash paste to cover the old writing. Let me think awhile." Muirne got out the pen and bottle of ink stowed carefully underneath the airing cupboard, and sat down to carefully scratch out the letter her mother dictated.

Chapter 10

It took several days for the letter to reach Glasgow, during which Gillan and Neil had stayed to make sure there were not other opportunities to be had that would suit either of them better. They looked in at the taverns, at the factories supplying the new-fangled steam engines with crossbar tracks, and at the docks on the River Clyde where men stood loading and unloading freight.

"Now that's something I could do," said Neil, brightening at the thought of work out in the open, with other men.

Gillan nodded, and sought the dock for the man who looked like a boss. There was a small structure with one window back of the paths down to the river that looked promising. They went and knocked, and were met a moment later by a man who looked as if he'd just woken up. His clothes were in some disarray, and there was an odd smell about him.

"Good afternoon, sir. We were wondering—"

"Wondering about a job then?" The man's eyes narrowed as he glanced at Neil and Gillan. Neil avoided his gaze, which is why he caught sight of the ribbon on the floor, and the ladies' shoes peeking from behind a curtain at the back. Before his mind could process what that could mean, the man replied.

"I could take this lad on, as I can build him up to the work, but not you, you're not big enough for it," he said. The impersonal tone of this cut allowed Gillan to absorb it with a slow blink, as he took in that he and this man were the same height.

"And is it different owners up and down the river, or all one?" he asked.

"All different, but they'll tell you all the same thing. Got to be tall and strong, not bent over from farming work."

Gillan hung his head, appearing more bent over than ever. Neil felt ashamed for him.

"Thank you, sir." They turned away. Gillan's slight limp seemed even more pronounced for the short walk.

In a few paces, Neil had put together the pieces of what he'd seen, and wanted to tell Gillan that they did not want to work for this man anyway. "Father, did you notice—"

But Gillan did not want to talk. "Not now, Neil. Let's away home." And they walked home with a bit of cloud over their heads.

That night they said their goodbyes and gave their excuses as to why they had to go home: harvest, no need for a move right away, a daughter to see married. Jenny, and Charlie when he came home, accepted this reasoning with no qualms, and it made for a happy party around the table for tea that night, as the sun stretched long into the evening.

The next morning the pair set out early, laden with food and little presents of ointments and hankies for the women at home, and wooden carvings for Alisdair. They had sat down for their own solitary noon meal in the moor east of the city when Gillan finally spoke of the attitude of the navvy down on the banks.

"Ye mind, I know that I am not a great big honk of a man, but I'm enough to do for a family, the fishing, the farming. I served my king and am no longer in my best form, it's true, but there's no shame in that." He paused to consider, or perhaps convince himself. "I'm glad we're going back, Neil, since I don't think we're either of us suited to the factory or the dock work or whatever else in the city."

"Did you see, Father, that the man at the docks was hiding a woman?"

A tiny smile appeared on Gillan's face. "Didja see 'er then?"

"No, just some ribbon and her shoes under the curtain."

"Ach, well, just as well, since there is another reason: your mother would have my hide if she knew you were consortin' with the likes o' him!" And they had a good laugh, happy to be returning home where folk knew how to behave.

However they'd not gone far after that when they heard a rider galloping along the road, hallo-ing as he went. Neil and Gillan stopped to watch; they were astonished to see it was their Charlie, on a borrowed horse, come to seek them. Gillan's heart immediately dropped to his feet.

"It's not Sheila or the children, is it?" he asked before Charlie had stopped the horse. He was anxious to discover the news that had had his brother-in-law ride after them at such a pace.

"Whoa, whoa. I don't know, she's sent a note, your Sheila, by the express."

"The express!" said Neil, astonished. That would have taken money. She must really have wanted, or needed, to catch them before they left Aunt Jenny's. Neil read the words aloud, seeing his sister's handwriting but hearing his mother's tone in the careful restraint.

"*Dear Gillan,*

We have just had the news from the Rev. Mr. McManus that we are meant to move as well. A tacksman must have refused to deliver the notices back a month ago. Anyway, Mr. McManus does not know if it would be possible to stay even if we manage to pay the rents, so I am going tomorrow morning to ask the Laird about it.

I will send another letter then, not express, to tell you the answer. Meanwhile, you may as well stay in Glasgow with Jenny, as it may turn out better for us to stay split up. Muirne and Sheena and I will do for the harvest, if need be.

Your loving Sheila

There was a stunned, disbelieving pause after Neil finished. The hard blowing of the horse was the only sound.

"It looks as if we are to stay a bit longer at your table, Charlie, if it'd be no trouble," said Gillan.

Charlie looked from Gillan to Neil and back. "Aye, it's nae trouble. But what does it mean? Can ye no—"

"No, it does sound very bad. We may yet lose the croft. I may yet be working at yon mill with ye, Charlie," he said with an attempt to make light of the risk.

"Well," said Charlie, not sure how to comfort someone after such inconclusive news. "I'm sure Jenny'll be happy to have ye back for another while, and we shall pray for good news to come next."

Neil was hardly listening to them. His heart broke at the thought of his mother and sisters, even wee Sheena, out in the fields at the barley. They would have to be working longer than the men, as it would be smaller loads and more trips to the hay loft to bring in the stacks. *Dawn till dusk*, he thought. *And here I am complaining about a nine-hour day with a bit of noise.*

They turned back, Charlie leading the horse, and the two older men chatting about the factory work Gillan would try for. Along the way, Gillan spoke to Neil, "If you prefer the river log job, you can try your hand at that. We can at least see what the pay is at a different operation."

Neil knew he was trying to be very fair to him, and ducked his head. "Aye, I'll look to it tomorrow."

After another few miles, Neil asked, "How long do you think it will take for Mother's next letter? She must have been to see the Laird already."

"True," said Gillan. "I think the regular post takes three or four days, lad, so we shouldna have long to wait."

Suddenly, August stretched like a prison sentence in front of Neil. He wished to be able to step back and have this one last summer month on the island. If indeed they were to be tossed aside no matter the rents they could pay, then they would likely move here, to the city. His heart yearned to be back by the sea to help his mother and sisters with the harvest, and see the familiar sights one last time.

But it was not to be. Four days later they received the letter. Sheila used the same restrained, practical tone as before, but they could well imagine what she left out. How humiliating it had been to plead to keep her home, promising to pay to keep what was theirs, with no man to stand for her.

And the denial. Gillan had no doubt there were more details to that which his wife had withheld, but he did not press her in his reply. If the Laird had indeed turned 'English gentleman,' and chosen to live on his income in London rather than with his clan on the island, then it was probably best they did clear out before any worse troubles befell them.

* * *

As the menfolk were receiving and digesting the news of

the letter, Sheila and her three children at Dalcriadh were busy preparing for the mammoth task ahead. In a few days the barley would be thick with spikes, and they were readying the tools, clearing space next to the blackhouse for the stacks to stay dry, and hurrying to neighbors in the dark evenings to ask whether they would have need of their barley come the end of September.

Many were in the same boat, and would need to leave their crops behind. A few said they'd be staying and trusting to their luck and their faith, and these could spare a few coins in exchange for the extra grain. The time came for them to visit the Eglunds, and Muirne was dreading it, but determined to treat it as a challenge to her character that she leave her pride behind as she did what was necessary for her family.

Sheila's knock was answered by Alex's young wife, Polly, who registered a slight shock at seeing them, but asked them in politely. She'd come over from the mainland, a Seceder from an Argyll congregation, after his first wife had died young. They went through the niceties and Sheila came round to their point in visiting: the news they'd had from the Laird, and their current plan to move to Glasgow once the harvest was in. As they would not be taking it all with them, would the Eglunds have a need for some extra this winter, and be able to give them something for their journey and their plans to start over in the city?

Polly, Sheila could tell, was about to give some slight excuse to say no, but before she could, her husband spoke up from a dark corner of their house where he'd been listening. "And why isn't it yer man here to ask, Mrs. MacLean? I should think it'd be his duty."

Sheila colored; he clearly meant to embarrass her. Muirne responded for her. "My father and brother are already in Glasgow looking for work with some family there, Mr.

Eglund. They would be here if they could, but there is little time left for all the journeying, so we will join them there as soon as the harvest is in."

Polly's eyes looked at them pityingly, but her husband continued his taunt. "Is that it, then? Well, I shall wish you luck finding a husband after your face and figure have been ruined doing the men's job for them," he said.

Muirne stared, her mouth agape. Never would she have expected such unkindness from a neighbor. So much the better she had refused the offer to marry his son. His words hung in the air, stark and inexcusable. Muirne turned abruptly to Polly, thanking her for hearing them out, and she and her mother rose and went out, feeling the man's daggers at their backs.

"My!" Muirne gasped after they had walked a few steps outside. "If that was not the rudest—"

"Hush, Muirne. It's no good thinking on it. We'll just forget them. We're done visiting tonight, and it's time to get back to Alisdair and Sheena. She should have the porridge ready by now."

Muirne nodded, but her breath continued to come in little gasps as she walked. She resolved to write about it to Neil. He'd know how it felt, and offer sympathy. Besides, he would have all sorts of news from the factory where he was working, meeting new people. Muirne's heart eased, thinking of him, and she looked forward to writing a letter by rushlight when she got home.

Chapter 11

August, usually the bonniest month of the year, was pale and muggy and oppressive on the island. The MacLean women struggled in the field under the glare of the sun, the drops of rain that thankfully did not gather speed, and the clegs that flew about their faces to torment them as they cut and gathered the barley.

Muirne had read between the lines of Neil's last letter that he yearned to come home to Mull. She in turn wished to be done with the harvest so they could be together again, and be free of the heavy wooden tools and wire used to bind up the sheaves. Time and again she'd looked out to see her father or Gillan doing these tasks and it had seemed so effortless, but in her arms the bundles were awkward, and oftentimes the sheaves fell out before she could twist the wire around the full circumference. Starting over frustrated her to the point of angry tears.

What was more frustrating, however, was seeing Robbie Eglund, who'd never come around before, pass by their fields, touching his cap as he went. It was clearly meant to taunt her, and she ground her teeth in fury as she swung the scythe,

almost taking off her leg in one sweep. After that she reminded herself to be more careful, no matter the taunts she received. *I'll no' change my mind and accept him, if that's what he was
thinking.*

Each evening, all three women collapsed after a porridge
supper, tired to their bones from the day's work. Only
Alisdair, at six not able to lift any of the tools, stayed home or
ran and fetched for them. He also was now in charge of milking the cow and feeding the hens, after they had left for the
field rows.

It was almost three weeks before they saw the end in
sight. September loomed close by. They knew from their
letters that the men had both started jobs, but in different
places: Gillan in the same cotton mill as Charlie, Neil as a
freightloader on the Clyde. They were all curious about this, as
it seemed very odd and out of form for Neil to choose some
place other than beside his stepfather. There must not have
been enough spaces or something of that sort. Sheila wanted
only that they do a good job, earn a good wage, and find them
a solid enough house. She prayed for this each night before
bed. Muirne saw that her mother's dream of paying the rents
with her weaving had dissolved and floated away when the
Laird said no amount of money would allow them to stay: they
must make way for more efficient farming methods and live-
stock production. He was indeed turning 'English gentleman.'

As September came and the women worked to deliver the
barley stooks to neighbors that could spare some recompense,
Robbie no longer appeared at the end of the day, for which
Muirne was thankful. They had four more small loads left to
deliver, which they had figured to do on the morn, when,
returning, they saw men hanging about their front door.
Muirne turned her head to see her mother from under the
empty creel she carried.

"Inspectors, likely." Sheila seemed calm, but Muirne's heartbeat quickened as she thought of Alisdair inside. The three of them tossed aside their empty creels and ran down the hill to the house. As they had feared, they saw one of the men coming out of the house. *Where was Alisdair?*

"Hallo, gentlemen," she called from a distance as they caught up to the yard. "We've been out all day with the harvesting. Can I help you with anything?"

There were three of them, and they were dressed well in plain dark wool suits. They carried scrolls and sheaves of paper in a case that evidently they had been consulting before the women had arrived. One of them looked up; it was Alex Eglund. Another caught her eye, and Sheila fought down her panic to face him. This man she would treat as the messenger, and not Eglund, the toad.

"We are here inspecting for Laird of Torloisk, Mrs. MacLean. It seems you were meant to leave three days ago, when your harvest was in. Is not that so?"

"Well, sir, we have been preparing to leave, as demanded." Her voice took on a hard edge. "But as we are moving to the city, we've had to deliver it to neighbors who could purchase the stores from us. We are set to go in two days' time," she finished quietly.

"That is not what was specified in the notice of eviction, Mrs. MacLean, though, was it?" His tone was patient, as if he were talking to someone soft in the head.

"Well, what would be the point of stooking up the barley as the Laird allowed, then letting it rot? I'm only—"

The back of his hand connected with her cheek in a loud crack, and she barely stuck out her left hand in time to stop her head hitting the side of the house. Her right hand flew to her jaw, where she felt blood from inside her mouth. She spat it out, looking up to see her Alisdair in the doorway. His eyes were wide and afraid. Sheila coughed to cover the temper that came immediately on the heels of the pain.

Before Alisdair could scream, Muirne darted forward and scooped him up, holding him in her arms as she kept her back facing the house. "Can we leave in the morning then? Would that satisfy you?" she asked brusquely. She was thinking they could notify their closest neighbor to collect their remaining barley stooks on the morrow, as their situation had changed. And instead of the wagon they'd meant to borrow to transport their things, they would need to fit everything in the creels.

The stranger interrupted her thoughts with his reply. "No," he said loudly. "It would not."

"You were meant to be out; you shall be out," he said, and Muirne noticed a frisson of excitement pass through Eglund's body. The third man she could not make out in the shadow.

"We are here to tear down this structure, and the easiest way to do that is firing it. So if you've anything you want of value from it, hurry to it while we prepare our torches."

Muirne felt a scream die in her throat. Her mother rushed in, grabbing their pile of blankets by the bed and dumping it outside in the yard, a small distance from the door. "I'll get the hens in their cage," whispered Sheena, her eyes limpid and wide, obviously in shock.

Muirne set Alisdair down, telling him to stay with their pile of goods, away from the house, and away from those men. He nodded and she rushed in, looking wildly about. Her eyes blurred with tears as she tried to consider what was most important in this dear, old house. She wiped them away and made a grab for the iron pot over the fire.

The bedding was out, the cooking utensils were out, the hens and milk cow were caged and tethered by the smoke house. *The smokehouse!* thought Muirne, but she looked to see Sheena dash in and wrap their bounty of fish in a small apron, adding it to the pile of belongings. Muirne went in herself, grabbing the heavier salted mutton and bacon, deep under the chest.

Muirne skittered back into the house again and helped Sheila to lug out the wooden chest. They placed it farthest from the house as their eyes darted over to where the men stood. They had soaked rags in some sort of rancid fat and were now making a show of looking for their matches. Muirne choked back a sob as she ran back in, grabbing the few pictures off the wall, the rags from the holes in the walls, the spoons and the basin and her father's spare plaid.

As she passed through the doorway, she smelled the first whiffs of smoke. They had started from the back of the house, where it sat against the hill. She sought her mother's eyes. *The loom*, she mouthed. Her mother nodded, and they dove in once more, rushing to the left corner of the house where the loom stood.

"Should we break it down, or—"

"Nae time, let's just pull it through. It'll fit yet."

They struggled, pushing and pulling the large awkward wooden frame forward to the door. It bunched and creaked, not liking the sideways movement. Muirne took the front side and pulled it backwards through the door, but suddenly tripped and fell on her rump. She looked up to see one of the men laughing at her. She swiped away the tears of frustration and screamed, "Mama!"

For it looked as if the flames were inside the house now, and her mother trapped behind the loom, which took up the doorway. She scrambled to her feet, grabbed hold, and pulled to. She felt her mother twist one of the legs so it would fit through on the diagonal, and changed her grip to match its weight. Pulled again, and finally it was free of the doorway.

Sheila stumbled out, and they managed to get the loom

out of the reach of the fire. Alisdair held onto the rope, but the milk cow, frightened by the noise and heat, was pulling him away into the darkness. Muirne quickly covered its head with a cloth and led it back with shushing sounds. Sheena kept the overturned creel pressed to the earth so that none of the hens could escape. The four of them bowed their heads together briefly, holding hands while Sheila gave a broken prayer of thanks. The fire crackled away, smothering her words.

When they looked up, the men were gone.

Chapter 12

Muirne felt Sheila make a motion toward their nearest neighbors, the Taylors to the east. But as she headed over their way, she stopped. She saw little flickering lights where the Taylors' house stood. They would find no shelter with the neighbors this night. Those men were visiting everybody they knew.

"All right," Sheila said. Then again: "All right, everyone?" Nods and gulps around their small huddle. "Let's all do something so that we can batten down for the night, then. Sheena, you go and fetch our creels that we dropped up the hill, fetch them back here. Muirne, could you go quickly to the Taylors to see if they're out as well? Mind ye, be careful, I can see the f-flames from here." Another breath of horror troubled her tongue.

"Alisdair, you stand guard over that cow and these hens, now, y'hear? And I'll be going over to Serena McCall's to pass on the word about the last deliveries tomorrow. They can't have fired *her*." As Muirne turned to strike out down the hill, she heard her mother mutter: "Although if they've thrown out women and children, they'll have no fear to do the same with the widow-witch."

"The smoke shed is still there, Mama," Sheena volunteered. "If the wind picks up, we can all fit in there to stay warm the night." Sheila's quick thought was that their house on fire would probably keep them plenty warm, but again Muirne caught her look and understood it. They kept their eyes averted from the sight, a crackling mass some thirty feet away.

"Good girl, then that's what we'll do. All right." And they split up to do their tasks and deliver their messages, all studiously avoiding looking at the mass of flame beyond their pile of worldly goods.

* * *

The weeks that the women had spent gathering in the harvest had seen the men learning their new rules quickly and settling into their own routines. It was the first of September when Neil thought he had finally earned his place in the Franklin Freight Company. Although the teasing about his youth and his highland ways continued, Neil chose to take it in good humor, and tentatively ribbed some of the men about their own misfortunes.

Instead of the routine making it easier, however, he found it more and more difficult to rouse himself at four to make his way to the docks. His limbs felt weary and leaden each night at the supper table, and though Gillan and Charlie and others saw his pallor and sluggishness, they told him he'd soon toughen up to where he wouldn't mind the pace. Neil was not so sure.

But at least he was not in the mill. He thanked God for that every night as he said his prayers, and prayed for his stepfather, who looked beaten down by the loading job he was now doing. Gillan spoke not a word of complaint, and smiled more often than he had on the island, which told Neil more than any other sign that his spirit was flagging.

Being Charlie's brother-in-law helped, however. Gillan was friendly with some of the other men in the line with him, which was something Neil did not have. No, Neil spent the day escaping into his mind, silent to those around him unless advice or instruction was needed. He imagined his mother and sisters cutting the barley and digging up the spuds, packing up a borrowed wagon, traveling with all their goods down here alone. He saw in his mind's eye the bracken red on the hills behind them as they left, the moss being gathered for use on the way out.

The one new delight he had in their new neighborhood of Hutchesontown was his return home each day. The half-hour's walk took him past many taverns and workshops, but there was one in particular he had noticed for weeks. His notice had first been caught by the curving figure of a young woman as she set down a large creel in the alley by the Dog and Duck Pub. She moved awkwardly with its weight, but then turned and saw him after setting it down. She looked him up and down with an appraising gaze, then flounced back into the tavern. He'd barked a short laugh after the door shut, amused at such cool possession.

After that, Neil kept an eye out, but she didn't come out again while he passed. Instead, he saw her in the second-story window, watching for him. Her attention always took the tiredness out of him for a few moments. He walked past and sneaked a glance up. Each time he glimpsed fair skin and long dark hair before the figure stepped back into the shadow. She wore her hair straight instead of curled like so many of the town ladies. He pictured her cool smirk as she dropped the curtain on him, and a small smile crossed his face.

He said nothing of this exchange at the supper table with

his stepfather and Aunt Jenny's family, but it was something he thought of idly at night after his prayers were said before he drifted off to sleep. *Perhaps*, he thought, *I could find a reason to go into the tavern.*

When the news reached them, Gillan had just worked his sixth day and was relaxing on a chair after dinner as he talked to Jenny in the kitchen. She was making the porridge for the morning's breakfast. The children were in bed or practicing their letters in the sitting room and Charlie and Neil were talking in low voices by the fire, when a knock came at the door.

It was late for the postmen to be on their rounds, but Neil, who answered the door, saw that it was no postman, but a poorly young man who looked like an islander. His clothes were homespun, and his shoes were of the hard-to-turn cured leather that they made on Mull. Neil looked at him with curiosity. "Yes?"

"I was coming faster to the city, and asked to bring this message from yer family. Ye are the MacLeans of Dalcriadh?" he asked.

"Aye."

"Then I am sorry, and here is the letter. Good night to ye," he said and turned on his heel.

"What could that mean?" said Gillan behind him. "Open the letter, Neil. Read us what it says."

Neil lifted the flap free of the plant tar they used to seal envelopes, and unfolded his mother's letter. "Dearest Gillan and Neil," he read.

> *Dearest Gillan and Neil,*
> *We are on the road to join you in Glasgow, and I have asked this nice family man with the horse and cart to deliver the news before we arrive so that ye may be pre-*

pared. We meant to take two more days before leaving, but were visited by the inspectors, including one Alex Eglund, and they have burned the house down. We got most everything with us, but are passing slow with all the baggage and no cart. We tried to go first to my cousins in Corran, but they have an attack of the typhus, and we canna stay here. All told, we expect to arrive no sooner than Michaelmas.

The children are all fine, but all our neighbors suffered the same, so we could not sell as much barley as might be. Our store of money is less than hoped for, but still something better than nothing, to find a house near Jenny. I hope I have done as you might, had you been here, mo cridhe. We will be with you soon.

Your loving Sheila

Neil's voice had started out normal, then gone to a whisper. He couldn't believe what he was reading. *Burned down? Had they been in it? Had they been given notice? Why had Eglund been there?* Neil's gut burned with anger and powerlessness at the news of his family's desperate flight.

Gillan, listening, could not take it in either. He snapped the letter from Neil's hands as soon as he said "Your loving" and stared at the signature. Jenny went to his side and gripped his hand. "I know there were things said of the northeast evictions forty years ago, and those we heard about in Argyll twenty years past, but—"

Jenny interrupted. "But the children are all well. We must give thanks for that."

"And Mama?" Neil rasped.

"She must be all right, sure she wrote her own letter?"

"No, it's Muirne wrote this letter for her. Her hand is better," Neil supplied. He cleared his throat. "But she would have said something."

God, if she'd been hurt—

"I wonder where they are now. Bad about the typhus. Waste of three days' journey, that. The ten days to Michaelmas will be a long slog, with all that baggage and the wee one. So she wrote from Corran, Neil?" Jenny asked.

"Aye."

"Top of Loch Linnhe. They've still a long way ahead. Do ye want us to send one of our older ones on the road to meet them? We can go at least as far as Goolrick on a horse, nae problem."

Gillan spoke. "You say Corran is on the far side of Loch Linnhe, and it took four days for that man to reach us from there. And he had a cart, which means they'll only be about halfway, if even that." He looked to Charlie to confirm his distance calculations.

"Aye, if they're moving like we think they are, but really there's no telling," Charlie warned. "I don't think ye can safely leave the mill yet, ye're still learning, and the boss would look on it as shirking. Send someone," he urged.

"My family is defenseless on the road, in the hills, with all our household on their backs—" Gillan's voice shook.

"I'll go, Father. I'll go as far as the meeting of the highland roads at Crianlarich, and wait for them there, for it's sure they've no passed that far yet." He turned to Charlie. "Could you borrow that horse for me this night? And leave a message Monday at the dock?"

"Aye."

"Then I'll go get my plaid and be off, as soon as I can." His eyes shone; his body vibrated. He saw that Gillan was torn between wanting to go with him and not wanting to face the possibility of losing his family.

"Aye, Neil," Gillan's voice was rough. "I'll send the message. You be careful now, you'll be no good to your mother if that horse runs itself ragged or ye get thrown, ye mind? God's luck go with ye now." He turned to walk out the back door to the small yard where the privy stood.

"I'll take ye to Carson's now, Neil, if you're ready."

Neil dashed over to the corner where he slept, scooped up his plaid, patted his pockets to make sure he had his clothes all sorted, then followed Charlie out into the night.

* * *

Neil rode the shaggy, grey highland pony slowly through the eastern outskirts of the city. He accustomed himself to the feel of the hard wooden slats of the pack saddle that could be felt even under a thick horsehair blanket. He was careful to avoid the men who were leaving the taverns early, so drunk they were falling over and clutching anything to hand. He minded his stepfather's warning, and guarded the beast carefully. First, however, he had a destination in town.

He stopped below the window of the Dog and Duck, and dismounted to grab a few pebbles from the road. He threw them up at the window pane on at at time, where they made a small *ping*. After the third one, a face appeared at the window, and though it was dark, she held a rushlight in her hand. He saw her face fully: it was beautiful bathed in the soft yellow light of the lantern.

After seeing who it was, and that he had a horse with him, she gave a wave and left the window. The side door to the tavern was unbarred a few moments later, and she peered out. "It's you," she said. "What is it ye want?" She spoke practically, ignoring any question of whether or not they should be talking.

Her manner, though, betrayed some hesitancy, and Neil

knew he'd been bold to come here. He reassured himself: it was on his way, and he needed food. Also, he wanted a thought to cheer him, to replace the horrors he imagined for his family. He kept a respectful distance from her.

"I am on an urgent errand this night. My father has sent me to collect my family, as they are unchaperoned on the road from Fort William. I hoped you might help me with a meal for the road, if you could spare it."

Her look of wariness fell away. "Your mother?"

He nodded. "Two younger sisters and a wee brother as well."

"A'right," she said, a look of pain and sympathy crossing her face. "But what is your name?"

"Neil. Neil MacLean."

"Mine is Pleasance Cameron, but everybody calls me Letty." There was a pause as they each took a deep breath. *The chasm has been crossed!* thought Neil. Then Letty spoke again. "I'll away for your supper then." She gave him a slight smile before closing the door.

Neil turned his attention to the horse, who was lipping the weeds at the edge of the road. His vision was filled with his first close view of Letty: a turned-up nose, freckles, a high forehead, and an expressive mouth. Her looks pleased him, and he wondered what she thought of him. *Well, she is giving me a free meal*, he thought with a grin. He scanned the road and straightened, bringing his attention back to the potential dangers of the city at this time of evening. He thought then of the wickedness to be found even on his island, and started humming a tune to keep his sense of betrayal at bay.

Letty was back before long, and handed him a low basket wrapped and tied with a cloth. It was warm, and he looked up to thank her. Her cornflower blue eyes sparkled in the light from the lamp at the front door. Her gaze wavered, then dropped to his chest. "I do hope your urgent errand goes well," she said.

"Thank you." He drew her gaze upward by waiting. "Thank you, Letty. God will it be so. Good night then."

"Good night. Safe journey," she called to him as he settled himself back upon the horse and slipped into the darkness.

Chapter 13

It was easy for Neil to navigate by the city's lights for the first twenty miles. Then, he trusted the horse to continue on the broad path that made up the road north to Loch Lomond. As long as he did not veer too far right, he was not worried about going astray in the night.

However, he was feeling his tiredness creep up over him, now that the urgent shock of terror from the news and the warm glow from meeting Letty had both left him. He debated briefly whether to simply tie himself to the horse and keep going but worried that the animal might stop. He decided to stop and sleep for a nap, then eat something. He reasoned that the meal would waken him better than anything else.

Ten more miles up the road he stopped and pulled the horse aside, hobbling two of its legs with the bit of rope he'd brought. It immediately started chomping on the grass. Neil wrapped himself up in the plaid, curled up, and thought to himself, *Only an hour, only an hour.* He fell into sleep like someone walking off a cliff.

It was hours later that he woke. It was still dark, but Neil could feel the change in the air around and the chatter of birds that were getting ready for the day. He judged it to be about three o'clock. The basket was no longer warm, of course, but he delighted in the slices of roast meat and two small salted potatoes Letty'd packed. He whistled once, low and long, and heard the sputter of his horse blowing through her lips, as if she were laughing at him. *Well*, he thought, *if that's how you express gratitude, I'll no be stopping to let you eat any more grass, ye wee rascal.* He smiled to himself, then whistled again, two short, low blasts. He heard the plodding hooves and met the mare halfway, speaking low and holding his hands out to the grey apparition.

He set out again, and by the time the first lightness in the east could be detected, he'd arrived at the west shore of Loch Lomond. Here, for the first time since he'd seen the lights of Glasgow, there were other travelers. He judged it too soon for his mother to have reached there yet, so did not bother asking if anyone had seen his family. They looked like they were going about local business.

One man had a cart with jars of milk, the cream sloshing out of several as his horse stumbled a few times. The driver was grumbling, glancing back at his load and cursing the horse. Another horseman trotted past, a finely-dressed clergyman, perhaps out on an errand for his patrons. Two fishermen walked together, each holding two long handles with metal tines pointing sideways at the top. Neil wondered if they were after trout with those cleeks, or on their way to the sea for the skate. He nodded acknowledgement of all whom he passed.

As day broke full on him, the sleepiness left and some of the urgency returned. He clucked his mare into a trot for long periods, trying to cover more ground. He guessed that they would be traveling only by day, laden as they were and not knowing the road. So they would be up and moving now. He had said he would wait at Crianlarich, since that would be the logical point of intercepting them, but his heart wanted to continue, not sit waiting. The problem was he didn't know if they would come through one of the glens from Glencoe, or travel down the east shore of Loch Linnhe. He supposed the latter was safer, but they were probably going on advice from other travelers and his mother's intuition. Not a bad guide, but definitely not something he could predict.

He sighed, deciding to make camp at Crianlarich that night and to wait there the next day at least. By the time he reached the end of the long Sabbath, his back ached and his stomach was growling; he'd finished the bannocks and fried pie from Letty's basket for his noon meal. Instead of avoiding the next outcropping of buildings huddled together near the crossroads, he went up to knock at the door of a small stone-built cottage next to what looked like a kirk.

There he found a meal with the minister's family, the wife saying as how she knew her Christian duty well enough. He was well-filled when he hopped up onto his horse again, and thanked the family with a wave before trotting up the road.

Mindful of the warnings of his stepfather, he led the horse off the road at the point where he could see the western approach. He hobbled her feet again and sat to watch the last light leave the sky. He thought of the day he left Mull, when he'd looked back to see the same brilliant sunset over the island. His heart was heavy, but he prayed for his family on their way, that they not meet with trouble before he could protect them.

* * *

The night was cold, September starting to turn its pretty head and blow the autumn winds that would bring stinging rain and ice to the highlands. Neil curled himself tighter into a ball, but did not sleep long. He awoke with the sounds of the birds stirring, perhaps two o'clock, and gave the whistle for the horse. She ambled over a few moments later, and he used a few handfuls of grass to rub against her coat, cleaning off the sweat from the day before. The work warmed his hands.

Neil wished he could find shelter from the wind, but the land was treeless. The best he could do was work his way farther off the road to where he remembered seeing the rise of a small hill. As soon as he felt the ground rise under his feet, he also felt the wind drop. He could hear it still, rushing around the small tussock, but he dropped gratefully down and kept the horse nearby. He could lay on his right side on the slight incline of the hill and still keep his gaze to the west. He watched for any lights or movement in the shadowy vale before succumbing again to sleep.

His skin was cool and he was shaking a bit when he woke up, crouched over his knees. Pale pink stretches of light reached out from the east, and now the road was visible. Few people were on it that day though, and soon it was raining, a light rain, but steady. Neil thought about his post on the river. He hoped he'd still have it when he returned, for he liked it well enough and did not want to work indoors at the mill. The very thought of it made his throat start to close up, but he forced his thoughts to where his mother might be right now, struggling. He would do anything to protect them, even work in that bloody mill.

The first person he saw was mounted on a hardy highland pony. A dog trotted at its heels. Neil deemed it time to start asking for help, and raised his hand high in salute, hailing the rider down at the bend in the road.

"Good day to ye, sir," Neil said.

"And ye," the highlander returned.

"I am waiting for some of my family that are traveling

from Mull. Have you seen three women and a little boy walking this way?"

The man's eyes betrayed no reaction, but his words softened. "Nay, but God go with them, and thee." He nodded, Neil thanked him, and he walked on. Three more men reacted the same way when Neil posed his question to them throughout the day. Pity it was he saw in their faces. Either they had had their families removed as well, or they feared it might happen to them. No travelers this way had been well-dressed. *How did the wealthy manage to get from north to south then?* He'd seen no carriages. Just the one mail coach going north, making a great racket with its four horses and great big wheels.

It was nearing suppertime on the Monday, and Neil was wrestling with the decision to continue waiting in the smirr at Crianlarich, or whether to strike out to find them sooner. If only one of the travelers had seen them, he'd have a hint as to which way they were coming. Before he could decide, another horse came into view.

It walked with a quick step, as if nearing home. Neil saw that there were in fact two riders, a big man and a smaller woman, riding in front. He stepped out to hail them, and the horse plunged sideways. The man kept his seat, a trained rider, but the woman clutched the mane in front of her with a death grip. Neil saw the man speak some words low in her ear before turning murderous eyes on him. From twenty feet away, Neil still felt his heart quail from that look.

"And what do you want then? We've nothing to give or steal, if that's what you're after."

"No, sir, good e'en, sir, good e'en, lady," replied Neil, trying to remember his manners. "I am looking for news of my family on the road from Mull. Have you seen three women and a little boy on your way?"

At his question the woman looked up at him. "Yes. We

passed them near Ballachulish early yesterday. They were moving—they had to go quite slowly. From there, they'd come through Glencoe. They'll probably spend tonight there."

Glencoe. Witness to clan betrayal and government treachery. Scene of the massacre of 1692, when almost a hundred Scots perished. Valley filled with angry and unforgiving spirits.

"Thank you!" Neil all but sang out. "Thank you very much. I am sorry for scaring your horse. A safe journey to you both," Neil called out over his shoulder as he whistled for his horse and picked up the basket and his plaid and stowed them in his pack behind. *At last, a sign.* He ignored the shiver that ran low up his spine at the mention of Glencoe, and rode at a gallop to the north.

Chapter 14

Muirne's pain came and went in flashes: when the bite at her shoulders from the heavy creel got to be nearly unbearable, her attention would be pulled to the burning at her wrist, where she carried the loops of bags of cloth and linens rescued from the blackhouse. She looked in the blueing of the light and saw her sister Sheena was dropping tears from the tip of her nose. Their feet, normally calloused and serviceable, all had burst blisters from the roads and cuts from the rough bracken they'd scrambled over, fearful of losing the way.

She felt the permanent grooves on her shoulders where the heavy creel base had been sitting, every day for almost a week now. Her hands shook from alternating clutching the front of the basket to keep it balanced, and the fingers felt like claws as she flexed them painfully. She hid her hands when she felt her mother watching her.

Muirne motioned to Sheena. "Let's go down to the burn to fetch water for supper and some for our hands, eh?"

"Do ye look out for any willow trees beside it then, for the leaves make a good numbing herb," their mother said. "We can make a paste of it for after supper."

"Yes, Mama," replied Muirne.

The night was going to be cold and windy again. There were no trees in the glen for the wind to shake, but there was the strange scudding noise that was the wind whipping through the upper hills. It would soon make its way down to the corrie in which they'd made camp. Sheila got out the griddle for making supper and looked to where Alisdair had stopped in his tracks and knelt down to the ground with his burden.

They'd made him up a pack with a plaid on his back, but his job was to collect any kindling they could find along the way for the fire at the day's end. There was not much, but the small pile he'd been able to spy out would have to do them for a supper fire.

"Come here to me, Alisdair." He came, as if in a trance, the pack still tied to his back. Sheila released it and set it down gently, then hugged her to him. Gradually he melted back into a little boy, and he burrowed in for a closer embrace. After a few moments, Sheila whispered to him. "Time now to be doing your job and building up the fire, m'lad." She felt his little body shake, and sigh, and then straighten.

"Yes, Mama."

Sheila removed a few more of the old potatoes from a sack, put them next to the leeks she'd collected at their last stopping-place. Soup it would be, with the last of the fresh-killed hen meat, tonight. She lugged the kitchen pot over near where Alisdair sat building the fire, and started scrubbing at each of the items before tossing them in. When the girls came back with the water in their clay pot, most of it was dumped into the stewpot, with the rest reserved for the morning's porridge.

* * *

They heard the hoofbeats in the late evening long before anyone appeared, and immediately they took up the defensive position their mother had taught them the first day. They crouched in front of their piled belongings, Sheila standing in front of them. It was rather late, and only the last of summer's long light was visible to the west from the valley entrance.

From their position in the corrie, a ways up from the main glen road, Sheila could easily see the main road through Glencoe. By the time the rider was even with them, however, it was too dark to see who it was. His head was turning this way and that, searching. Finally he slowed, seeming to peer their way.

"Hallo? Anybody there?"

"Is that—Neil, is that you?" Muirne asked, jumping up. She felt Sheena's hand grasp her foot.

"Muirne! Mother?" The figure immediately jumped off the horse and scrambled toward them. Their fire had long died, but they didn't need its light to recognize his voice and his walk as he clambered over the rocky ground.

"Are ye all right? Is everyone well?" Neil asked, as he was engulfed in tearful hugs and laughs of relief.

"We are, they are, God help us. But why—how—how did you know to find us here, Neil? How long have ye been—"

"It's all right, Mother. I'm only four days from home. I chanced to meet someone who'd seen you back at Ballachulish early yesterday, and they told me which way you'd be coming through. Thank God I've found you."

"Aye." Sheila looked briefly up toward the darkening sky, but said nothing more.

"I've been praying that it wouldn't break the children's health to make this journey, praying that there would be no early September snow, as there sometimes is. But now we have another pair of arms, a man's arms, with us." She smiled approval at Neil's courage, her hand clutching his arm.

"And a horse as well, and you're within four days of shelter, or maybe a bit more," Neil told them, nodding.

But it had been close, Muirne thought, looking at her mother. She put the thought away, and met Neil's gaze. He knew.

* * *

Neil watched his family closely when they moved off the next morning, leaving the glen behind and turning south. In the initial round of storytelling last night, none of them had touched on the burning of their house. It was clear they were exhausted, and when the initial excitement at Neil's arrival wore off, they'd fallen asleep quickly. Now in the light, he saw just how depleted his sisters had become from the week of hard travel. And his mother, though she saved her breath to refrain from appearing short of it.

They redistributed the loads in the creels, with Neil crafting two sacks from his traveling blankets and laying them atop the horse for balance. He caught the smiles between Muirne and Sheena as they shouldered their baskets and realized how light they felt now. But still, the base sat on the same sore points of their shoulders, and after a while, they were once again head down, teeth gritted. They continued on the same schedule as before even with the new distribution, and stopped every hour for a few minutes to straighten their backs.

These short rests were when they talked, and Neil heard of the night visit, or 'inspection.' His stomach roiled with anger again as he heard how they'd been so carelessly tossed out of their own home. *Surely that was not the action of an honorable laird*, he thought. He heard of the milk cow left with neighbors who could be trusted and the hens who were killed and eaten in the past week. He heard of other neighbors' houses they'd passed, where nothing remained but smoking timbers and blackened pots. In turn, he told them of the jobs he and Gillan had taken, the people they'd met, and stories recounted at the supper table in the past few weeks. He had them all laughing at some of the escapades on the docks.

They were able to set a pace a bit faster than before, and reached the place where Neil had camped before at Crianlarich just after sunset the second day. Alisdair still held the job of collecting any sticks for a fire, but the winding road south toward Glasgow seemed picked clean, well-traversed as it was, and so they had no fire that night. They shared a bit of cold smoked fish from a pack, and slept out in the fields by the road, using their pile of belongings as a wind break, all snuggled together.

It took them five days to reach Jenny's house in Hutchesontown. They were met by a bustling Jenny, who brought out a special side of smoked salmon to be braised with the abundance of vegetables from her garden. The smell of it made Muirne's mouth water freely, so long it had been since she'd had a real meal. Gillan hung back in the house at first. He was choked up until Sheila came to put her arms around him, and then tears of relief flowed freely down his cheeks.

They ranged themselves around the fireplace and fell to sleep immediately, bellies full and glad to be at home with family, free of the burden of all their worldly possessions. With a great effort, Muirne stayed awake to tell Neil what had taken place in more detail. They held hands as she told him, and he saw what she'd seen in her retelling. She spoke in barely a whisper, mindful of the younger children asleep, and their parents on the other side of the wall. After such an unburdening of the soul, Muirne wept a little and fell asleep quickly, even curled against the wall. Neil crossed his arms against his chest, not feeling the warmth from the fire as Muirne's words sunk in.

* * *

Neil woke up earlier than the others in the sitting room. He was stiff from riding and sleeping sitting up, but he tried to stretch out the soreness as he helped himself to porridge on the stove and dressed for work. Gillan had told him he thought it would be all right after one week to go back to work and explain what had happened with his family, but Neil was feeling nervous anyway. He did not want to end up at the cotton mill.

But Gillan was right; he'd chosen a good company, and the foreman listened to his short tale silently before nodding, saying that he understood, he'd gotten the note, and his post had not been filled. Neil heaved a sigh of gratitude, nodding to Mr. Carter his thanks, and took up his duties just as before. Some of the men had eyed him with distaste, but at the dinner hour, he revealed what had taken him away for the week, and they clucked in sympathy, shaking their heads at the madness of the lairds and the changing times. A barrier, it seemed, had been breached.

Many of them were highlanders or islanders like him, and had come down from the hills and glens in the last year or two. Others were older transplants, having come out of the north a generation or two ago, after the 'Forty-Five. Glasgow was growing even then, although it wasn't until the past thirty years that the trade on the River Clyde had expanded so quickly that it was hard to hire labor fast enough to keep up with demand.

Besides freight, Neil was hearing that ship-building further west on the river was a booming industry. It was just as physically demanding, but took longer to learn, and so you had better security—you couldn't be replaced easily. Neil turned this over in his mind, resolving to check out some of the ship-building yards on his day off to see if he could manage a job there. Perhaps even Gillan could find a job there as well, and they could work together.

On his way home, he did not forget to stop in at the tavern and pay a call to thank Letty for her help. He wanted her to know his duty had been discharged, and his mother and younger siblings were all now safe and together. Letty's eyes went wide even with this brief retelling of the errand that had taken him away, and her forehead creased with concern.

"Don't be worried," he said. "It's all right now, thanks in part to you."

"I'm so sorry for it though," she said. "I do hope things will go better with you now." She crossed her arms.

"Today has been going well, for me, at any rate," he teased, and she blushed. She looked down, hiding her gaze. He admired her eyelashes, dark and long against her pale skin. She looked so different when she spoke to him from her heart—a very different picture from her early cool appraisal.

She looked up at him. "Oh, ye think so, do you?"

There was a teasing jibe in her tone, and he felt drawn in by the beauty of her. There was nothing left for it. Her eyes held an appeal he could not turn away from. Neil bent, and gently kissed her cheek. Letty stood stock-still as he did so, then her hand flew to her cheek where his lips had touched her. Their eyes met and it was a long moment before either moved.

Letty let her hand down and looked about to speak when her father raised a hoarse grumbling cry from the tavern room. She answered; the spell was broken. Neil dipped his head and bid her good night. His body fairly glowed with energy as she nodded and closed the door. He imagined what she had been about to say, all possibilities relating to how she felt just as he did. He started planning his next opportunity to see her, and floated above the earth on his walk home.

Chapter 15

Life took on a new shape. Sheila looked for a house for the family, and Jenny provided her with plenty of advice. It only took a few days of searching for her to find one close by in Laurieston at a reasonable rate that would allow Jenny and Charlie the use of their parlor again. The new place had the same setup as Jenny and Charlie's: two separate rooms for beds, a kitchen with a stove, and a sitting room with a fireplace at the wall. The privy was shared out back in the yard with the block of houses.

There was no place for a vegetable garden in the new place, but Sheila was kept busy with other tasks. They found a school for Sheena and Alisdair both, paid for in the church rates. They attended the kirk that Jenny and Charlie went to, and met some of the families in their yard that went with them each Sunday. Neil went with Charlie to one of the shipbuilding outfits further west of the city and was hired on as paid apprentice. But over all this settling-in activity, there was a feeling of impermanence. Sheila finally put a name to it one day in early November, after six weeks had gone by in their new home.

"We're country people, it's clear enough," she said, when the younger children were in bed, and she was knitting at the fireside. Neil and Muirne were out at a friend's ceilidh for the night. "Neil may do very well learning the ship-building, and you're doing well enough at the mill with Charlie, but I ken ye don't love it."

Gillan had snorted at this. "And how can I not love something that puts food on the table for my family, and a roof over their heads?"

"You don't love it the way you loved putting out and taking in the crops, and fishing in the sea. Oh, well," she revised. "Maybe you never loved keeping the nets in condition, but you felt it was good, honest work and you said when and how and where."

"And isn't this good, honest work I'm doing?" Gillan asked. "What would you have me do here? We're in a city, on a river, crowded with folks coming in from the countryside. It's not like there are folk clamoring for people to come work their land and become crofters."

"Not here," she said.

"No, not here," he repeated in a different tone. "And I'll not go halfway 'round the world looking for something that's gone, impossible, fantasy now, d'ye hear? I don't know what rumors ye've heard of the settlements in the Americas or wherever, but we'll stick with what we know and manage to keep the family together." Gillan's voice grew quiet. "I couldn't stand to hear of ye in such trouble again, d'ye ken that?"

"Aye," Sheila replied softly.

But she kept her ears open for opportunities nonetheless, and a short time later, one landed square in her lap.

Sheila and Muirne were paying a morning visit to Mrs. Murray, a woman Sheila had met at kirk and struck up a friendship with immediately. Isabel Murray had come from Mull to care for family one year and ended up marrying up and staying in the city. She'd been there five years now, and had two young children. Her husband worked at the same mill as Charlie and Gillan, but he was in charge of the hiring and wage-giving and seeing that all the government laws were followed.

Mrs. Murray was telling Sheila of a recent stramash over a strike. Of course, organized groups were illegal, but that hadn't stopped a group of men from walking out in high summer as the cotton production was just getting up again since the war years. It would have been devastating to stop the work then, and so Mr. Murray had commissioned a foreign agent to hire and transport eighty men out of Ireland to come work in the place of the men who were striking to teach them a lesson.

"And this 'foreign agent,' Sheila asked, "he goes only to Ireland, or to other foreign places as well?"

"Oh, from my husband's description, it sounds like he's been all over!" Mrs. Murray laughed and pondered the details. "I know he's even been to Australia once, but did not like it there. Disliked it so much in fact that he refused to deal with any fellow agents there, since he couldn't trust that they wouldn't be putting transported criminals back on a boat here with new names. The gall! When you think of it," she clucked her tongue in disapprobation.

Sheila put in delicately, "And the Americas?"

"Oh, them. Yes, I believe Harry's—I mean, Mr. Young, that is—" she cleared her throat, clearly self-conscious at what she'd revealed. "Mr. Young, my husband's agent, has been to Canada, the Maritimes, I believe, and Boston, on several occasions. I suppose that means that they've been successful scouting trips." Her voice fluttered. Sheila reached over and put her hand on the woman's wrist to still her knitting.

"Do you think you could ask Harry if he hears of any land opportunities in the Americas, to let us know?"

"Surely, I could. He's a devoted friend, working with my husband so closely and all—"

Sheila patted her wrist. "It's all right, you needn't worry."

They exchanged a glance, with fear and relief mixed on one side, and pity and hope on the other. As Muirne watched this exchange, she felt a slight prickle of foreboding. Was her mother truly thinking of leaving for the Americas?

* * *

It took some time for Mrs. Murray to come back with any news, and by that time, Sheila had also discreetly asked their minister, both the teachers at Sheena and Alisdair's school, and several others she knew with foreign connections, whether they could pass on any news of settlements or open land in the new territories. Sheila saw that while Neil was coping well enough learning his new trade and paying visits to his tavern girl, it was not the learning that she had hoped for him. And as for Gillan, the days inside the mill were breaking down his health, now that they were no longer tempered with outside work since the weather had turned cold and wet.

The fiber-congested air inside was making Gillan cough wretchedly. His chest constricted at intervals when she lay her head on it at night, as if he clenched the coughs down not to disturb her. But he couldn't fall asleep like that, surely? Perhaps that was why he took the swig of whisky laced with some other substance each night. He said the mill doctor had given it to him, that everyone at the mill took it at night.

Muirne kept busy helping her mother, but made no intimate friends. She stayed close to home, ran errands for her mother, and read the few books that she could get ahold of in the parish library. She felt uncomfortable with how people acted in the city, and talked to Neil about it one day.

He came home from the docks and plopped down into the spindly chair at the table to await supper. His face was relaxed, his eyes closed, and as Muirne watched, a small smile crept in. She tugged his sleeve and indicated the door. He heaved himself back up and followed her out, repeating his exaggerated manner of sitting on the ground in the front yard, where some straggling roses tried to grow. "What is it, Muirne?"

Muirne hemmed and hawed a moment. "You remember saying about how Miss Letty changed from a city person to a real person?"

Neil's expression of insouciance vanished and he sat up. He spoke low. "Yes. Why?"

"What is it about the city? Why do people go to such lengths, and play at being things they are not? I don't understand why we can't have gatherings like we did at home—if we had friends, I mean."

"We do have friends, Muirne. Wasn't Mother just out visiting Mrs. Murray? And there are Aunt Jenny's neighbors, who invited you to that outing—"

"But Mrs. Murray—" Muirne bit her bottom lip. "It's true, the girls next door, especially Marjorie, are very kind. But the other folk I meet, they just don't seem real, or practical, or— I don't know what I mean, only that people like Mrs. Murray don't inspire me to confide in them."

"Maybe you have to wait. Maybe it takes—something real —to make them forget their city manners. Like Letty." His voice softened.

Muirne crouched down to Neil's level. She saw the stars in his eyes and reached out a hand to push him off balance. "You."

"Hey!" Neil rolled over onto the dirt and jumped up to brush himself off. "You'll find someone, Muirne. Dinna worry."

"Find someone? Is it back to that again, then? Oh, Neil, if only there was some way I could. I'd love to be able to help, but I didn't notice any man at kirk that was not married and old enough. Well, there was that Joseph..." She let her voice trail off and rolled her eyes at Neil. Joseph had been the old codger who fell asleep at the last kirk meeting and entertained everyone with his practically-musical snoring pattern.

"Ah, no, he must be near seventy! Surely there are some good young men in the parish," Neil chided.

"Well, there are a handful of good-for-nothings whose mamas want to be rid of them, but not one man I saw who was in want of a wife that could actually provide for her. They're all snatched up," she said. She looked directly at Neil. "I'd help if I could, Neil, but..."

"Ye've done all right, Muirne. You're our mother's right hand, sure enough. Dinna worry about the other. It'll come out all right in the end."

Muirne sighed. Neil didn't know what would happen any more than she did, but he didn't worry about it as much. She'd try to adopt the same attitude.

* * *

News finally came to Sheila from her queries, and when it did, she heard it twice in the same day. First, the male schoolteacher paid them a call on a Sunday afternoon shortly before Christmas. He exuded good cheer, and even though the prospect of a thin Christmas loomed before them, the MacLeans smiled at his youthful energy as he sat with them around their rickety table.

"I have heard," began Mr. Cartwright, after the niceties had been exchanged, "that there is a new settlement party to be launched in the new year to reinforce the one started by the *Prince William*."

As no faces showed recognition, he explained. "The *Prince William* was the ship that sailed from here seven years past to Nova Scotia: New Scotland. It's one of the provinces of Canada, named by the Scots who have made it their home. Now, I hear it is very cold—"

This brought up a laugh, as they were experiencing one of the coldest Novembers on record in Scotland. "Oh, aye?" said Neil. "I think we'd be well prepared, then."

Gillan was standing off from this conversation, aloof and detached. He asked Mr. Cartwright the question but looked straight at Sheila. "And how much would it be for the ship's passage, and for the land once ye got there, sir?"

"Well, that is the interesting part," Mr. Cartwright replied, pulling a rolled piece of paper from his pocket and spreading it out on the table. "It says that the ship passage is £5 a person if ye can provide your own meal for five weeks. And it says that British citizens in good standing are allowed a fair plot of land that they can clear and make useful, for nothing!"

This statement was greeted with gasps and scoldings, for such a thing certainly could not be true. "No, it is," Mr. Cartwright insisted. "It seems they've adopted the Americans' public lands model to colonize the wilderness and the natives." Sheila's eyebrows raised.

"Yes, you'll have to get more information on the dangers, it seems," he said, his enthusiasm moderated a bit. He brightened again. "But I bet you there will be enough people in this next ship that you'll be able to settle together and have some safety in numbers if the native tribes are hostile. They may not be. You will just have to write and enquire. But I will have done my duty in bringing you the news, and can wish you the best of luck." He grinned broadly in a decidedly un-schoolmaster-like manner, then shook a glaring Gillan's hand. He bowed to Sheila, and took his leave.

Gillan appeared unable to speak until he crooked a finger at Sheila, and they went to sit in the box bed with the curtain drawn. The bevy of whispered words were indistinguishable, but Sheila emerged after a minute with a grim expression, smoothing her apron and retreating to the stove. Gillan went over to his chair to stare at the fire.

The family should have been cowed by this subdued conference, but instead they were abuzz with speculation about the new ship, which Mr. Cartwright's notice had called the *Amidou*. Gillan stiffly rose and went out, saying he'd go down to the pub with Charlie. In his wake came Mrs. Murray, with her baby daughter in tow.

Mrs. Murray skipped the niceties altogether, opening her visit with, "Mrs. MacLean, I have *such* good news for you from Harry!" And she in turn brought out a rolled piece of paper containing the same news as before: "SAIL TO CANADA, £9 BOARD, £5 OWN MEAL, ABOARD THE *AMIDOU*."

When the younger children broke into loud laughter, Sheila hurried to explain they'd had the news from their schoolmaster just this afternoon, but perhaps Mrs. Murray knew more about the situation in Canada?

"Indeed I do. Mr. Young has explained that they need hardy folk, as the winters are very harsh there in the Maritimes, but that you could be sure of Scots neighbors and your right to worship as you like, as well as the sixty acres promised in the settlement incentive."

"The what?" asked Sheila. She told them that there had been an expedition ship two years before, but the settlement needed reinforcements, especially in order to keep the region firmly under British control.

The visit was finished before too long. Sheila went to set up the dough for the next day's bread. It came together in her hands naturally, sticky but pliant enough when warmed. Muirne watched her as she kneaded and turned it on the table, kneaded and turned.

She took most of her cues from her mother: when to allow informality, how to convince Gillan of a course of action, when to demand an apology, how to calm Sheena after a nightmare. All these things she'd learned from observing her mother, never explicitly being told one thing or another. But now, Sheila spoke not a word about the radical changes confronting them. Muirne tried to examine her own thoughts, as she knew her mother was doing, with her kneading and turning.

Father seems afraid. Afraid for us, I imagine. Mother seems worried too, but more about what will happen to us if we keep on as we are, not about the unknown. Which is harder, when you come down to it? After you've been torn from the place you were planted, what pain is there in continuing to drift for a little while longer? Why not see more of the world before settling for this noisy, bone-rattling city existence? I certainly don't care for it. And Neil seemed to be doing well with the shipwrights, but he might do just as well in this New Scotland. And perhaps that Letty of his would come too, if he asked her.

"What are you thinking of, Mother?" Muirne asked.

"Oh, just chewing on the news of the *Amidou*." She paused in her kneading to plop the dough in the metal tin and set it on the shelf in the wall near the chimney. "What's in your thoughts, Muirne? Would ye stay or go?"

"Go," she said immediately.

"Why so quick?"

"Because we're a family for the country." She met her

mother's gaze seriously. "I can see Father's failing. He breathes in that fluff all day. I've only been by the cotton yard a couple of times, but when I peeked my head in at the door, I could hardly see through it. It's a wonder they've not all got cotton wadding in their lungs. I don't know how the others stand it."

"Aye. It does seem to affect him more. But for yourself? There's nothing to keep you here in Scotland, then?"

"Oh, of course I'd rather stay here, Mama, but there's no place for us anymore, is there?" Muirne's gaze dropped to the hearth. She saw their blackhouse again, engulfed in flames.

"You're right," Sheila said softly, the same sight imprinted against her closed eyelids for a brief second. "It's just that your father didn't see it happen, so it's harder for him to let go."

Chapter 16

Christmas approached with little fanfare. Even with the two men's wages, the rent of the house and food for the table ate up almost all the income for the MacLeans. Their winter store was sadly diminished, as they'd had to leave all the kail and cabbage, and most of the neeps and potatoes in the ground when they left. The salted and smoked food, the fish and pork, was carefully rationed out by Sheila. She did not want to use any of their precious coin savings; she was hoarding it for their passage on the ship.

The poster had not said when the *Amidou* would sail, but it was likely not before winter storms were past and calm weather was at least a possibility. With this in mind, Sheila had once again taken out her loom, piece by piece, even the singed bits. She gathered what wool she could find, cleaning it as best she was able, and spinning it by the firelight in the evenings, then weaving the threads into sturdy blankets and clothing that she could sell. Muirne joined her sometimes, watching and taking a hand in.

Sheila had not taught her how to set up the warp, but she had picked up the rhythm of passing the shuttle through the shed and pulling the beater down, passing it back, and repeating the process. Sheila had confided in Muirne her first plan to sell, and so she did with this second. Muirne asked what she could do to contribute, beyond working the weft. Sheila taught her how to make decorative baskets from rushes. They collected the rushes in the mornings after breakfast by the small burn that was untouched by the mill waste, and plaited them in the evenings after supper.

When Sheena was let off from day school a few days before Christmas, the three of them made a round of the houses by the grand park just south of the city. They called from the street like fishwives, proclaiming their baskets and woven cloth the best this side of the Tyne. It was almost like play-acting, and they enjoyed the activity together. Sheila was disappointed by how little they made Christmas week, perhaps because the cloth was not properly waulked. If she'd been at home on Mull, no doubt she could have gotten together a group of her women friends for a waulking, where the cloth was pulled and stretched while wet to make it tighter. There would have been a dozen or so friends around a table, and the singing of special songs.

But no matter, Sheila was determined to keep going. They had enough for three people's passage: £15, the result of their savings after a year of ups and downs. "If it is not this ship, it will be the next," Sheila vowed to Muirne.

Gillan took no notice of their activities, or at least did not let on. He returned from the mill, and Neil returned from the docks at about the same time. If one was early at the crossroads before their little street, he waited for the other. There were a few moments then, to communicate any large or small thing that had happened at work that was not to be discussed in front of the women. So far, it was merely an opportunity for Gillan to chuck Neil in the shoulder and tease him about the man he'd become.

A few times now, Neil had been a quarter of an hour late, and he had begged Gillan's pardon, he'd made a brief visit to Miss Letty. That just gave Gillan more ammunition for teasing, but he didn't do it in front of everyone, knowing that the boy would come to it, telling the family his intentions in his own time.

* * *

The day before Christmas, Neil's head was swarming. He'd heard from Muirne about the selling of the blankets and the baskets, and his mother's hopes to leave Scotland. He was getting on fine with the men at the dockyard, and felt well enough suited to the hard work, but he wondered how they were to ever settle in, if they were only just scraping by. Would they ever build a new house of their own? Not if they didn't own the land. Maybe settling in the Americas would be worth it, if they got to start over.

The option of further schooling was no longer on the table. They would have to hope that Sheena and Alisdair got even as much education as he had. He would teach them to read himself if he had to, but when? He left before sunrise and came home in time for supper, then had a few minutes to relax before falling asleep.

School, his siblings, land, time. The routine of his new life and its worries buzzed around his head until he had to shake himself. He stopped in the street, and looked up to find the Dog and Duck Pub. At this hour, there were plenty of customers dropping by for their drop of ale after work, or workers coming to order their supper if they did not have a wife at home. Neil stood and watched the flow of people for a minute before he saw Letty through the front window. She was setting down a wooden trencher with a large piece of roast meat before two gentlemen. They were a tad overdressed for the quality of the establishment, Neil thought. Letty's usual serving apron covered a dark green dress with white trim at the neck. Her hair was held back with a green kerchief.

As she turned, the gentleman on the left caught her arm. He said something to her, and Neil felt his fists clench and his blood race. She deftly removed her arm from his grip and threw him a sardonic glance, before looking up and seeing Neil outside.

Letty's face blanched. She hurried away, and the gentleman turned to see what had caused her about-face. He took in Neil standing in the street, glaring at him through the window, tossed off a comment that made his companion laugh, then turned back to his meal.

Neil continued glaring at them until Letty came through the side door, wrapping a shawl around herself. She was upset, if her jerky movements and frustrated puffs of air were any indication. He stepped out of the street to where she stood near the door.

"Letty, are you well? What was—?"

"What was what, Neil?" She raised a hard pair of eyes to his. "Me doing my job and humoring the customers? What do you think?"

"It looked like that man was being too forward, that's all. I wouldn't allow someone to be rude to you like that."

"Oh, you wouldn't, eh?" She said it with a dry, disbelieving humor, and Neil felt the cold mask of her city manners fall between them.

"Letty, please. I want to—that is, I'd like to—" He stopped and cleared his throat. "Letty, I wonder if you would —"

"Oh!" she cried out, and flung herself at him. This was no

chaste kiss like the ones he'd been leaving her with. Letty had her arms round his neck, one hand in his hair and the other pulling him down to her mouth. She kissed him passionately, and he responded. Her breasts pushed against his chest, and he reached around to pull her closer. His loins responded as well, and he felt himself swelling, aching to push farther into her.

He gasped at this thought and broke contact, stepping back and almost tripping over the barrels lined up outside the tavern. He put a hand back to stop himself and straightened. Letty gaped, waiting for him to explain his sudden breaking away.

"Letty," he said softly. She came to him more calmly then, and he rubbed his right hand over her back. "I'm sorry. I should never have—"

"I don't care. Neil, what were you going to say?" He saw the hope in her eyes then, a hint of a smile. He felt emboldened again, but tried to hold his body firmly in check.

"Letty, would you come to America if I were to go?"

"I—what?" Her hopeful face had transformed into creases of worry and open-mouthed fear. "America?"

"Aye—or Canada. My family have been thinking—"

"Canada? Sail off? But, Neil—" She reined in her discomposure, smoothing her forehead and pressing her lips together. Her voice dropped to a low growl and her gaze remained downcast as well. "I thought you were going to ask for permission to go *courting.*"

"Well, of course, there's that as well," Neil said, laughing. He grasped her left arm and dipped his head down to put himself in her line of vision. Reluctantly she met his gaze. His confidence pushed him to bubble over. "But Letty, there's a chance we could—"

"I can't leave. I don't want to hear about it. You can't ask it of me! Don't—don't come here anymore, Neil." She shook

herself and his hands lifted in shock. She walked resolutely
back into the tavern, and Neil was left standing in the cold, his
hands outstretched and his face registering just how lost he
felt.

* * *

Neil was several minutes late meeting his stepfather at the
crossroads. Gillan was not surprised, and waited composedly
on one of the white-painted rocks, watching the people scurry
along. A large carriage trundled by with two long buckboards
on each side of the driver, open instead of a proper roof. It
was pulled by a pair of sweaty draft horses, and the party of
people on top looked as if they were having a gay time of it.
Happy chatter, with the slow cadence of a day well spent in
energetic pursuits, reached Gillan's ear as he sat on his rock at
the side of the road.

"...*Greenock never looked so well*..."

"...*shall always be in my memory*..."

"...*the best holiday*..."

After the omnibus roared past, it stopped for a passenger
to alight and return to her home nearby. Gillan pondered the
episode. Some of the men at work had talked of these holiday
omnibuses, that take you away for the day and bring you back
for a fee lower than a hired cab, since it was a shared con-
veyance. It seemed a popular pursuit here, no doubt because
people liked to get away from their work and forget their
misery. Gillan's heart constricted a bit as he thought that. *Oh,
for my work at home*, he pined. Of course, Sheila'd been right
when she talked of him not being made to work in the guts of
a machine. But what could he do? He needed to support his
family.

At last, the tread of Neil's well-worn shoes interrupted his reverie. Neil looked up from his feet to Gillan's waiting gaze, but his expression was inscrutable.

"Not had a good session with Letty, then?"

"No, I was not with her this time. She was busy."

"Well, then—"

"I cannot say, Father. I have been walking. That—is all I can say for now."

Gillan scanned Neil's face for signs of trouble. Had he taken drink? Had a shock? Been thrown out of the tavern by Letty's father? He saw evidence of none of these things, only Neil's effort to keep his face neutral, while a vast mountain of sadness ate at his heart. Gillan's own mountain threatened to bury him when he saw that. Without speaking, they both turned toward home.

* * *

While Christmas fell in the middle of the week that year, the managers at the mill had done them the great favor of closing for the day, and so the next morning, the family went off to kirk together. Gillan noticed Neil's continued downcast face, but waited to question him. If it was a lovers' quarrel, he'd explain as soon as his gloom was shaken off.

The service was not a long one, and many people were in a good mood, having had a special meal the night before, and seeing the prospect of another one before them. For the MacLeans, it was a time for giving thanks that they survived. Indeed, Gillan had not got all the news of his family's journey out of Sheila, and he suspected there was something she did not share, that Neil had seen or been part of. It had marked them. Gillan saw it especially in the way that Muirne looked at Neil like he was her savior, the way Sheila proudly gazed on her son.

For the first time in a long while, Gillan felt left out of the family circle, the way he had when he and Sheila had first married, and he'd had to prove himself a father to the three small children from her first marriage. He shook those thoughts out of his head and concentrated on the final benediction. All of a sudden, he knew what would fix it: *I'll take them on one of those omnibus holidays!*

It was too late to do today, but he marked the spot where he'd seen the passenger alight and had vaguely recognized the lady; he would find her and ask how to request a place. As soon as he'd thought of it, he stood a little taller, and reached for his wife's hand. She looked up at him from the side, surprised. He merely smiled and looked back to the front. She looked back toward the minister as well, wondering what had come over her husband, but giving thanks that it was lifting his melancholy.

After the service, Sheila had planned to take the step of appealing to the parish authorities for food, as she knew she only had the bit of barley harvested and few of their smoked fish to last them through another month. The loss of their vegetable store was a blow from which they could not recover this season. She sought out one of the church board members' wives and explained her need.

If she had expected kindness on this day of Christ's birth, she would have to keep looking, as the lady's expression changed to one of repugnance as she realized what Sheila was asking for. "Yes, yes, we can put your name on the rolls. Another MacLean, is it?" she said idly, marking it down with her fountain pen on a ready piece of paper in her reticule.

"It's bread and a strong broth we provide, and ye can pick it up yoursel's every Monday and Friday."

"Thank you, ma'am, and best wishes for Christmas, ma'am."

She ducked her head and headed back to her family, her cheeks stinging a little, but the weight on her chest lessened a bit. When she reached Gillan and saw how nicely turned out her family was, what good manners her children had, her spirits rose even higher. She combed her fingers through Alisdair's lank hair, looking up to find Gillan's gaze.

"Shall we go?"

Chapter 17

The next day Gillan did manage to hunt down the figure he'd seen getting down from the omnibus. It was a Mrs. Jones in the street across the main trunk road, and she gave him the information readily enough, wishing him a happy Christmas as well.

He planned it for the Sunday after Christmas. Instead of kirk, he would take them on a holiday to Greenock, where they would be in a much better frame of mind to be thankful to God for all His blessings, anyway. When he told them on the Saturday before, they clapped with delight at his idea.

"Now, make sure that ye pack well in your warmest, and keep the warm stones at your feet," he managed before he was covered in hugs from his two daughters and young son.

"Eh, now, let him be. We've got to be up and washed and dressed. Did ye no hear?" Neil poked at Alisdair, who was hanging onto Gillan's leg.

"Yes, yes! I hear'd it. Just wait!" And he scampered out to the privy and then the pump to wash. Neil grinned at the high-pitched cry, and delighted himself in watching his sisters and mother fall to, hunting for their heaviest capes and the extra plaids.

They were off early the next morning, and easily acquaint-ed themselves with the other passengers seated on the buck-board slats. As each person entered, the driver collected the fee, a few shillings each, and wished them a merry holiday.

"And have you been to Greenock a'fore, sir?" the large matron beside Gillan asked. He shook his head. "Ah, it's beau-tiful to be by the sea," she said with a sigh.

It was a frosty morning, although there was no snow on the ground, and the company shared out the blankets, amass-ing body warmth through chatter and laughter. With the horses at a brisk trot, it took them above two hours to make the seaside town. The driver collected the stones people had brought and promised to set them in the fire at the public house where he was headed. "See you then at three o'clock!" he shouted to each party as they set off.

The MacLeans made their way leisurely through the main road of the town to wander down the dunes to the sea. It was churning white and green, and there were many ships of all stripes and shapes to observe, as the Port of Glasgow was not far off the mouth of the river.

Sheila and Muirne carried their baskets with provisions, while Sheena had their large quilt folded under both arms. They fanned out and pointed out different sights on the water to each other. Neil saw that Gillan had drifted farthest to the right, north towards the river, and stopped. He saw his father's hands in his pockets, his back rigid with tension.

Neil called to him but he did not hear. Worried, Neil jogged over to him, touched his shoulder. "Father, what's wrong?"

For an answer, Gillan merely nodded ahead of him. Turn-ing, Neil saw what he had seen that had rattled him so. With the last winter storm on the coast, wreaths of tangled kelp stems were strewn across the bank and up above on the hills. They were not set out for drying; in fact, it looked like some had been torched where they were, but they had not burned long so close to the waves.

The initial reaction Neil had was a surge of pride: *What bounty we have on our shores!* But then he realized it was sitting to rot and float away, and he understood his stepfather's rigidity. It was fury, both at the turn of events and at his impotence to stand up to them. *What a waste.* He pulled at his sleeve, willing him to come away before the girls came to look for him as well.

"Aye, 'tis a waste, Father, but dinna dwell on it today. You've had a fine idea for a holiday, and I shan't waste it, or ruin it for the others. Let's go."

Gillan nodded. His eyes were moist with tears. He clasped Neil's arm. "Aye, I'll come. I jis'—"

He did not finish his thought, but Neil knew what he meant. They shook off the feeling of rage that had fallen on them both at the sight of their former livelihood going to rot on the beach. Neil cleared his throat. "I asked Letty if she'd be up for travel to the New World if I was to go. She said no."

Gillan turned to look at Neil, his eyebrows lifted.

"I thought I may as well get all the sad news out at once." Neil explained. "Now we can enjoy ourselves, then."

Neil gave him a brief smile. Gillan shook his head slowly, following. Within sight of the rest of the party, Gillan made a great effort to appear cheerful. He threw himself down on the sand near where Alisdair was seated, digging in the sand for crabs or clams, and asked to be buried.

With glee, Alisdair made a move to slop the wet sand at his father, and Gillan rolled out of the way in time. He had them all laughing again soon.

Chapter 18

The trip to the shore buoyed everyone's spirits. Then it was time to make plans for Hogmanay, the celebration of the new year. This always involved a grand affair of a meal, a large variety of drinking games for the men, and First Footing, with special presents to be given in the darkness after midnight. It was something the MacLean children usually looked forward to for weeks on the island but had not held out much hope for this year: Hogmanay depended on the friends you had.

True, Jenny and Charlie's family would host a good party, but Muirne pined for their own village's celebration, where Katie Miller would be slipping the whisky to the younger lads, and Mrs. McCall would be howling down the plagues of Heaven on anyone out of their beds. Those familiar notes of anticipation crept back, all the more attractive as they approached the holiday.

Sheila and Muirne debated whether to give some of their baskets as gifts or keep them to sell. Could they afford it? Yes, it was decided. They were packed with sachets of herbs picked along the river, jellies of gooseberries gathered from brambles, and spicy ginger biscuits, that wonderful holiday treat. Never mind that they were receiving their broth and meal from the parish store, the women were determined to continue their tradition of generosity on this day.

They managed to procure most of a shoulder of lamb, and Sheila made sure it was in the pot all day, long enough to become tender and richly flavored with its own fat and the luxurious spices she had come by: white pepper and coriander. She reminded herself that this was the one time in the year when they celebrated so, and that every other coin they made was going to necessities or to their ship passage fund. They would make it up, somehow.

Hogmanay started on the Wednesday, so that many of Gillan's and Neil's fellow workmen left before the ending bell had been rung. The highlanders that made up the shipbuilding crews, the islanders that made up the weavers and machinists and engineers—they all were going to keep their traditional rite sacred. Neil, having waited for a cue to when he might leave without repercussions, felt a bit of pride swell his chest, as he followed a knot of other men out the large warehouse gate.

His mother had somehow managed a feast, and the sun had only just set. With the darkness coming early, there would be many hours of storytelling, feasting, and singing to go before it was midnight and the new year welcomed in. They had not yet spoken of which houses they would go visit, but it was in Neil's mind to visit Letty's house. While she had said no to accompanying him across the sea, it was only common courtesy to wish your acquaintances well in the new year.

They began with *A Chaorain, A Chaorain!* and joined together, dancing and singing after the meal. It was snug and warm in the house, filled as it was with good cheer. Eventually, the time was come to suit up for the first footing. Sheila would stay home with the two younger children, and the older two would go out to hallo their neighbors. Sheena rubbed the fog off the window pane and exclaimed, "It's snowed!"

The others came rushing over to see, and indeed, a soft white powder was covering everything they could see in the circle of light cast by their door torch, prepared earlier for the visitors who might come. The big white flakes still floated down serenely, and Neil's stomach clenched before he realized they reminded him of the cotton in the mill. He tried to let go of the tension in his spine. He still felt such fear at the possibility of having to work there, but was not sure why. It was a feeling of premonition perhaps, since it did not attach to Gillan, only himself. God knows he felt sorry for Gillan working there, but there wasn't the cold fear about it. Neil shrugged again, shaking it off.

They weren't sure of the etiquette of First Footing here in Laurieston, their little neighborhood next to Hutchesontown where Jenny lived, but Gillan meant to visit those closest to them first; his setting foot on the threshold would be a sign of good luck to come for the new year for that family. What if they had already been visited? Well then, they could still present the basket of gifts and pass on a dram of the home-made quality whisky bottle Gillan carried.

They visited first the six houses in their own close. They weren't on social terms with any of these families yet, but they were still surprised to see not a single lit torch at a door, nor a light from inside. The silence in the close disconcerted the little group until Gillan turned to them from the last door at which there was no answer and suggested a visit to Jenny's street. They knew at least two families there would be celebrating. Spirits lifted, they walked the half-mile and found lights blazing and sounds of merriment escaping through the windows.

They knocked at the Atchesons' door and were pleased to

learn they were still the first to come by. It was, after all, only half past twelve. They took their time making toasts and singing songs at each house, inching their way closer to Jenny's house. Gillan left it for last, since he knew they would stay for a long spell to sing and drink everyone's better fortune in the new year.

Neil tugged on Gillan's sleeve, cocking his head to the north. "Could we no' try Letty's first before Auntie's? They're likely to have visitors already, but it would only be a moment, and she'd get to see you."

Gillan straightened his shoulders and puffed out his chest, seeing Neil's intention to show this girl his wealth: his family. He nodded; it would do very well. The tavern was only five minutes' walk up the road, and the merry band all covered the distance quickly. Gillan had his torch in one hand, whisky in the other, while Neil and Muirne walked with arms linked, suffused with warmth from within against the cold air at their cheeks and snow beneath their feet.

The tavern looked still to be open on this night, with its front room lights ablaze and its chimney smoking away. Neil looked at Gillan and shrugged. "Maybe they're providing a feast for the neighbors," he said, although he doubted it, with visions of how curmudgeonly Letty's father appeared. *Still, perhaps for the holiday*, Neil allowed.

Neil knocked on the door. In answer, a scowling, wrinkled face appeared at the window briefly before yanking the curtains closed at first one pane, then the other. The silence stretched for a moment, then two, and still no one answered the door. Neil was speechless. *Refusing to receive visitors to bless your house—it was just not done. What were they on about?* Neil felt a hand on his sleeve: Muirne.

"If they don't want us, we should leave," she whispered to Neil. He saw she was scared, put off by the ill treatment.

Saints! Neil thought to himself. *This isn't how I thought it would go.* And so sighing, he turned away, and they followed, walking slowly back to Jenny's.

Neil did not look back, but Muirne did, and she saw a pale face peering out from the first-floor window. She didn't catch more than a flash, but figured it was the girl who Neil had been talking to for these past several months. *Why had she not come down? Why was she hiding? I shall pay her a call the first week of the new year, and size her up then*, she thought.

The short gloom was dispelled as soon as they regained Jenny's street, and saw her house all aglow with torchlight and holly, the windows steamed up with the warmth within. A family from their own island, after all, knew how to welcome a guest who came with blessings and gifts to hand. They finished up their rounds, smiling and carousing a bit with the neighbors already enjoying Jenny and Charlie's hospitality.

Gillan looked into his bottle. "I see there are about two drops left, so for the sake of all that is good, please tell me you've not run out." His grin was wide and silly, and he wove a bit on the threshold.

Jenny made a sound somewhere between a grunt and a giggle, welcoming her brother first with a dubious glance, then open arms. They embraced, Gillan saying the blessing of the new year to her. They stayed that way a long time, in the way of those who have been overexcited and do well with a moment to calm themselves. Charlie smiled, Muirne's eyes brimmed with happy tears, and the younger children of the house, who'd either been allowed to stay up, or just woken up with the ruckus, howled with excitement.

There was indeed more whisky. After many rounds of singing and stuffing themselves with almond sweets, they made to go. Jenny waved them off with a last dram. "It'll keep you warm all the way into your beds," she said. "Up Helly A!

Look!"

And sure enough, down at the end of their street, even in the snow, there was a miniature ship built, ablaze with fire, and several men dancing about it, singing high and loud. This was a tradition from the Shetlands, and it appeared the next close held a fair pack of them. One of the ship-bearers looked their way at Jenny's shout, and raised his torch to them in silent salute.

The MacLeans were glad to stand witness to the ritual burning, and see the clansmen, honoring their Viking roots, destroying the past and making way for the future. Muirne held Neil's hand, her one glance confirming that she was yet glad their mother was not here to be so close to the flaming structure. After a few minutes, Gillan spoke. "Clearing away the old to make room for the new. Aye. Well, let's away home, lads and lasses. There will be work again early tomorrow."

They made their way home. Gillan extinguished his torch in the light layer of snow piled by their door and set it to the side of their step. The torch in the bracket next to their own door was still burning, if feebly. They toddled in, suddenly yawning and tired, but not too far gone to see their mother. She was seated at the table with a candle. Sheena dozed at her side, her head resting on Sheila's arm.

"What, are you waiting up for us, lovely wife?" Gillan asked. A note of nervous worry had crept into his chuckle. All four felt the presence of some sadness in the stillness in Sheila's body.

"Aye, of course," she replied. "No one's been to call on us, so I'm still awaiting my tall, dark stranger to come and bless the house."

"Well! It's a good thing I was first to cross the sill then!" said Gillan, who had dark hair, whereas her first husband's children all had blonde or reddish-blonde hair. Gillan rushed to her side to kiss her cheek, cupping her face in his hand, feeling the evidence of weeping. They'd been gone almost three hours, and no one had visited for the new year.

Sheena stirred, and Muirne took her hand and squeezed it. Gillan spoke again, "Well, let's have it then, gather round for the last one."

He motioned for them to circle Sheila and grasp hands. "Lord, we invite you into this home in the New Year. Let it be a place of joy, of love, and of faith in You. Help us to live good lives following the example of Your Son. And help us when we are in need," he finished in a garbled voice. He cleared his throat. "Anyone else?"

"We've had a wonderful time visiting our neighbors, Mother," Muirne said quietly. "I wish you could have come." She leaned across the circle and put her arms around her mother's shoulders. Sheena hugged her waist, and Neil leaned over them all. Gillan placed a kiss on the top of her head.

"There now," he said. "That should be able to cure anything."

Sheila smiled, her head still down. "Aye."

Chapter 19

Wintry days piled on after that, with the men's work pace slowing but little to accommodate the weather patterns and delays of ships on their rounds. Sheila had found every chink in their little cottage by now, plugging the holes with the rags she'd torn from their own blackhouse walls and moss gathered from the small burn by the western road to Paisley. The fire was now always going by nightfall to welcome the men back to the house after their long day, as well as give light for the needlework Muirne had taken on to earn extra money.

She was no expert, but she took the pieces that needed time to sort out, rather than those that needed to be show-pieces in a front parlor. She'd met a woman at one of Aunt Jenny's ceilidhs who did piecework regularly and asked if she could help with any of the more practical bits, and that is how she'd gotten this side work. Muirne felt proud to find another way to contribute, even if she often had to retrace her work and redo stitches in the tablecloths and pillowcases.

By the end of February, their friend Mrs. Murray had again come in with a notice. "Am I first with the news this time?" she asked. Assured that she was, she brimmed with excitement. "The *Amidou*, it's set a date for the settlement party. It's to be early April, the 9th. Look right here at what I found!"

She pulled a wrinkled paper from her reticule. "AMIDOU SAILING FOR NOVA SCOTIA, NEW SETTLEMENTS ARRANGED, APRIL 9th, INQUIRE FOR TICKETS BY APRIL 3rd." There were other details in smaller type, but Sheila looked up at Mrs. Murray. "That is certainly very useful news, Anna. Thank you for bringing it to us. Did you only just see this paper?"

"Only just. But you're not the only family I promised news of the sailing, so I'll have to be off again right away."

Sheila rose with her, noting that the self-important woman folded the paper back up and tucked it into her bag. "And how shall I find out the other details, Mrs. Murray? Was there somewhere I could find a similar notice?"

"Oh, yes, of course. They're all along the riverside. Just ask your Neil, he works there, doesn't he? He should be able to pluck one off a tree."

With that, she flounced out. Sheila felt the beginning of a headache coming on. Mrs. Murray was more an acquaintance than a friend, and her infrequent visits always tended to have this effect. *Maybe it was the way she always thought she was doing you a favor by coming*, Sheila thought. Whatever it was, it had started to rub her the wrong way. In one way though, she was thankful. *April 3rd.*

That gave her almost two months. Sheila now looked at all their possessions, carried with such pain over the long distance from Mull. She decided to confront Gillan about his noncommittal attitude to the idea. She waited for an evening hour when the younger children were abed and he was not instantly asleep. She caught his attention at the table where he was picking out the stones from his shoe soles and beckoned him over to the corner seat where she was sewing. He pulled over one of the stools and sat in front of her, and for a moment Sheila was distracted, seeing the way his eyes lingered on her ears. His next move would be to tuck a stray hair behind her ear, she knew. Before his hand got past his thigh however, she spoke directly.

"Gillan, I've been wanting to ask you about something."

"And what is that?"

"Why do you never speak about taking the ship? You seem not to want to leave here, but not to be in love with your job, either." She looked at him, enquiring. Neil's ears perked up at this question, as he very much wanted to hear the answer as well. He sat extremely still at his post near the fire, where he was reading a tract borrowed from the parish library.

"I do not love it except that it puts food on the table and a roof over our heads," he said. "And a ship to the Americas? I am trying not to put fool hopes into the heads of the children. If this is our lot, then we shouldn't go filling them up with dreams of faraway places and free land and all the rest of it. 'Twill only make the living here harder."

"But what if we can do it, what if we managed the money for the fares? Wouldn't you be happier there, with the forests, and the sea, and the clean air to breathe, a patch of land ours to claim as we would?"

"I might very well be. But did ye hear how much it is? Five pounds! And the six of us? We'll never save that sort of money."

"I've already enough saved for three tickets and more, Gil. From the weaving and the barley before we left." She said this quietly, but he started, and grabbed hold of her elbows.

"Ye've what?"

"Shh, don't wake them." Her eyes indicated the sleeping

forms of Sheena and Alisdair on the floor of the sitting room. Her eyes skimmed over Neil's head as she continued, and his ears perked up.

"We had those few pounds saved for Neil's school, and then I was trying my hardest in the summer to weave for the fair, and that went pretty well, but we had to leave anyway, and—"

Her voice hiccupped and she started shaking. Neil glanced over to see her whole back trembling. His mother was finding it hard to breathe. He looked away, listening intensely to what his stepfather would say.

"Easy now, Sheila, dinna fash yerself so. D'ye mean ye did have the rents all made up, even with the terrible yield from the ash?"

Sheila kept her head bent but nodded.

"Oh, mo nighean, what a wonder you are." He wrapped an arm around her side, his other hand cradling her neck, and he rocked her back and forth. Neil glanced at them again, sensing a private moment, but wanting desperately to hear the outcome of theis discussion of leaving Scotland altogether.

"Why did ye never tell me afore?"

Sheila drew in a slow, measured breath that wheezed, and Neil jumped up to dip a cup into the water pail and come to his mother with it. "'Cuz I didna want to get—yer hopes—up. I wanted to wait—until I had it all, or al—almost." She took a brief sip and closed her eyes.

"You wee rascal. What a hoard!" Neil looked at Gillan's face but he had eyes only for Sheila. "Do ye want it that much, mo cridhe? Leaving everything behind?"

Neil watched his mother. She handed the cup back to Neil and laid a hand on his. She looked at him, then at Gillan, as she lay her other hand on his. "Aye."

Gillan finally looked over at Neil, kneeling between them.

He cleared his throat. "Then we've the three left to save up for, eh? By April, is it? A little more than six weeks. Mmm..."

Both Neil and Sheila had their gazes trained on Gillan's, waiting for his judgment.

"We'll try it. If you've the heart to hope for it, I'll do it for you." He gathered her up again, and rubbed her back with one hand while she calmed down the agitation of long-suppressed emotion. After a few moments, he pulled away to look her in the eye.

"We shall do it, mo cridhe. I shall see what I can do for extra time at the mill."

"And I at the yards," Neil put in, his voice quiet but firm.

Gil turned slightly to acknowledge him again. "And we'll move back in with Jenny to save the rent of this place for March. We shall see that money in six weeks."

Sheila let go a last shaky sigh, and smiled at him. "Six weeks," she repeated.

* * *

The time sped by. Gillan told Jenny and Charlie of the plan as well, and they agreed to host them for the final month. It was risky, since if the boss learned of his intended departure, Gillan might be forced to give over his post, and they might not make the full thirty pounds in time. But Gillan had committed to believing it would happen. He, too, started passing his eye over all they had. What could fetch a fair price, with everyone around so impoverished? These were cruel decisions.

His father's tools? No, they'd very likely need those to build with in Canada. His mother's jet brooch, which he'd given to Sheila when he asked her to marry him? Of course not. Their plates? Aye, they could do without all of them, although they were no so very fine. Sheila's lace shawl, that she'd had made by an old woman on the island who knew the ways of Belgian lace-makers? Never.

Their few last treasures. He knew Sheila was doing the same, as night after night, he followed her eyes, casting around the little sitting room and coming back to her own plate in defeat. She was still at the loom every night, weaving, and he saw Muirne bent over mending tasks beside her in the firelight. Neil had taken up running messages in the evening for the municipal captain of police, as he'd learned that apprentices could only get a set fee no matter how long they worked. For a couple hours he earned a few shillings, not bad at all, although he could only burn the candle at both ends for a little longer before his attention at his job failed and he made a careless mistake.

Sheena had taken to searching the fields several miles south of town for kindling and turf-pieces so they would not have to use their money for coal or turf. Alisdair went with her to help carry. It seemed everyone had a function, and was pulling hard for those five weeks. They must have seemed either quite the industrious family, or quite the avaricious one, to any neighbors who cared to look. But as evidenced by the first footing, it seemed none did.

They took this in stride, instead joining in the rowdy ceilidhs at Jenny's house many Saturday nights, when other friends dropped in. Gillan would greet them, and Jenny would introduce him and his family. On one of these occasions, it was Letty's father who came by.

He had the unfortunate name, in that neighborhood, of George, for it was the name of the former king gone mad and the current Prince Regent, a generally despised fop. The man did not let on that he knew it was unpopular, seeming unaware of the tiny damper in energy that went round when he was introduced.

"George Cameron, aye, pleased to make yer acquaintance. Now, have ye heard that song of Jenny's porter, yet? That is one of my favorites." And so saying, he launched into a sprightly tune. Gillan wondered how he had been able to get away from his Saturday custom duties at the tavern, and Neil wondered if he knew of his visits to Letty.

That question was well settled, as, during the song, Mr. Cameron sang a verse about the porter being brewed by the barman's daughter, and stared straight at Neil as he did so. Then it was *hup* to the next verse, and the thinly-veiled malice dissipated. *Was it malice?* Neil wondered. *Or simply spite and possession?* He could not be sure, but he had not been by the tavern for several weeks, and did not plan to return by that way again, now that they had made the decision to sail and he was occupied by all the messenger runs in the evenings.

Mr. Cameron made no other move toward him, but got up to sing another song later in the night, which concerned a lass wasting away for her love. It was a sad ballad, and his voice was a decent one, so the company listened attentively. Neil watched to see if his eye would be turned on him again. Sure enough, for the last verse, George Cameron turned on him, and hurled out the words with feeling.

> *He has gain away, gain away*
> *Never to be seen more*
> *And I shall ne'ever be the same*
> *Lass as before*

Neil shifted uncomfortably. Was the man implying he'd made Letty unhappy by stopping his visits? She'd been the one to say no, so he didn't think it his place to insist. He'd been taught by his father, and then by Gillan, that an honorable man did not insist once a lady had declared her intent. And then the treatment at Hogmanay, where the man had turned his back on well-wishing guests!

Neil kept his head down as the others clapped for Mr. Cameron's song. The man left soon after, and Neil felt a pang of guilt, or regret; he was not sure. All he knew was though he was committed to emigrating with his family, some part of him wished he could bring Letty along, too.

Chapter 20

"How much is it, then?"

Sheena had the task of counting all the silver and copper coins amassed in the family treasury this time, and she was apparently taking too long for everyone else.

"Stop interrupting, you're making me lose count!" she cried, frustrated. She went back to the neat piles of each pound. There were twenty-four piles, spread out all across the uneven table, and the leftover pile sat in front of her. "Twenty-four pounds, eight shillings, and sixpence," she pronounced.

It was a lot, more than any of them had ever seen together at once. It was also the reason that the blankets had been commandeered to cover the windows while it was counted, for to do otherwise would have invited trouble.

"That still leaves more than five pounds," Muirne said softly. It was March twenty-first, and it seemed impossible that they would have done all this work to still not make enough for those six fares.

"Now wait, just wait," said Neil, as he rooted around in his pockets. Finally his face lighted up when his hand was in his jacket pocket, and he produced from its depths with great flourish several five-shilling notes and two half-crowns.

"Neil!" Sheila exclaimed. "Where did you get that?"

"Well, you've already had my pay from the messengering. This was something extra I got from side work off of that. Don't worry; I didna break any laws," he said, smiling at his mother. She asked no more, but pushed the other coins out of the way to make room for the pile of papers.

"Four pounds left then," she sighed. It still felt unconquerable after their last efforts.

"Now wait then," Gillan said. "It seems Neil stole my idea for a grand finale, but I will not be trumped. I've got final rights to contribute." Saying this, he laid two pound notes on top of Neil's pile.

"And that," he said, pre-empting his wife's question, "is from my extra hours for the past two weeks at the mill." He gave a great smile at this, but was suddenly seized by a fit of coughing. This had become a common occurrence, and Muirne was ready with a cup of water from the well bucket before he had brought his head up to ask for it.

"Now, now, it'll do ye nae good to earn all this money if ye can't keep yer health," Sheila told him, wagging her finger at him. He nodded, trying to soothe his throat by clutching at it with his hand and making smoothing down motions.

"So. Two pounds. Twelve days. Or no—Two pounds minus two shillings and sixpence, which makes—"

Sheena looked up. "One pound, seventeen shillings, and sixpence!"

Muirne nodded her head. "Very good, Sheena."

Sheila shook her head in wonder at them all. "You have all done so well. God's grace is upon us, I feel it, and He will help us in this final wee while, too." She smiled at each of her children, last at Gillan. "Just keep your chin up and those ideas coming. And remember, you'll get to sleep however long ye like on the ship," she said with a glance at Neil. It was a tease, but she had started to worry over how exhausted he was these past few weeks.

Muirne squeezed his shoulder, and murmured in his ear. "So how did you get that money, anyway?"

"I won a bet," was all he would say, with a tired smile.

His mother gave him a stern look, and started to transfer all the little piles of coins into their hiding place, the large tray hidden at the bottom of their trunk. It was not very large, but full of their clothes and linens, fitted with iron fastenings, it had been an awful burden for any of them to carry down the glens. Sheila had settled for tying a rope from its handle to her waist and dragging it behind her. She was glad they still had it now, though. And she was glad that it would be Gillan carrying it on their next journey.

* * *

The time had come, Sheila knew. There were only a few more days. She took her knitted bag over to the pawn shop on a Monday afternoon. First she drew out the jewelry, the jet brooch from Gillan, her mother's gold ring, which had been hers at her first marriage, and the tiny silver locket given to her by Alec, her first husband.

The shop owner nodded to her as she came in, then watched as she laid out her jewelry on the counter. "I can gi'e ye four and six for all of 'em," he said, as impartially as one could.

It had been a rapid calculation, and Sheila was surprised. "So—" but she did not finish her thought. *So little?* "All right then. And what about this?"

She took out the wooden pieces slowly, placing them carefully on the table in front of the shop owner. After four of the legs, he still had not realized what it was. Next was the long arm that held the hooks for the harnesses, and finally, understanding dawned on his face.

"Well, isn't that handy, a loom ye can break down to travel with." His glance traveled up to meet hers briefly before returning to the goods on the table. "So ye're no travelin' yerself then?"

"No, I am, but we're short of the fare. I thought this might make up the difference. One can always build a new one, even if it takes a while."

"Aye, well. This is a first-rate model, I can see. I could gi'e ye a guinea fer dat," he said, a little less impartially.

That meant only thirteen shillings to go, and Neil and Gillan would likely have that from their side work in the last week. "Done," she pronounced.

The shop owner handed over the money. Sheila bent over quickly to retrieve the purse under her skirts, and stuffed the money into it. She let it drop back to where it hung by the string around her waist. She glanced up at the owner, who had watched as she did all this. She blushed a little.

"You can never be too careful."

"Aye, you're right there, mistress. Good luck to ye then, and Godspeed."

* * *

"Absolutely not. You have to pay for one of them things, and I'll not part with any of this money until I convert it into six bleeding tickets for that ship!" Sheila shrieked.

"Sheila, mo nighean," Gillan said quietly. "What if something happens to us on the ship, and there's no one to hand to take care of the children? We need to leave behind a will, to make sure they're taken care of."

Sheila's breath caught. She closed her eyes into a squint. "But we are so close," she moaned. She opened her eyes. Gillan stood in front of her, his look one of understanding. "A'right," she said. "Jus' promise me we'll still make it."

His eyes tugged down at the corners; she knew he could promise no such thing.

He left to go with Charlie to see the man who took care of the regulations at the mill. He was a lawyer, and they hoped he would not charge them too much to perform the duties of a notary on a will. Sheila spent the time at home grinding their dearly bought supply of oats into meal, a task she had switched over to as soon as she'd sold her loom. It was a good task for when there was the worry upon you. Like churning butter, you either exorcised the demon, or ended up too exhausted to care.

When Gillan returned, it was with his last wages as well as the copy of the will.

"He dinna charge me a penny," Gillan said.

"Good man, that Robertson," Charlie added.

Sheila felt her shoulders descend several inches as she breathed out. "And did ye sight Neil as ye came back?"

"No, but he'll likely be a few more days at the docks, as he can hide his intentions longer."

"Hm," Sheila replied, absently nodding her head as she watched Gillan lay out the coins onto the table. Her eyes did a quick count. "Nine shillings more. We are so close."

Gillan came around to put his arm around her. "We shall make it, dinna worry. Now," he said, his tone straightening and putting on its martial clothes. "What of our other tasks? How is the meal coming?"

"It is coming," Sheila replied. "There's plenty of time to keep doing it just in the evenings."

"All right, and what about the list. Was Muirne able to

find out any other families who'll be on the *Amidou?*"

"None of them have come back yet today from their errands. But they should be along soon, it is just the hour for—"

The door opened, and Muirne rushed in. She had a
healthy glow, her cheeks pink from the cold but her eyes
dancing. "You'll never guess who's on the list, Mama!"

"If I'll never guess, ye may as well tell me then, silly
goose. Come on, out with it," Sheila teased. Muirne came to
the table and spied the coins laid out. She stopped and looked
up at Gillan. "Are we there yet, Father?"

Gillan shook his head. "No, but very close. Sit down, we'll
hear your news all together." No sooner had they sat than
Alisdair came in, back from morning lessons at kirk. Jenny
and her brood were out visiting, but would rejoin them for
supper. Gillan settled Alisdair on the bench next to him, and
Muirne finally said what news was fresh on her mind.

"The Wilsons from Kilninian are coming! Not just Orly
and Robert, but their relations too from across the bay on
Gometra, and the parents. I did not see their address or I
would have paid them a call on the way home, but that means
at least they are well and fit to travel. Isn't it wonderful?"

Sheila stilled her first reactions to the name, which
brought back the image of the fire sighted away off in the
darkness, the realization that they would find no shelter with
neighbors, that they were all being chased away and burnt out.
Gillan, who sat to one side of her on the bench, felt her sudden stillness. "What is it, mo gràdh?" he whispered.

"Nothing," she said, willing herself to picture the Wilsons
she knew well. They were all right then, and had found their
way through the autumn and winter to the same boat as they
had. Orly had been pregnant in the summer, she wondered if
the child had come through all right. She met Muirne's eyes.
"Was there a sixth child listed for Orly and Robert?"

Muirne shook her head sadly.

"She lost the baby, then. That is some sad news among the good news that they are still alive and together as a family."

"Anyone else we know, lass?" Gillan asked.

"I think so. There were several Alexander MacLeans listed, but they were—they were listed solely, so I'm not sure if they are the MacLeans we know from Achnacraig…" Her voice drifted off. It was a common enough name, but if it was unaccompanied by the wife and daughters they knew, it was ill news indeed.

"And then there was also listed an Elizabeth Stewart, no other name, and no address."

"That's also a common name, but you're thinking it might be your Lizzie from kirk?" Sheila asked.

Muirne nodded. "Just a feeling."

"Mm," Sheila replied. "Well, that is some interesting news to consider. I will be glad to meet up with the Wilsons again. They are a large merry band, that's for sure."

Gillan concurred. "Well done, Muirne. Glad you could do that errand for us. Still a few last tasks left to do." Saying that, he rose from the bench, putting Alisdair to the side. "When'll dinner be ready, Sheila?"

"Och, I've been grinding the meal, it'll take me a few minutes for the tattie scones and a few more for the soup broth. Give me half an hour then."

"Alright, I'm going out for a bit."

Muirne helped with the soup and it was bubbling as they discussed the news, themselves bubbling over with nervous enthusiasm for the journey to be taken in seven days.

Chapter 21

"I wish we could have visited the family graves one last time," Gillan said.

"Aye, or my family's," Sheila agreed.

It was the third of April, and they had just bought their tickets. Neil's side work from the Saturday half-day was enough for them to come on Monday, carefully carrying all those pound notes and coins, to turn them into six very valuable pieces of paper. Their names were also written down in the manifest. Others would be able to see them as passengers, just as they had looked for acquaintances and friends earlier. They gave Jenny's address for their last six days in Scotland.

They had received a little more information about the sea voyage upon buying their tickets. Sheila and Gillan returned home and sat in Jenny's sitting room, relaying the details as she readied the supper for them all.

"Six weeks' provision is needed," Gillan said, ticking off the points on his fingers. "Meal as well as citrus, so we don't fall sick of the scurvy."

"Citrus? What's that?" Sheena asked.

"Lemons and oranges and quince. Something for the

scurvy."

Sheila let out a bark of a laugh. "And where do they expect us to get these in January in Scotland, or afford them, any
road?"

"Well, the officer did recommend dried pieces to chew
on. I think I know a place where they put up the marmalade,
and we can take a few jars of it, courtesy of that Robertson
from the mill."

"Oh, right. Good, then. What else?"

"They take on the water for all passengers, but it may be
good to keep a store if you think you may need more. They do
not provide water for washing, only drinking. And—no privy,
just chamber pots ye throw into the ocean. So, no washing
that, at least."

"Euch," Sheena exclaimed.

"Surely ye can use the sea-water for washing a pot
though," Sheila said.

"Ah, probably right there." Gillan smiled at her. "Let's see,
anything else—"

"How much room for our bags? And where are we to
sleep?" Muirne asked. Even though they did not have much
left, it was a concern.

"They did not say there was a limit, but they'll no' be
carrying it on for ye, so I guess that's the self-enforced limit.
And as for sleeping, each family will have a marked-off piece
of floor, to prevent crowding. They're each divided off by a
railing, the man said. You get what you pay for, so I'm thinking
it'll only be a bare space. If I knew anyone with a hammock I
would try to buy it, but they may have them on board."

"At some expense though, I'll bet," Muirne said, rolling
her eyes.

"Well," Sheila said, when it looked as though Gillan had
finished. "Five days."

There was quiet around the table where they sat. The noise of spoons on plates clinked from the kitchen, where Jenny'd set up her children for tonight's dinner. Neil, who so far had added nothing to the discussion, spoke up.

"Aye, five days. Sail on Friday. It is hard to believe, no?"

"Many are the blessings," Gillan started.

Neil coughed loudly, interrupting the flow of words. "I had rather say, Father, that we've done well, with the Lord's help, helping ourselves." This was a breach of manners, but Sheila looked at her son, so stretched past his limits, and let it pass.

"Neil, why don't you go have a lay down." In truth, he looked rather ill. His eyes were red-streaked from fatigue, the skin smudged with grey underneath. His pallor alarmed Sheila, who had not really noted it until just then.

"Aye, think I will," he said.

There was quiet after that. Gillan could see they were still brimming with questions, but decided to wait. He murmured to Sheila. "He should go tell his work he's leaving tomorrow, so he can rest before departure. We don't want him to be after catching something, and we've got our tickets now, so."

Sheila nodded. What was there left to do? Sewing their few valuables into the clothes they'd be wearing. Packing their meal and flour. Finding containers for extra water. Saying goodbye.

Chapter 22

The morning dawned, April 9th. The rising sun found crowds of people who'd been waiting since dark had fallen, to be first on the ship, or to get a ticket at a cheaper price. The MacLeans stood together, each guarding a creel or a chest or a sack. They were dressed in their warmest clothes, but still the cold of the early spring morning seeped in.

Neil, seeing Muirne shivering, came close to put an arm around her. "It's Scotland trying to tell us goodbye," he said, which made her smile.

"Either that or trying to come with us," she quipped. She looked over at her brother in the teal-grey light. He did not look much better, despite the days of rest and Jenny's good food. Muirne wondered if there was to be a health inspection, this side or the other. She sent a quick prayer for Neil to keep in good health.

There was more waiting, as the ship's crew sought to make room for more passengers to increase the profit from the voyage. In fact, it was past noon and they were all famished when they were visited by Charlie, who'd brought along oatcakes smeared with homemade preserves, and bacon rolls.

Other groups looked on enviously, or sent a messenger to procure their own food, as they devoured it all quickly.

"How did ye know we'd not sailed?" Gillan asked.

"How do ye know the sky's blue?" Charlie replied. "We've seen a few friends off now, and they always manage to wait till the end of the day. Not sure why. Leastwise, you're not standing there for weeks, as I heard happened before. They've only just started leaving at scheduled times, so you're lucky," he said with a grin.

Jenny had come up behind him. Even though they'd already said goodbye, apparently she had also known there would be a wait. She brought little presents for each person. A tin of tea for Sheila, a tiny sachet of lavender and sage for her brother, three little books for the older children, and playing cards for Alisdair. Jenny and Gillan hugged fiercely.

"You take care of that beautiful family," she said to him.

"And you yours, Jenny. Thank you. God bless ye, sister."

They all heard a loud, low horn. "See? How lucky ye are," Charlie said. "Not even three o'clock, and they're starting with the passengers. Fair winds!" He hugged or touched the shoulders of each again, as did Jenny. It was obvious they could not bear to turn away, so Gillan, his eyes full of held-back tears, pulled his plaid over his head and hoisted their wooden chest. "Time to walk on, lads and lasses. Here we are."

They joined the slow-moving, shuffling line. Every third step Sheila slipped her hand into the folds of her arisaid to feel the shape of the tickets. They arrived at the ticket-taker's seat and handed over the papers. He ripped a tear almost all the way through each, checking each person's identity before handing them back. A careless nod, and they were on board. Someone directed them to follow the crowd down below decks, and there they saw the berths with the marked off lines for large parcels. Otherwise, it was first come, first pick.

They shuffled through with all their bags, not wanting to relinquish any of it, and settled on a patch in the middle of the ship. Gillan explained that it might be the best place for avoiding the rocking of the ship. They unrolled the bedding they had brought and laid claim to the space. Sheila motioned for them to go back up on the open deck to see off the boat. "I'll see to the things. I've said my goodbyes, but ye might like to see us pull away from the docks." Muirne elected to stay with her mother, not feeling up to watching the land pull away so slowly that it looked possible to swim back.

When the others had left, Sheila pulled out Jenny's gift of tea. She opened it, and saw nestled in among the black crackled leaves, a tiny envelope. She opened it carefully, and saw the bit of sand, and the variety of seeds inside. Her eyes filled, and her hands dropped with the box into her lap. Muirne came over and sat beside her, glancing in.

The seeds and bit of soil must have been part of Jenny's own store, taken from the island, in hopes that they'd have land again someday. Sheila stifled a sob, which captured the attention of several onlookers, still arranging their own bags and bedding. Muirne put her arm around her and lay her head against her shoulder. She stared into the dark creaking depths of the ship, seeing the long empty days stretch in front of them.

One man looked over kindly. "Dinna fash, mistress. We shall make it across this wide ocean, and have a new start. I know it."

Muirne was more irritated with his optimism than thankful for his kindness at the moment, but it helped interrupt her sad thoughts. She nodded in his direction, not really being able to see him through the blur of tears. Her mother's labored breathing eased, and she hoped Neil was able to wave to Jenny and Charlie. She felt exhausted all of a sudden, and laid across their bags. Leaving a hand on her mother's foot, she fell into an instant doze.

Up on the deck, the rest of the family were standing, waiting for the signal of movement. Every once in a while they waved at those on shore, grinning or smiling. The minutes stretched on as they watched the last people in line filter up the plank and have their tickets torn. The parties who had waited to see if they could get on at a discount, mostly single men or women with children, were now arguing with the ticket-taker. Apparently he was having none of it.

Neil was watching the action, feeling quite detached and queer, when he heard his name. *Someone else's Neil?* he wondered. But no, he spied Letty, running forward through the crowd, waving her green kerchief in the air.

"Letty!" he called back, waving an arm. She stopped suddenly, putting her hands to her mouth.

"You are going then?" she called.

"I guess so!" he said, earning a few chuckles from those around him observing the exchange.

"I—I shall miss you," she stuttered. "Write to me, won't you?"

"I—" but then it was Neil's turn to stumble. *Why didn't she ask me before?* "Aye, I will."

Letty clasped her hands in front of her then, her face the picture of longing. Neil was looking at her, wondering where they had gone wrong, then started as he heard the loud, low horn again, signaling some new action for the crew. He held up his hand, and Letty did the same, the other on her heart. Neil felt a tickle coming up his throat, and turned to cough into his elbow. When he looked up, Letty was gone. The harbor whistles started then, and he felt the ship move.

Neil's eyes darted around the dock, where knots of people

were lingering. He found his aunt and uncle one last time, waving and shouting their goodbyes along with the other hundreds of people on shore. He saw no more of the green kerchief. The feeling drained out of his arms. Feeling like he might throw himself over the railing, he clamped down on the rail a moment, then went below to find his family.

Chapter 23

Neil soon learned what was required on the ship: as much fresh air as possible, eating and drinking as little as possible, and staying quiet and still when down below. Moving around made the floorboards creak and echo around the open hold. It was bad enough with the coughing and retching noises, as people adjusted to the sea's motion, but then there was also the babies' crying and the shouting of some of the families, who did not bother to be discreet about their affairs. Neil was surprised to note that some couples did not bother to be discreet about other activities either: groans at night were clearly audible but never assigned an owner in the mornings.

The first night, they were within sight of the shores of Dumfries with clear weather, so he stayed on deck to watch the few gaslights in the villages as they grew indistinct, one by one. He knew his place was here with his family, but he struggled to understand the appearance of Letty at the last moment. *Had she just found out about the ship? Had she been trying to discourage me leaving, but wanted me still?* Neil knew the sensible thing for her to have done was to tell him she loved him and given him the choice, if she did not want to emigrate.

But she had not done that; she'd pulled back and hidden any evidence of affection, given him the notion that she was not interested in him in the least.

He drifted in and out of sleep, awoken by the unfamiliar sounds of the sails flapping and the rigging creaking above him. *Five to six weeks it would take. Then I can send her a letter, but what will I say? 'Thanks for coming to see me off and putting me in a right state of confusion?'* His lips quirked in a slight smile. *Ach, well. I suppose what they say about love is true, then. It makes ye do mad things.*

Neil woke from his dozing before the sun had lightened the horizon. The sailors' activity overhead had increased in volume. They yelled back and forth to one another, but he didn't understand a word of what they were saying, even though he'd been brought up on fishing boats. He went down below deck, where already the smell of the unwashed mass of people assailed his nose.

No light reached down through the hatch, even when it was day. He picked his way carefully through the sleeping forms, finally locating his own patch. He looked down on his mother, curled up and clutching the little tin of tea. Gillan lay behind her, then Alisdair. On the other pile of blankets huddled Sheena and Muirne. Muirne was awake, he saw, as what little light there was caught her eye and glinted. She poked out an arm from under the blankets, inviting him under. He lay down on his back next to her, and she half-turned to whisper to him.

"So what can you see, up there then?"

"It's just the stars and the black sea. No' that exciting."

"Did you sleep? You still look something awful, you know."

"Thanks," he said, laughter in his tone. "I did sleep, a bit."

"Are you well, Neil? Is something troubling you?"

Trust Muirne to notice his hastily hidden melancholy. "It's

no' important. Jus'—I was just confused seeing Letty there, that's all. I'd thought she didn't want me."

"Letty? She came?" Neil related the brief moment they'd had. He almost doubted its happening, but for the memory of the bystanders' laughter when he'd first replied.

Muirne reached up her hand, looking for his. It was on his chest, but he moved it to where she could reach. She squeezed it.

"Of course she'd want you. She just didn't want all of us."

"Or to leave her family. Although her father—"

"He didna seem the affectionate kind, no, but perhaps she's just afraid of the unknown." Muirne paused, then said, "I am." Neil gave her hand a squeeze back.

"Well, at least we're together this time," he said. A vision of how he'd found them in Glencoe: ragged, dispirited, and exhausted, came to him then, and he took in a quick breath, then let it out slowly. He turned to his sister. "Is she cold?"

Sheena was shivering in her sleep. "Aye. We've no more blankets, though. I think it's just the shock of the first day," she whispered.

Neil rolled out from under the blanket and crept to the other side. He settled himself between Alisdair and Sheena, tucking the blankets to create a snug little nest for Sheena. He looked across, where he could see Muirne's eyes still glinting.

"Dinna fash. We shall make it." Muirne echoed the old passenger's words to her mother to settle her brother. It seemed to work. He'd told her that he'd asked Letty to come with him, but that he'd mucked it up somehow, and been rebuffed. She'd offered to go talk to the girl herself, but Neil had refused the offer. Now they were well on their way, but a tendril of the old world had been flung out to sink its hooks into Neil. He'd let it chew on his insides unless he had something else to think about.

Well, Muirne laughed to herself. *There is plenty to think about on this ship, and plenty of time to do naught else.*

* * *

Before long, the three older children had found good use for their little books. Neil wrote in his about his confusion and hopes for the new land. Muirne wrote in hers about the daily events that made her laugh so she would be able to look back on the voyage and remember its pleasanter points, instead of just the smells and aches and hardships.

Sheena sketched places and people from home, then asked Muirne for help in writing the names of those she missed. Occasionally she would appear at Neil's elbow, asking about the location of a certain rock on their beach, or when the last time was that they had thatched the roof on the blackhouse. They were easy questions for Neil to supply the answers to, but it clutched at his heart each time.

Muirne made sure to include her sister in her writing, telling her of some little incident to distract her. And it was quite easy for Muirne to create incidents, Neil noticed, since there were a good number of young men among the two hundred passengers, and they'd certainly taken notice of the young women. Muirne, with her long golden hair and piercing blue eyes, stood out.

She teased some of the older boys into showing her tricks at cards, which amused Alisdair. And she walked the upper deck around the two masts during the calm weather days to be able to converse with some of the other families, like the Wilsons. She brought back stories and whispered them to Sheena and Alisdair before they fell asleep each night. Neil knew for certain she was making most of them up when she brought the cailleach and magic into the stories, but thought it was doing them all a bit of good.

Once, Neil had interrupted a troubling scene: Muirne, back to the open air of the side deck; Alisdair, his arms wound through the piles of netting used for night fishing; and a tall young man with bright red hair, looming over Muirne. He saw her hand clutch convulsively at the rigging support behind her.

"And what has Alisdair got himself into now, then?" he asked.

Muirne's eyes found his and he noticed her rapid breathing, too. *What might have happened if I hadn't come upon them?*

The young man turned and smiled, a bit knowingly for Neil's taste. "Oh, he's after trying that Chinese rope game I was teaching yesterday. But with the netting."

"Careful, Alisdair. Don't want to mess up the fishing. We might be out of a dinner that way." Neil went to help Alisdair extricate himself and saw under his lashes Muirne recovering herself. She had a hand to her belly, then scrubbed the back of it against the side of her dress. The red-headed youth seemed not to notice. He nodded to acknowledge Neil and strolled off.

"And who was that?" Neil asked once he'd disappeared behind the ship's forecastle.

"A Gordon. One of several I've met so far. I think——" She cleared her throat. "Let's go down, shall we? I've had enough of the sea air for today."

They went down and it wasn't long before Sheena occupied Alisdair enough that Muirne could relate the details.

"He very craftily got Alisdair going on the pile of nets so he could corner me, like some animal in the woods!" she whispered. "I'll be more careful next time."

Neil was listening, but remembering being in that young Gordon's place not too long ago.

"What is it? Neil? You don't blame me?"

His eyes focused back on her face. "What? No!" he whispered. "I was just remembering feeling like a wild animal myself. Part of the problem with Letty," he added. Her look asked for more details. "I just didn't ask her in the right way. She kissed me, and I rushed in—you know." He looked sheepish.

"She kissed *you*?"

"Aye. She thought I was asking permission to go courting, which I would have done, but—she wasnae prepared for the sailing."

His regret was palpable. Muirne held back her other questions.

* * *

Gillan and Sheila followed the same rules for ship life that Neil had set down for himself, with the addition of time for private conversation. The married couple seemed to have a standing appointment for a hurried, whispered discussion each evening before supper. It seemed to Muirne to involve her mother prodding her stepfather about something, which he shook his head at. It ended in Sheila leaving for the ship's caboose. Sheila was obliged to trudge over to the small galley in the caboose and wait in line to make her family's meals. The cooking fire and large, shared griddle made the line move fast, but even so, others were there who took a long time cooking their meals, and altercations sometimes broke out.

In mid-April, after their first week at sea, Muirne asked her mother what they were talking about, one night after supper was finished and Gillan had gone out to empty the slops bucket. He'd taken the small brandy bottle with him.

"Oh, he's just having a bit of trouble deciding where to

settle in the new colony, that's all, dear. We didna have any replies to our letters afore we left, so he's not sure which is the better course—to stay or to continue with another boat up to the capital." Sheila sniffed. Muirne thought she caught a note of impatience in it.

"He's got plenty of time though. And I'll keep up the asking." She smiled at Muirne briefly before taking off her apron and outer dress and rolling under the quilt that she shared with Gillan. At that moment, he stumbled into the little area marked off with their bags and parcels. Muirne smiled back at her mother and nestled into her corner with Sheena.

That evening, they had their first spring squall. Everyone was directed to stay below deck as the crew strained to navigate safely though the storm. Their ship held over two hundred passengers; having them all stuffed down on the lower deck for over fourteen hours was bad enough. *But I wouldn't like being up there right now any more, so,* Neil reminded himself, hearing the shouts and curses of the sailors, feeling the pitch and heave of the ship against the waves.

Chapter 24

Another week went by, then another. The rations they had brought, stretched so thinly, made them resort to imagining the feasts they wished they could partake in. The Wilsons, with their large family of eight gathered with the MacLeans most nights, where one of the entertainments was conjuring up a fantastic meal to describe to the others, which only made them hungrier.

The passengers had established their patterns of sociability quickly. Some stayed close together under the deck and others walked topside, taking breaks from the dank, sickly air below. After several brief storms, the hold had taken on a permanent smell of putrid sickness, but at least there had been no fever on board as yet.

"I shall always remember this April," Muirne pronounced one evening as they watched the sun set. Low, blue-grey clouds were reflected in the water and hid the orange-tinted sun. Its light poured down to the water in a triangle, as if a gaslight were glowing down through the fog. "It's made me appreciate the things around me more—the ones I usually don't notice, like a sunset." She turned to Sheena. "What do you think you'll remember from this month?"

Something passed over Sheena's face, but she quickly looked down to hide it. "I'm trying to remember everything I can about home," she said, so quietly that Muirne could barely hear her. "That's what I want to remember."

Muirne put her arm around her sister, stroking the side of her arm instead of replying.

One of the young men came around the walk, and his face lit up when he saw the two girls. Muirne remembered this one's name was Tom. He didn't loom, and conducted himself affably. She remembered he was one of the very few passengers who came alone. "Hello, Tom. Done with your sums?"

"Hello, Muirne. And Sheena. It's Sheena, is it?" Sheena nodded, a small smile appearing. "And yes, I have done with my 'sums,' as you call them, but I assure you they're much more important than schoolwork. They're mathematical puzzles, and if I can solve one, I earn a place in the largest college in the colony, in Montreal."

"And how long have ye been working on it?" Muirne asked.

"Oh, six weeks. And who knows how many more I've got on this ship?"

"Oh, don't say that," Sheena said with a groan. "I'm ready to walk on land again."

"Are you one to be getting seasick then? You don't look too bad."

"No, not seasick, just—land sick."

Tom smiled as if he understood. He sat down a little apart from them, and Muirne thought about how it could still be pleasant to share someone's company, even if you had little choice.

She asked Tom what he would remember of this April. "Besides this mathematical proof? I'm not sure. Some lovely company, perhaps." He grinned at her. She was on her guard to be careful, but couldn't help melting a little under his kind attention.

When he sought her out each late afternoon in time for the sunset, she started to entertain thoughts of courting and marriage. But he constantly talked of school, and said nothing of settling down. She let it pass, willing herself to be content with his distracting presence and easy camaraderie.

* * *

When five weeks had passed of similar routines, there began to be a crowd in the foredeck each morning. Mainly men, but with a few women and some of the braver younger children as well. They craned their necks to peer across the horizon, searching for land. They kept as silent as possible to hear what the crew members called to one another, in case they spoke of land. It was its own fever, the hunger to be off the water and move on with their lives, for it seemed that as long as they were trapped on that ship, they were suspended, in limbo.

A different crowd gathered in the same place each evening. This one was different each night, as the number of passengers who had succumbed to the fever onboard grew in number. A Church of Scotland minister came to do for all the Protestant families, and—a curious figure for the MacLean children—a priest was present for the Catholic burials at sea.

Gillan had been improving for most of the voyage, with the cotton cough lifting its hold on him as long as he stayed in the fresh air. When he was below deck, it seemed to close back in on him, and his dry wheeze could be heard among the chorus of coughing, or retching when there was a storm on. They didn't have any real medicine that could help it, but Sheila had done her best, lacing the foul-tasting water with small nips of the brandy, and heating it through in the ship kitchen. But the wee bottle was empty now.

Neil had tried introducing himself to a few of the other older boys on the ship, making sure they knew he was Muirne's brother. It was more important to protect his sister than make friends on this voyage, and anyway, his head was filled with thoughts of his life in this New Scotland. His little book was almost completely full, as he wrote on the front and back of each page, with no space between the lines. With three pages left, he resolved to do more thinking than writing, although he was more often interrupted while mulling over his thoughts. He longed for more paper.

The Sundays on the ship fascinated Muirne, and they were the source of some of the musings in her journal. They saw little knots of folks together worshipping, and made a game of guessing which kirk they belonged to by observing them closely. The large group early in the morning, crossing themselves and kneeling precariously on the tilting deck—those would be the Catholics. Muirne spied Tom in their number, and pointed him out to Sheena and Alisdair, who were following her game. It surprised her a bit. She'd always thought Catholics must be a wild-eyed slavering lot, from how they were described by the Reverend Lachlan MacManus. Neil listened in on their game of predictions.

"And those ones that have been waiting for the forecastle position for an age, I bet they're Seceders. What do you think, Alisdair?"

The little boy squinted, shielding the side of his face from the sun with a grubby hand. "Alisdair! When was the last time you washed your hands?" They were filthy, his pale skin showing through only in the slices of wrinkle and crease at knuckle and palm.

Her exclamation attracted the attention of several people

nearby, so Muirne lowered her voice. "You go back to Mama right now and scrub your hands with the dry rushes if there's no water. Then you can come back and find out if they're Seceders for us, a'right?"

His downcast face lit up at that, and he popped off to the hatch to find his mother below.

"Wasn't your Robbie a Seceder, Muirne? Is that bad?"

"He wasna 'my' Robbie, Sheena; you know that. And yes, the Eglunds are Seceders. There's something they disagree with the Kirk about, and we don't see any reason for it. Unreasonable, is what it is." Muirne's hand found its way back to Sheena's hair, and she stroked the dark blonde locks, not wanting to say more.

* * *

"It's a curse!" someone had shouted. Two days shy of six weeks, and the people still gathered each morning to spy out the horizon and hamper the crew's movements. One of them had seen the floating mass before anyone else, and watching it come in, had realized it was all stained red.

"An ill omen!" The person shouting was a tall, thin man all in black, wearing a suit cut from heavy cloth. He had been in the small knot of people waiting for the Catholics to move on. Muirne watched as he continued calling out. They had not been Seceders, as she had guessed. Neil had crept stealthily around from the other side to listen to what they were saying once they started their service. *Relief Church*, he'd said. *Well now, what was that? Something you didna come across every day in Glasgow,* thought Muirne. *And even less when we get to Canada, perhaps.*

By then, almost everyone could see the hulking piece of ice floating a hundred yards off the starboard side. Blood-red ice, bobbing in the dark grey water. Her skin crawled and she couldn't suppress a shiver. *What do we know about this land, anyway?* She searched out the gaze of her brother, who stood several paces to her right, closer to the railing.

Neil squinted at the water. *Blood-red ice—what did that signify?* He backed away and came to Muirne's side. There were fearful murmurings in the crowd, and he was going to suggest getting out of there in case people panicked in the small space when they heard a cackle from above. Neil looked up, along with forty other people.

One of the crew was leaning over the rigging, holding his side, and cackling with laughter. "Every time," they heard him say. The captain shouted up at him from the middle deck and he straightened, but the grin was still plastered on his face.

"Cap'n wants me to tell you that that there is our first PEI iceberg," he rattled off as if he'd had it memorized. "Prince Edward Island has a very red clay soil, and in the spring when the bay comes unfrozen, chunks of ice full of the clay soil float off into the sea. That there's one o' them."

He turned away from them again, chuckling. Neil and Muirne looked at each other. "What a terrible eejit, scaring the people like that," Muirne said. Others in the crowd were too shocked or ashamed to speak. Neil saw the vulnerability of them all, with no knowledge of the place to which they were headed. *They'll be at the mercy of their handlers*, he thought. *Red icebergs, indeed.*

Chapter 25

The next days brought more icebergs, and the ship had to take care to steer clear of the larger ones. They were not the 'curse of the sea' someone had called them, but they were still a dangerous mass to be avoided. Neil and Muirne related the story to their family below deck. Neil felt his stepfather stiffen with insult when he heard how the sailor had laughed at them all.

"Tha's no' right," Gillan said. Sheila shook her head, clucking.

"But you know what it means, don't ye?" Neil asked. They looked at him. "We're near land!" A smile of relief broke out on his mother's face. Neil continued. "The crew has not warned us of the progress for some time, but we must be close in. I bet we'll be sighting the channels and islands any time now."

"Where are we stopping at first, Gil?" Sheila asked.

"They come in on the north side of Nova Scotia, call at the Port of Pictou, then proceed up the St. Lawrence River to the capital. It'll depend on the weather when they go on, but we shall have to see the situation in Pictou before deciding," he recited, as if he'd reasoned it out before.

"Of course," Sheila replied.

Neil caught Muirne's eye and they retreated to a corner of their six-foot stretch of floor. She whispered to him. "What do *you* want to do, Neil?"

"I dinna know. I canna tell if it would be better to go to the capital and find a sailing or shipbuilding outfit, or stay on the outer island to get a farm going. They said there was still land to claim for farming in Nova Scotia, so that might be the way of it."

"Unless they were lying," Muirne said.

Neil gave a sharp sigh. "We will find what we find," he said. "I wonder about the Scots already there," he wondered aloud. "And who else is there. Do you suppose there are natives up here as well?"

Muirne let go a small gasp. "I haven't thought of that since before Christmas!" she said. "Safety in numbers, Mr. Cartwright said." She pulled her knees up closer to her chest where she sat, wrapping her arms around her legs. Neil felt the shiver run through her frame. He leaned over so that their sides touched. "Dinna fash. I'm sure the Scots from before will have taken care of 'em." His face had a small smile on it. Muirne sighed, the many possibilities still racing through her head about what they would find once they arrived. Wouldn't be long now.

* * *

That night they stayed moored in one place, swaying as the waves rocked the boat wildly. They must be very close, thought Neil. In order to remain above deck, he bundled himself up in as many layers as he'd brought, and placed his back against several of the large rain barrels as a wind-break.

He hoped to see the light come up and reveal the land they'd been searching for.

He was not disappointed. The dark blue of the early morning was chased up and over the sky by the lightening pink, and as he followed its progress, the ship plowed away from it. His eyes picked up the birds that came out to meet the ship, another sign land was close by. Finally, he thought he saw a gash of black on the horizon that was not just the water meeting the sky. Sure enough, it grew bigger, floating off to their left as the crew tacked off to the right.

He thought about going down to fetch Muirne or Alisdair, but couldn't bring himself to take his eyes off the sight. Over six weeks, and all of April gone, spent in pursuit of this dream of new land. His small journal had been full for days, and it held his doubts and fears, his confused hopes.

Neil wondered whether or not history would repeat itself. When he'd mentioned other Scots to his sister, he'd been thinking of how they'd known each other back at home, known who was important, whose job it was to organize the clan. It might be very different here, but the only thing Neil could think of was meeting up and talking with the older settlers to see where they came from, and find someone who would help the MacLeans because of kinship ties. It was better that than charity from the kirk, although they would need that as well.

Neil's thoughts drifted to their utter poverty now. Back on Mull, he hadn't felt so vulnerable, as they had the house, and the land, and the laird, and the family and neighbors. Even in Glasgow, they'd had connections for a job and family and the kirk to turn to. But here, who did they know from home? No one but the Wilsons, who'd decided to go on to Quebec City.

No one owed them anything. And did they have any savings to purchase the land they might find to farm? None at all: it had all gone for passage fare.

We still have each other, and we're resourceful, Neil thought. *When we're together,* he amended, as the terrible thought of his mother and sisters and brother alone in the glen came upon him again. *We must not split up,* he reasoned. The talk of continuing up the river to Montreal was now foolishness in his mind, but he could not say that to Gillan, who seemed committed to the possibility.

The light pink had turned to white, and the cold winds continued to blow them toward the land on the left, with the sailors maneuvering to keep the ship steady on its course between Cape Breton Island and Prince Edward Island. These were names Neil had learned from one of Muirne's interested young men, who shared a well-creased, waxen map of eastern Canada showing where they would be landing and where the great St. Lawrence River wound its way through the continent.

It was a bit nerve-wracking, to entertain these young men, since he had to walk a fine line: being courteous to acquaintances on the ship and fiercely protecting his sister. Neil wished they would just leave her alone, but on a small ship during a long confinement in close quarters, he knew she appreciated the diversion.

Nonetheless, he had made one friend: a John MacPherson. He was nineteen years old and on the boat with his three sisters. Their parents had died in a fire, the young man had explained briefly, and Neil did not ask whether it had been set in a croft house. His family came from further north, up in Sutherland, farmers of oats and potatoes. Theirs had been a winding road, from the eastern coast below Wick to emigrating to Aberdeen, to being thrown out yet again. They had not been used to sailing on their farm, and found the motion of the seas not to their liking. John and one sister fared better than the other two, who'd been ill most of the voyage. John and his middle sister Elsbeth had tended to them with water and broth, and they were very weak.

As Neil listened, he realized how lucky his family were, all six of them without the seasickness. *Maybe I should be thanking God after all*, he thought.

Chapter 26

John joined Neil just in time to hear the halloo of "Land Ho-o-o" from above. He'd been about to sit down with Neil, but upon hearing it, straightened back up. "I've got to go tell Elsbeth," he said. Then he shaded his eyes, peering out into the glare. "Sure enough," he whispered to himself.

"Aye, the Lord be thankit," Neil replied. "Now just let us off!"

John turned to spare him a smile before hurrying back toward the hatch. He returned fifteen minutes later with his sister Elsbeth. She was tall for a woman, and thin. She had a long face, which was usually pinched with anxiety, but today Neil saw it relaxed with wonder, and relief. Tears sprang to her eyes. *She must be exhausted, caring for two sisters all this time,* thought Neil.

Others gathered around Neil's prime spot to view the land coming in close, then passing by. The black gash became tall hills and shadowed sea cliffs. He spied lines of trees, looking like infinity to his unaccustomed eye. Families murmured excitedly, and he realized he should have gone down by now to tell his own, but he could not bear to give up his place.

Eventually, as the swaths of trees cleared, he saw little clusters of buildings on the low-lying land close to shore.

"Neil?" a small voice was calling.

"Here, Sheena," he replied, staying in his crouch against the barrels and peering down through the crowd of legs and shawls and plaids.

"Neil!" Sheena had found him. She came to his side and stopped to look out. "Is that—are we really—"

"Yes, that is land sighted, and I do believe it is our New Scotland. Now, what part of it, I haven't a clue. Everyone all right below?"

Sheena's eyes were big, taking in the long lines of forest, but she snapped back to attention after a moment. "Aye. Ma jis' wanted to have you close to see what the shoutin' was about."

"A'right." Reluctantly Neil followed her back down, holding his breath at the smell that still overwhelmed his senses. He told his family what had been sighted. They all grew excited, restless to hear instructions from the crew, if they were really that close to their destination port.

Neil wondered if anyone would meet them. He thought of the letters his parents had written, the people their minister had known, those of Charlie's relatives that had been consulted. They had received no reply from any of them, throughout the long autumn, winter, and spring in Glasgow. If they had, they might have a better idea of where to stay or how to settle on a piece of available land.

But no, no answers had he seen. And no decision would Gillan commit to before he had laid eyes on Pictou.

* * *

Eventually the crowd of people lost the singular tension that held it together and dispersed to different parts of the deck and quarters, waiting for the announcement from the captain. Half of the MacLeans stayed below with their belongings, while Neil came back up with Muirne and Alisdair to show them the sight. Finally the captain went down below to announce the arrival time in three quarters of an hour, and the process for the customs house and all. Everyone readied themselves and their belongings, but prepared for a long wait anyway, by now used to the delays of the sea.

"Just think of all that meal we no longer have to carry, Alisdair, since we ate it all up!" Muirne said. Neil met her eyes, looking disapproving, or troubled. Muirne's gaiety subsided. Their thoughts both turned to where their next meal would come from, with the oats completely gone. They'd nearly finished up the last of the potatoes and bartered ship biscuit, and were almost out of provisions. Others who'd run out already had been forced to accept ship provisions on loan conditions. No doubt the shipping company had figured how to make the most out of each passenger.

"Do you suppose anyone will be there to meet us?" Muirne asked, voicing Neil's earlier thought. They turned back to help with the packing and loading of bags and creels below deck.

"I don't know. I hope so. Otherwise," and his voice lowered for her ears alone, "we'll be starting out here hat in hand at the kirk."

Muirne bit her lip; she knew. She'd hoped for a new start here, but it might very well be a new start with nothing at all and no help. That had been the risk. It had been better than Gillan coughing to death in the mill, however, and the children getting sent straight there with no schooling.

"Well, I'll still pray for someone to be there meeting us," she said. Little Alisdair was watching the exchange and took her hand, tugging it.

"I will too," he said.

* * *

The unloading commenced very slowly, and by the time the dinghy came back for a second party to be processed, it was dark, so they were forced to wait until the next day to resume. A frustrated, strangled sigh went round the parties waiting on deck, but at least they could stay above deck that night, as it was unseasonably warm, not even freezing temperature. *May,* Muirne thought, *and it's warm if we're not freezing. How on earth will we manage?*

The MacLeans passed the night huddled in a pile on the deck. The few friends they'd made on the voyage had come round in the night or as the sun was rising to say their good-byes. One or two pressed addresses on slips of paper into their hands. When the sun came out, things started to move quickly. Several dinghies were sent out in order to load more people.

By the time they arrived at the customs house, their bellies were protesting loudly. Gillan gnawed on an old crust of barley cake, and they tried to wait in line in silence, but Alisdair was restless and Sheena felt faint. When Gillan finally went to the front of the line at quarter to eleven, they were ushered into a side office with an employee.

There were two chairs in front of the desk. Gillan and Sheila sat down in them, Alisdair leaned against his mother's side, and the other children stood behind. The employee, who introduced himself as Mr. Balwhidder, sat on the other side of the desk. He opened a drawer and pulled out candies wrapped in wax paper, setting a handful on the desk.

"Is that tablet?" Alisdair asked.

"No, it's called taffy. Here, have a taste, and wait a bit

before chewing it."

Alisdair looked to his mother for confirmation before saying thank you and unwrapping one. He popped it into his mouth, and immediately his whole mouth filled with saliva at its sweetness. His little jaw moved up and down slowly, his eyes registering surprise at the slow stickiness.

He tried to say "Thank you, it's very good" to show his good manners, but it came out, "Rakey, shferra coo."

Mr. Balwhidder smiled tolerantly. Evidently this was how he put people at ease. "Please, everyone try one. Welcome to Pictou and Nova Scotia. We hope you'll become valued citizens of our country in time. And now for business," he said as everyone but Gillan took one and nodded their thanks.

"Is anyone here to meet you and stand witness for your settlement?"

Sheila looked at Gillan, who coughed. He was actually covering a laugh at the look of her, since she had stuck her ball of taffy in one cheek. She spoke for them, her speech only mildly garbled. "We have written multiple letters to relatives and acquaintances, Mr. Balwhidder, but we had no reply before we left Glasgow. They might be here in fact, but us not able to recognize them, even if we could see through the gates with all the crowds of people out there."

"I see. And is your plan to stay here then, or continue west with another ship up the St. Lawrence?"

Here was the moment. Sheila looked back to Gillan, who had composed his features by now. "We plan to stay here for the moment, and look into the land market, afore deciding anything more permanent."

"I see," Mr. Balwhidder said again. "And what line of work are you in, sir?"

"At our home I was fisherman, farmer, and we burned the kelp as well." There was a brief flicker of movement in Mr.

Balwhidder's posture at the mention of the kelp. *I wonder what he's got against kelp-burners*, Neil thought, and shifted his own stance. "When we moved into the city for the past half a year, I did loading and pulling work at a cotton mill and Neil here loaded freight from the ships on the docks. He was also start-ing to learn the shipbuilding craft."

There was pride in the last remark, and Mr. Balwhidder responded to it. "Well, we don't have much of a shipbuilding industry here, as there is ice so much of the year, but that might be something to see about upriver. Further south and inland, they may have better drydock situations." He said this to Neil, who merely nodded in return. *I'd rather stay and farm the land*, he was thinking, but gave no indication in his expres-sion.

"And excuse the delicate question, but if you've no certain relatives or friends with whom you can stay, have you brought enough silver to establish yourselves? It is May, but we will still have some mighty bad storms to get through, and ye'll need shelter and fuel sure enough." Before they could muster a reply, he added, "Fuel is easy enough here, much better than in Scotland, but the shelter must be very hardy if ye are to sur-vive."

Gillan replied after a pause. "We've almost no money left, as we used it all for passage. But we've all that's necessary for a household, and could work for another if it means we have that shelter for the first wee while."

Mr. Balwhidder inclined his head, then sat thinking. "To which kirk do ye belong?"

"Church of Scotland," said Gillan.

There was another brief flicker in his eyes. The family were all aware from the man's speech that Mr. Balwhidder was from a much higher station than they were, and their safety might depend on his mercy. Was he not Church of Scotland as well? They held their collective breath, until Alisdair starting choking on the taffy.

"Well, I can give you direction to apply for work with the Presbyterian minister, but they have been overset of late with incomers, especially former kelp processors. Ye may have to travel before finding a satisfactory situation." He paused, then raised his eyes to Gillan's. "Would you work with Catholics, or would that be a problem?"

"No, sir, no problem. I've worked with mony a type of man," Gillan replied.

"Well then, maybe you'll be able to find a more permanent situation over in Antigonish. It is about 60 miles east of Pictou, and has a good scattering of houses congregated together. Up to you, of course, but there are still a good many chances for summer work up Antigonish way. They're all Scots up there as well, mainly from Moidart and Morar. Now, if you find ye've no place to stay once you exit the gates, here is a boarding house that takes in new folks just off the boat. Ye can work out some sort of deal with Mrs. Conaghey to work for your room, but I'll leave that to you. She's worked with many a new arrival."

Mr. Balwhidder then brought them all the papers they would have to fill out and sign in order to stay in the town. As he was talking them over with Gillan, the children were each taken out, one at a time, for a brief health inspection. When they were all done, it was Sheila's and then Gillan's turn, and they all came back with a clean bill except Gillian, who was recorded as having "fluid in the lungs due to catarrh." It would not stop him entering the colony, thankfully.

Indeed, it was so much pleasanter an experience than they were expecting, that when they walked out of the gates, they were all a bit dazed. The lack of water and food contributed to their light-headedness, but so did the relief of being off the ship and away with their goods, together.

"Now," said Sheila, with a light tone. "Where to?" They stood against a stone wall bordering the harbor, beyond the crowds pressing against the opening gate for a glimpse of loved ones. Muirne was looking over the crowd of hundreds, dressed in warm, dark clothes. "I'm trying to see if there's anyone we know," she said. "But it's quite impossible the way everyone is moving and blocking each other."

"Perhaps we should find the boarding house first," Sheila said.

"All right, everyone. Up we go, and stay close." Gillan said. "It's off in search of Mrs. Conaghey. We'll ask first in town," and he pointed down the street where a sign stood crookedly, declaring "TOWN" to be to the right. They hoisted their creels and the chest for the umpteenth time, and set out. Before they reached the sign, Sheena had dropped behind and set down her creel. She cried, "Wait!" and they all stopped and turned back to look at her. "What is it, Sheena?"

She dropped to her knees, and placed her arms on the ground where it was soft and grassy. She raised her head. "We should give thanks," she said.

"Aye," said Gillan, smiling. He set the chest down, walked to where she knelt, and lowered himself down beside her. The others ranged themselves around in a circle. Their eyes walked around, meeting and grinning, still giddy from the arrival, the easy processing, the bit of sugar on an empty stomach.

"You go ahead, Sheena. Say our prayer for us," said her mother.

And they bent, praying to the earth with the words of an eleven-year-old girl, thanking the good Lord for their safe crossing, their good health, and the nice man who had welcomed them. Before standing, they all joined hands. Sheila teared up, and she sniffed; they laughed, and the spell of seriousness was broken. They were in the new land, and would see what it had to offer them.

Chapter 27

Mrs. Conaghey turned out to be a Scots-Irish widow from Ulster, and a brisk, fastidious soul. Her husband had died the first week after their arrival in Canada in '15, so she'd had to take care of herself for a good many years. She had work for Gillan and Neil to do that would cover their rent while they looked for paying work, and chores for the women to do that would cover their board. Rooms were paid the week in advance, and board was tallied after each week, so if they felt the inclination to move up the river, they could do so without the loss of much time or money.

The room they took was about twelve foot square, which felt like a luxury after the cramped space between decks they'd just emerged from. There was room for sleeping when their baggage was ranged along one wall. There was one large window across from where they slept, and a little coal brazier stand next to the window. Obviously, it would be very cold during winter here, and the brazier would not be much help. Gillan and Sheila noted this, thinking that it wouldn't matter, since they would have their own situation come autumn, whether here or farther out.

At tea time that first day, Mrs. Conaghey persuaded them to have a small, dry meal, so that their stomachs wouldn't rebel against too-rich food so soon after their restricted diet at sea. They'd told her that their circumstances were much reduced, and she understood what they meant: they were near to starving. She knew how to advise them and how to accustom them to normal food so they wouldn't become ill.

After a few days, they were all feeling much restored on her broths and country bread, and the earth did not seem to roll and pitch under their feet as it first had. Neil and Muirne were very curious to explore Pictou, and one sunny afternoon they set out to do so. Leaving the large wooden multi-story boarding house, they headed back down the road towards the harbor, thinking that the main part of town would be that way.

Instead of shops and homes, the harbor road seemed to house shanties for sailors and warehouses. Muirne didn't mind the noisy gulls wheeling and diving for fish brought ashore by fishermen, but the shanties seemed to be squatting and listless, indicating lax householding. Women traveled between a few of these, and their clothes were garishly bright, if a bit ragged. Their walk spoke of wanton self-satisfaction. From the viewpoint on the hill, brother and sister looked down.

"Muirne, I think those are—"

"I know, Neil, they're fancy women, women of easy virtue. Obviously visiting the home of the sailors—or are they fishermen, d'ye think?"

Neil glanced at his sister, stepping a little closer. "Both, most likely. Let's head back around this way," he said, pointing inland from the harbor, where a road split off and vanished over a hill. "Perhaps there is more of town that way."

"All right," Muirne said, and shivered a little as she turned away. She dared not catch the eye of one of the women, for fear of seeing the reflection of her own thinly disguised desperation. What if her family had had to indenture to make the journey? It had been so close, so very close, but they hadn't given in.

For his own part, Neil felt as if cold water had been thrown on his sunny day. One of the fancy women had worn a green kerchief 'round her waist, and the image of Letty's waving hand at the ship had risen in his mind. *I was going to write to her, as soon as we arrived. Wasn't I?* Glasgow seemed a long way off from this hill in Pictou.

The road curved over the hill then plunged down into a shallow dell. Behind this lay a front street to their right with fine-looking buildings, and a high street to their left, flanking the larger hills beyond. Most buildings had a layer of white-wash, which needed a new coat following the last year of storms. Other than that, Neil noted well-maintained roofs and well-appointed windows. He and Muirne walked along the front street for a bit, soaking up the afternoon sun still pouring over the brow of the hill.

* * *

The actual town was nowhere near Glasgow's size, but more orderly than either Hutchesontown or Laurieston had been. Streets and corners formed the familiar blocks of houses and places of businesses. The view was quite nice down the front street and they paused to admire it.

"What would you do, Neil, if you had your choice?" Muirne asked.

Neil's eyes continued to scan the vista before them. He didn't need to ask what she meant. "I'd as soon get a plot of land to plow up for a farm as anything. Looks like we'll be felling trees, though, as they're everywhere."

Muirne followed his gaze up over the town to the hills,

which indeed showed unbroken expanses of tall trees, a house or two peeking out among them, visible only by their white paint. "But that's good, no? They don't seem to have peat here, just the coal from the mines and the charcoal they make from the trees." This she had gleaned from a conversation with Mrs. Conaghey.

"Mmph," Neil replied. "No, I dinna mind the trees or having to fell them at all. It'll be better, I think. And, perhaps —well."

He blushed and looked sheepish for a moment. Then he turned to Muirne then and gave her a wry smile.

"Maybe when we've a steading, or when things are more sure, I can write and ask Letty again. But what about you, Muirne? What would you do, an' ye had your way?"

He looked at his sister. She returned his slight smile about Letty, then looked away, out to the hills. Her eyes were narrowed against the sun's glare, and the breeze played with her pale hair, lifting it up and away. She turned to face him and it blew before her, obscuring her face. She smiled faintly, but spoke carefully to give her words weight.

"It seems I have a wind to follow. And it only obliges if I face the one way, Neil." She raked her hands over her hair, pulling it back and tying it with a leather thong. "There's no money for more schooling, and I've no interest in going to work in a mill, judging from your description of it."

Neil reached out to touch her elbow, shaking his head.

"So it's marriage, but where am I to meet a man? We know nobody here, and I've no employment. When we go to kirk on Sunday perhaps we'll find some kin there, but otherwise, I'll just waste away."

"Never," Neil said. "It may be at kirk, or it may be somewhere else, Muirne, but dinna worry over that. The Eglunds were not your only chance. You attract plenty of attention;

you'll find a good man, soon, I bet." She took his arm, squeezed it, and they continued their walk.

* * *

When they arrived home in time for supper, they had much to relate about the town layout, the businesses where they might look for work, the grand homes and the not-so-grand, where they might live if they did stay. Gillan said no more words on the matter, and the subject was dropped.

The next day, Gillan and Sheila ventured forth, while Muirne stayed at Mrs. Conaghey's with her chores. Sheena and Alisdair were set to task by Neil and his old school primer. Husband and wife saw some of the same sites, thinking some of the same thoughts, but Gillan had a more specific goal. He visited the house of the Presbyterian minister, and introduced himself and his wife. They talked of the voyage, the ways of the new community, the needs of the different regions.

"You're saying that all the summer freight will be towed upriver for unloading, and the merchants live in the capital rather than the first port?"

"Aye," said the minister, a Mr. Brown. "They profit from the tobacco trade with the Glaswegians, so they can afford some muckle houses, but it wouldn't be at all fashionable for them to reside here, provincial as we are. So they're in the capital at Quebec, even though their business often brings them downriver to us."

"I see," said Gillan. "And what of the land claims, are there more open stakes here or further west?"

"There are still land claims out here, and especially land that's already had a start but was abandoned. The winters—they are verra hard, it must be said." He said this with a glance at Sheila. "Does the mistress have a squad of braw children to help ye with the building and planting while we have the good weather?"

"I have four children, sir, but one is not yet grown to do heavy farming work, and two of them should really finish a few more years of school—"

"Of course, of course, there's the village school just north of Pictou, but you'd do best to have them working during the summer, as the good season is short, as you will see. If you go further north, say around Bras d'Or Lake, the schoolin' is harder to come by. You'd more likely be getting the books and teachin' 'em yerself, in the spare evenings."

"Hmm," said Gillan. Sheila looked at him, unable to guess what this particular 'hmm' meant.

"Would ye be knowing any other folk in Quebec who might be helpful in arranging employment?" Gillan asked. Sheila held her breath. *Back into the city*, she thought. *That's not why we came here.*

"I can write to a few and give you their names, but I couldn't promise anything." Gillan had a few more questions about the farm markets and which crops were grown, but the conversation was winding down. A few more pleasantries and remarks of gratitude, and they were done.

When they were out the door, Sheila managed several steps holding her tongue with difficulty. Then, without turning her head, she asked a question. "How would ye be thinking of going upriver, Gil?"

"How?" he repeated. "By boat, I suppose. And I'd take Neil with me, so we can both make the best wage we can over the summer. Then we'd come back and have a better situation while looking for a piece of land."

"Oh." *I hadn't looked at it that way.* "And why would we not try for a piece of land now so that we could harvest come summer's end?"

"Because we haven't any of the capital needed to buy it, Sheila. They're not giving it away completely free, ye ken?"

"Oh." *I thought they'd said it was, if you made the improvements on the land.* Sheila was quiet on the walk back, while Gillan occasionally threw out ideas about how he and Neil would find work, and how she and the other children would cope with the chores and Mrs. Conaghey in the meantime. Sheila tried to follow his reasoned-out plans, but felt the cold prickle of fear down her back instead. *Alone. And vulnerable again.*

Chapter 28

Tension reigned in the second-floor boarding room. Sheena and Alisdair had their lessons to copy on a black slate, but the others held their mouths in grimly set lines. They cleared their throats, attempting to dislodge the words that they swallowed instead of saying. A week had gone by; a routine had taken shape. The first Sunday, they chose the Reverend Maurice Brown's kirk to attend, and found it to be just like the service back home. That was a comfort.

Sheila had not told Neil what Gillan was considering, but he knew something was wrong between them, and waited for an opportunity to talk with his mother alone. It came after that first service at kirk, when Gillan was invited out with several other men of the kirk to take a turn and talk with them. As they walked the short distance back to the boarding house, Neil walked with his mother behind the others.

"What is it, Mother? What's wrong between you? Has he made a decision?"

"I think so, but maybe he's no' so sure, so he doesna say yet. Don't worry, Neil, he'll do what's best for all of us," Sheila said. Her eyes followed the road. Neil knew—by her not meeting his gaze or taking his hand—that she was not telling all she knew or guessed.

"Is he hiding something? Are you hiding it for him? Please, Mama, I can tell something worries ye."

She turned to him then, her brow wrinkling and her mouth in a dismayed frown. "We should all of us be happy fer the now, Neil," she said. "We've made it here after many a bad fright we would not make it at all." She gave a sharp sigh. "And if we have to go into town again to stow away some coin for the land, then that is what we'll do, or what some of us will do."

Neil digested this information with a frozen look on his face. "Ye mean he's talking of splitting up again? Is he off his head?"

"Wheesht, don't talk so of yer father," she said.

"I thought we were deciding whether to stay or to go, but some staying and some going, it's mad—"

"Wheesht, lad, don't say that. Have some respect."

"Ma, he didna see you on the road on yer own. And I didna see our house go up in the fire," he said as his eyes went glassy and his voice quivered. "I could no' leave ye again to face the same situation. I canna let ye alone without one of us, at least." At her pleading look, he added, "He's no' my father, it comes to that, but ye are my *mathair*, and I'm old enough to protect ye."

"Oh, Neil, don't—I'm sure we'll find something safe before ye go. I'm sure Gil will look out something for us, don't worry yourself." She tried to appear confident, but Neil knew she was scared. It was the way she looked straight ahead at this moment, her eyes large and her mouth clamped firmly down to keep it from quivering.

He left off the subject, but was glad to have found out which direction things were tending. *It looks like I'll have to do some looking out on my own.*

* * *

Their second week they celebrated Alisdair's birthday, and it was an occasion Mrs. Conaghey involved herself in, to their great relief and delight. She knew everyone, it seemed, and had invited several near neighbors for a great heaping setting-up of tea. Their friends the Wilsons were still in Pictou awaiting some kin to travel to Quebec with, and they had also made food to bring.

As this was the first community gathering since the *Amidou* had disembarked, Alisdair's birthday was really just an excuse to come together. Mrs. Conaghey put everything on the kitchen work-table as people arrived, and it fair groaned with the weight of the scones, tarts, breads, cured meats, soft cheeses, and bottles of local whisky brought as gifts.

"Ye do know Alisdair'll not be getting any of these yet?" Gillan asked as the next group entered with another bottle in hand.

"I'd hope not!" the man exclaimed. "Tha's good brandy, that is." He introduced himself as Mr. Farraday and his wife as Sarah. There were many people to meet during the celebration, as it was arranged on a Friday afternoon and the townsfolk would have closed their shops. The farmers from surrounding areas would not be able to make it until later, as they stayed out to work with the sun, but Mrs. Conaghey explained that they would come later.

"This is quite a to-do, Mrs. Conaghey, I cannot thank you enough for your help," Sheila said. "I think Alisdair will be around to thank ye soon as well, soon as his head is done being turned by all this attention."

Mrs. Conaghey laughed, and swatted her hand through the

air. "Oh no bother, Mrs. MacLean. These people were itching for an occasion to gather, can ye no' tell? Our May Day celebration was somewhat lacking, as there was terrible weather the week before yer ship arrived. No, I just gave them the excuse. It's glad I am ye're meeting them all. Tell me, you're looking for a piece of land to farm, isn't that right?"

"Well, yes, but I'm not so sure now whether we'll be able to do it this summer, or have to wait until next. Why, have ye any news?"

"Why ever would ye be wanting to wait?" Mrs. Conaghey asked, incredulous. "Aye, maybe yer man should be talking to some of the farmers as they come in the evening, for they'd be able to tell him which plots are empty or abandoned. There are a fair number abandoned, with some of the materials still left around and no one to take it up. I'm thinking you could take up one of those as doesn't have a claim and set to planting right away. But you'd have to get a better feel for where to look with some of the farmers."

Sheila nodded. Neil came up beside her, touched her elbow. "Y'see?" he whispered, then stepped away before she could scold him.

When the crowd had rotated through once and it was getting dark, there came another shift, the farmers and their families. There were about half a dozen that came through after sunset, and they were received readily, their hosts searching for information and advice. Alisdair had in the meanwhile imbibed some of the homemade punch and was sprawled out on the floor on one side of the table, giving everyone a laugh.

"Why, at seven, I was throwing back tumblers of whisky!" one of the farmers was saying with good humor. Sheila felt the warm glow of the fiery liquid in her own chest, and the kind regard of the people present. She saw Gillan animatedly discussing something across the kitchen and wondered if what he heard was changing his mind. She met Neil's gaze where he sat near Muirne, and he gave her an encouraging nod.

* * *

Mrs. Conaghey had indeed done a job of inviting the right people. Gillan had talked to some of the farmers about what they were planting. With the shift before, it had been about what trades were needed in the towns, both Pictou and the surrounding ones. He'd gotten a fair picture of where he might try apprenticing Neil, although he knew Neil might have his own ideas.

He was not ready to reveal it until he was certain of the details, but Gillan was aiming to find a trade for Neil that he could grow in, and earn a good wage at. They'd scatter for the summer when it would not be as hard on the rest of the family, then return for the hard weather. That way, they could learn more and perhaps see different regions around the island before committing money and their labor to a particular plot. He allowed himself a moment to dream of a croft again, picturing the cow and hens; his short respite was interrupted by someone's loud guffaw at close range.

The entertainment did not finish until near midnight, but Alisdair by that time had been removed to his own mat in the corner, and showed no signs of waking. Sheila looked around and saw that most everyone was asleep already. She'd been the one to show out the last guests, thanking the couple and promising to come to the next waulking to be held. Now she saw Gillan was waiting for her, his back against the wall, a candle in a holder at his side illuminating his tired face: eyes closed, a slight smile playing across his lips.

She undressed to her shift by the press, carefully laying out her clothes so they would air in the drawer, then picked her way across to him. She blew out the candle and leaned against him. "What are you so happy about?" she whispered.

No answer, but his head flopped in her direction. She cupped his cheek with her hand as he slowly slid sideways, his head coming to rest on her lap. She deftly lifted it up and wiggled herself down onto their bed, while he stayed curled up, even with the wall. *At least our heads are in the same place*, Sheila thought with a giggle. It died inside her as she was reminded of Gillan and Neil and their different ideas. She turned onto her side, facing away from the now-snoring Gillan.

What to do, not to be torn in two?

Chapter 29

In the event, Gillan and Neil had their own discussion that settled the matter.

Gillan took Neil aside one day before supper to have a word with him, away from the women. "Neil, I've considered our choices. The only way we'll get enough silver to buy a plot of land is to be laborers during the good-weather season. I've written to a friend of the Reverend's here, and the Reverend is fair sure he'll take us on at the cargo mill upriver. It's a big sawmill where—"

"I don't care what it is. You think I'm going to leave with you again, after what happened the last time? I'll not be leaving my family alone again, *Uncail*. How much worse is it going to be here where we know no one?"

Gillan's expression changed with Neil's use of the term Uncle, which was less respectful than calling him Father or even Stepfather. He blinked, and continued in a rough, desperate voice.

"The laird meant to burn them all out. There was nothing we could have done. It was bad that it happened after we'd been given assurances, that is true. But we've learned the lesson, and will not trust any of the high-class bastards around here." He darted a quick look toward the brazier and the cooking pot before continuing in a lower voice. "That's why we're here, Neil. And we'll do all right if we gather our resources before jumping into anything before we have a plan."

"You may have nae plan," Neil said testily.

"Neil," Gillan's voice held a warning.

"Why are you afraid to go out east? They said there were plots a-plenty, half-worked and abandoned. It's perfect. We jus' need to go up Antigonish way, talk to more people—"

"Ye'll do nae such thing. I'm doing this for *you*, Neil. For yer mother. D'ye think I want to go sell my health to another filthy, crowded place?" He switched tacks. "And for yourself, can ye not see the opportunity in a trade in a town, more surety than picking a living out of rocky or clay soil, at the mercy of a laird or a government, and the Lord's weather—"

Neil eyed him, not wanting to give in at any point but seeing the reasonableness of this argument. "Aye," he said. "There may be some trades good to enter now, if I'm not past age already, but never, if it is at the expense of my family." He paused, looking to see if Gillan felt the shame of not wanting to protect them himself. *How is it he thinks they'll be perfectly safe, after what they've already been through?*

"They are my family too, ken. And I wilna be without means to ensure they are safe. That was my promise on coming here."

So he wants the means to provide for them, while I want to protect them with my own self, thought Neil. *Then I guess we can both get what we want.* "Then we split ourselves up to make sure we achieve both our aims. You find the money; I'll be their protection."

Gillan grunted at him, not wanting to admit the reason in his son's plan any more than Neil had. After a moment spent looking out the window, he sighed, his shoulders shifting cautiously down. "A'right, Neil. We shall split ourselves, to achieve both our ends. It may take longer, and you may come to regret missing your chance, but I've said enough. Ye're yer own man now."

* * *

When Neil told his mother, she couldn't decide whom to glare at more, her son or her husband. Neil saw the conflicting emotions tearing through her: losing a husband, keeping a son, relief at not being left alone, fear how her husband would deal with all the risk on his own.

Gillan stayed long enough to hear Neil give the news, then ducked his head and left the room. Sheila pulled Neil close and clutched at him. "Thank you, Neil. For convincing him. It's glad I am you'll be here, my son."

Now that the decision had been taken, Gillan had more letters for Sheila to send, more people to see, a voyage to plan. Responsibilities shifted for their room fee, and Neil began to make his way overnight to farther and farther destinations, where he would spend the day talking to folk about the available land. Much of it was in the inland hills or forested land, hard to access and hard to tame. When he returned from these forays around the island, he related the important details he'd learned to all the family in front of the fire, then fell asleep instantly. His chores waited for him on his return, and the routine quickly began to wear him down again.

Gillan removed himself from the chore rotation and went out to do laboring work in order to gain some silver for the journey west. He came in at mealtimes, and talked to everyone sociably except Neil. Neil tried to take this lightly, but it did a job on his spirit, the same as his travels were doing to his body. Muirne often was the one to wake him after a long nap or a short night of sleep, and she did so by laying her cheek against his chest, and digging her hands under him for a hug. She'd give him a lopsided smile and tell him it was 'time for the day to begin again.'

In addition to her boarding chores, Muirne took over teaching Sheena and Alisdair, instructing them in reading and writing. They started in Gaelic, using the Bible and the small black slate. Chalk was hard to come by, but Sheena went to the schoolmaster's house and begged for the small castaway pieces.

The single men that boarded with Mrs. Conaghey were incessantly polite to Muirne, but when she ventured out, there were glances and shouts. One embarrassing episode had occurred when she looked up at one of the shouts because she'd been crossing the street, and thought it might announce an approaching vehicle. Instead of a carriage or a horseman, she saw two young blond men in workmen's aprons. One's face held a big grin, and he was being shoved in her direction by his friend. Fearing they would consider her attention an acknowledgement, she quickly averted her gaze and crossed the street, almost running into a buggy coming the other way.

The driver of the buggy, a sharp-eyed man of middle age with a large bushy mustache, reined the horses in. She was about to apologize when she saw his gaze flicker to the young men not far distant. He nodded at her to pass, keeping his gaze over her shoulder. She reached the other side of the road, flushed and unsettled from the whole encounter.

She wondered if it would be any better in a bigger city or in the country 'round about Pictou. She'd felt safe at home on their island, but was that because she'd been younger and less experienced? Or because they knew all their neighbors and shared the same code of civility? She hadn't thought it was a question of civility, but of common decency, but apparently, the Big City and the New Country had their own codes. She was relieved to know Neil would stay close by, even though it looked to be taking a toll on him to assume such a role so young.

* * *

They prepared for Gillan's leave-taking. He'd had the offer through Mr. Brown's friend confirmed, and would be setting off by St. Columba's Day. For his part, he did his round of thank-yous, making sure to leave what neighbors there were on good terms. It was agreed that the eldest Wilson boy would accompany him, to look out for any opportunities upriver. Gillan also updated the will they'd carried with them, leaving the document with a bank clerk.

The family felt the edge of Gillan's bitterness in these last few days, even when he made efforts to be involved. Sheila expressed her faith in his ability to earn the silver to find a good plot. She stayed down in the common kitchen for a long time, at the stove making oat bannocks and stovies that would keep for a few days of his journey.

Neil tried to stay out of his father's way, as he could feel the bridled hostility most acutely. It was a bustling, but not a happy household, despite the good situation they had found and the good weather that held. When Gillan had his food laid in, his few tools collected, and his spare shirt packed, he announced he was ready to leave that morning. He said farewell on the steps of the boarding house, promising to send word as soon as he could with any news.

Coming to Neil, he put his hand across to his shoulder. He seemed about to say something, but coughed instead and pulled him close. Neil pressed his arm around his stepfather, but kept his expression schooled to blankness, Muirne saw. It was painful, and she put her hand to her breastbone, which hurt with this break in the family. The last time she had felt the pain just there had been when they heard the news her father was gone.

Gillan saw his family's tears: they stayed in his mind's eye as he left to catch the boat that would take him up the St. Lawrence. He shook his head to free himself of the image a few times, then gave it up. His wife's anguished expression haunted him. He'd promised to make as much as he could, as quickly as possible, and spare nothing for his own keep, until they had enough for the new land west of the river, said to be flatter and more fertile.

Muirne heard his whispered words to her mother, and winced again at pain in her breastbone.

"When I return, it will be worth it."

Chapter 30

When Gillan left, Neil's journeying stopped. He was not sure
if it was temporary, but he could no longer leave for a night
and a day at a whim. For one, it would be leaving the other
four alone; for another, he could no longer go without sleep
to walk that far. And for a third, he had heard of a very good
possibility for them out east.

The next town over from them was New Glasgow, and
Neil had snorted at the name. *Not there, certainly*, he thought.
But when he approached the town from Pictou, there was a
ridge of land that he ascended slowly, only to see the whole of
the valley laid out before his eyes. It being June, Neil looked
and looked, the sun pouring down and the light glinting on the
water which wound its way through the settlements.

Instead of heading south to Truro or Halifax, where it was
lowland and fertile, he was forming a dream of finding a high
point for their new home, a place to look out to sea from,
maybe even eastward to look toward home. *Should I confide in
Muirne or wait until it is a closer possibility? Nay, I'll wait.*

He had a while to wait, for he had first to recover his
strength from the double schedule. This he had done in under

a week, but then Muirne had voiced a desire to accompany him on the overnight trip. They agreed it might be helpful for both to go, but then there were more preparations to make, as well as ensuring his mother was safe and well-stocked while they'd be gone. By now they had faith in their neighbors, and two of these agreed to stop by each morning to check in on them and help out if need be.

In a leave-taking uncomfortably close to their father's, Neil and Muirne set off. They were keen to see the acreage off the Sherbrooke Road that Neil had heard called a good prospect. Muirne was both excited and filled with trepidation, a mix which made her frequently glance around at the thick forest, so different from Scotland's barren volcanic hills and lowland valleys. They wore the same heavy plaids that had journeyed with the family from Mull, which were still in good repair despite their heavy service in the outdoors and on the ship. Long parts of the day saw them carrying them, as it was humid and warm, but they were thankful when they made camp for the night to have their warmth.

"Thank God for those hardy sheep," Neil said to her over their first campfire, outside New Glasgow. His grin won Muirne over and she relaxed a bit.

"I wish we had a way to recover a loom for Mama. She could do so much with one here, where people don't seem to have as much skill with their wool." This brought up a low laugh from Neil, as intended, since he knew she was thinking of a comical episode from kirk the week before. Someone they did not know had stood in front of the main door of the kirk as the folks filed out, wearing the long kilt, but it was atrociously woven, such that long strands hung down from many points, and floated around as he turned this way and that.

"Aye, I've been thinking on that too, and watching for any opportunity, but I haven't seen any weavers advertising in the town, have you?"

Muirne shook her head. "But how would we pay for it if we did find one? Are we not already doing all the wood chopping and coal gathering and water carrying for our room now? And yerself also the sanding and repairs and anything else that Mrs. Conaghey can think up for our board?"

"But if Mother had a loom, she could be earning money with it, and not having to scrub floors as now."

"Aye, but it's that first step: how to leap over that little mountain?"

* * *

They slept warm under the stars that night and the next. The third day, they reached the start of the hill path described to Neil, and began their ascent mid-morning. By noon, after fighting brush and brambles fiercely for a couple of hours, Neil called for a break. He could see Muirne's frustration, and they sat down to eat the oatcakes in their parcel and drink the water taken from the stream that morning.

When they started again, Muirne had regained some of her equanimity, but called out to Neil in good humor. "What was that big knife you said they had for cutting through the jungles in Africa? Ma-cherry?"

"Ma-chetty," he pronounced. "It's as long as a scimitar but straight, and cuts through vines and new growth like butter."

"And who told ye of this marvel?"

"Martin Wilson, while we were on the ship. As his older brother is going to run the smithy after their father, Martin's decided to go into the navy, but he's promised his mother to apply for a scholarship to one of the church schools in Quebec before he leaves."

"Tcha there," Muirne scolded as she lifted up her skirts to

stamp down another patch of thorny brambles. "Are you sure this is the way, Neil? It's nothing but brambles."

"Oh aye," he said. "Did ye notice that we've not had to be ducking through any tree branches? The brambles have only taken over where the trees were cut down for a path."

Muirne looked around, abashed she hadn't noticed something so simple. "Ow!" she cried out as her foot hit something forcefully and she put out her hands to break her fall. "Ooohh, the devil," she breathed as she recollected herself and saw all the thorns stuck to her palms.

"Tcha now," Neil said, imitating her scold a minute before. He laughed at the look she gave him. "What took your foot?"

"What else? A tree stump! Just as you were explaining about the cut-down trees."

Neil threw his head back to laugh freely at that, a kind of release for both of them in it. "It's only a short way before the crest. Come on, we're almost there." He helped her with the last of the thorns, and she pressed the cloth of her petticoat to her palms to staunch any blood coming up.

They struggled up as before, but Muirne could see the end of the ridge now, too. Neil reached it first and stood stock-still until she joined him. Where the path turned to run along the ridge, they stood under a grove of tall cedars. She gasped at the view and reached both hands outward to balance herself as she turned to gaze in all directions.

"We've got a view of the whole country here," Neil said. "It's quite handsome, wouldn't you say?"

Muirne was speechless. They gazed out to the west and south where the sun was just starting its long slow summer descent. There were other hills nearby, lakes glinting between them. Trees climbed high all around, and for the middle of the day, it seemed very quiet. Neil felt his spirit rise with the beauty of the landscape. Turning, he watched Muirne's eyes skim over the peaks and foothills, the delight evident in her open-mouthed wonder.

"I don't think I've ever been this high," she said.

"I know. Folks say the Cuillins are fair tall, but I think this is even higher."

"You said there was a cabin started here as well? Why would someone desert their claim here?" A shadow of doubt had come into her voice, he noticed.

"Well, let's find the site if we can. Maybe we'll see why there. If not, it's back to the town gossips again."

They made their way to the right, following the path of no trees again. Muirne laughed at this. "Aye, and I'm no' to ask how you won the favors of these town gossips, am I?"

"Mmph," Neil said emphatically. "I'm no' getting into trouble, so don't you worry," he said, preferring to be enigmatic for the moment rather than dispel his sister's visions of his being the romantic rover of Pictou.

They saw the clearance for the site first, as the rocks and shells stood out on the dark earth. Foundation and large logs were covered with moss and mushrooms. *Apparently it's wet even up here on the ridge*, Neil thought. Beyond the outlines of the cabin lay the stacks of wood meant for its walls. They were long poles stripped of bark, not milled at a lumber mill.

"Was this a very early settlement, Neil?"

A stillness had settled inside him at the sight, and her question broke his train of thought. "What was that?"

"I asked if it was a very early settlement, since the logs look all homemade, you know, stripped young trees from the forest around, instead of the long rectangular sides you see in town."

"I was just thinking the same thing," he told her. The stillness returned, and Muirne spoke quietly this time.

"It reminds me of our house, Neil."

"How d'ye mean? Ours was stone and daub, not wood logs like—" He stopped himself at her expression, which seemed appropriate for a cemetery.

"Not that way. I mean, our house probably looks like this now, burnt down and exposed for a year now. It's—" she searched for a word. "Lonely."

Neil reviewed the images that had been in his head ever since he'd been told in Glencoe of their blackhouse being burnt and abandoned. He'd imagined it burnt to cinders, the rocks strewn about. But Muirne had been there that morning, and now he understood that the men had not returned, confident that the lives of the tenants were destroyed enough. So there were likely corners standing. Hooks left in the walls. Shelves only turned over, still inside the outline of the house.

He turned away from Muirne and a sharp exclamation broke from him, "*Mo cridhe!*" His hands squeezed tight into fists, and he wished he could stop the new images from forming in his mind, but it was as if he was a bird swooping down for a better view of their own Dalcriadh, a year after they'd left.

Muirne looked at him, then focused her gaze upon the ground at her feet, the leaves collected there and the plants pushing up through the ground cover. When she'd mastered her own memories, she looked back up to Neil.

She was unsurprised to see his face screwed up and his nose running as he wept. The beautiful day shone down on them in the little clearing, taking no notice of their grief, finally aired.

Muirne stepped to his side and he put his arm around her shoulder. She looked out from the site to the north, where one could just glimpse the sea. She knew it must be the strait between Nova Scotia and New Brunswick, but she let it be the sea outside their home for a moment as she gazed, feeling

Neil's tears where her temple touched his chin.

Chapter 31

The first news they received from Gillan came two weeks after he had left. It was a fine hot June afternoon, and the MacLeans in Pictou were all occupied clearing the tangle of brambles and brush on that steeply pitched road to Sherbrooke. Faced with the choice of waiting for Gillan's news and subsequent money or starting on something that could gain them a place sooner, they chose the latter.

They borrowed scraps of leather to grasp the thorns with, and hacked at the plants with other borrowed implements: a scythe, a sickle, a saw. They were all old tools, blunt and little effective. Still, they'd been at it four days running and made recognizable progress when they were hailed by someone down the hill.

"Mistress MacLean!" the voice cried, carried upward easily by winds that cooled the brow of those working. Sheila stopped, turned back to look, and saw one of their neighbors from Pictou standing at the foot of the hill fifty feet distant, waving an arm with something white in his hand. Sheena took the opportunity to straighten her back from its bent position and sigh dramatically. She sat down in the cleared area, thankful for a rest.

Alisdair giggled, imitating her sigh and executed a dramatic swooping fall. Muirne looked at them, shaking her head, then laid down her saw and followed her mother and Neil down the hill. The neighbor was Mr. Macklemore, and he had a smile plastered across his face. "Has the town found a vein of gold under the streets then, Mr. Macklemore?" Sheila asked him.

He cackled at that, throwing back his head and showing his strong set of discolored teeth. "Ah no, Mrs. MacLean, but you've 'ad a letter from your Gillan these three days past, and I've only been able to bring it to you now that I'm on my way to visit a friend. He's got some horses to inspect. I might buy a few to bring back."

Muirne thought of his going to buy horses and felt a momentary twinge of envy for those already well settled, but let it pass. *Our time will come,* she told herself. *In the meantime, no use getting upset at the bragging of a good-natured blowhard.* He continued to regale them with the account of the letter's arrival and the decision of who should bring it to the family while they camped out here. Sheena much enjoyed the rest on the soft earth, choosing not to listen to the rambling account.

"I was honored to be the messenger," he said, amusement glinting from his eyes. "And since my friend with the horses lives near a town on the express route, I would be happy to transmit any news back to your husband if there is a reply needed." He waited then, rocking back on his heels and settling his folded hands on the paunch under his waistcoat.

Sheila acknowledged his effort in tracking them down and thanked him for the offer of returning her reply. She sat down to open the letter while he waited and beckoned to Neil. Muirne and Neil both moved closer, and Neil took the pages from her hands but held it out so they could all see the scrap of paper from their Gillan.

There was Sandy Wilson's splotchy quillwork in Gaelic across two pages. He wrote that Gillan had had two interviews in Tadoussac, a town along the north coast of the river where he had been deposited by the boat. It was an older town at the intersection of two rivers, and there seemed to be plenty of opportunities. He would consider these two posts, but intended to continue upriver into the city even if he was accepted, in effect delaying his start in order to have time to explore the capital.

He ended with endearments for Sheila and affection to all, and as Neil read that he could feel his stepfather's solid barrier still there between them. *Very well*, thought Neil. *I will just be proving him wrong by adopting this place and moving into it before he even knows what he's about. He'll see.*

No reply was needed, especially since the return direction would likely be wrong now. Gillan was most likely making his way on foot now to the capital, Quebec City. Sheila thanked Mr. Macklemore once again before he continued on his way. Sheila turned to see Sheena and Alisdair standing and watching the action down the hill. She grinned, then with her own dramatic sigh, swirled around and fell to the ground. Children were not the only ones who needed humor.

* * *

More days passed with no news, as the MacLeans restored the road to a troddable path. They had one more visit from a Pictou neighbor, who came to replenish their supply of oats and onions, compliments of Mrs. Conaghey, or rather their account with her. He'd thrown in a gooseberry tart that his wife had made, and they almost toppled him with their enthusiastic hugs and exclamations upon the discovery. True, there were gooseberries growing wild enough on the surrounding hills, but they were much too sour to enjoy, and there was the work of topping and tailing each one before you could cook and eat it.

They enjoyed the tart very much, and counted the days left until they would need to return to town to replenish the rest of their supplies. They subsisted on the water from the creek on the property, which was swift-running and clear, and they made nightly fires where Sheila cooked the skirlie in the griddle. Each took a turn telling stories to keep the attention off their aches and blisters. They had made a fair bit of headway by the mark of nine days, when they needed to go back.

Sheila stood back with Neil and surveyed their handiwork. It was soft dirt with plenty of roots scattered about. When the path turned to the right and went out of sight, it was also clear for a good fifty feet.

"When we come back it will need to be with shovels to dig out those roots," Sheila said.

"Aye, or a *cas-chrom*," he teased. They would not likely find their own island farming implements floating around this Pictou community, Scots though it was.

Sheila and the three children would return to town and the boarding house while Neil chased down more details of the property's owners and the law concerning possession, improvement, and ownership with the professional men in New Glasgow. While they waited for word, Sheila and the children might also be able to return some of the favors done them by the people of Pictou.

It took them the same two days it had taken Neil and Muirne to return to Pictou on foot. Sheena and Alisdair were growing up, no longer running roughshod all over the place but contributing to the household and learning how to behave in civilized company. On the way back, Sheila looked back to see Neil and Muirne with their heads together, laughing over some tale. She thought about the need to find a good lad for Muirne, but whom? She cast her mind over the people they'd met, all kind, but with a noticeable lack of marriageable sons. She would ask Mrs. Conaghey, who no doubt could hold forth on the subject, and perhaps already had done, in their absence.

Chapter 32

The return to town and Mrs. Conaghey's boarding house went smoothly. The welcome they received and the curious questions upon their return made Neil and Muirne feel grateful for this resting place, where people seemed to look out for one another. They compared it to Glasgow and their disastrous First Footing there, and saw that their mother did not seem as desperately lonely among their neighbors as she had been before.

They were all keeping so busy that it was easy to forget that Gillan was missing. His second letter came as a surprise the day after they returned. Neil was handed the letter by the town grocer, and he brought it home to read to his mother at supper.

"Dear Everyone," Neil read aloud at the table. "I did not find a satisfactory situation at either of the two posts in Tadoussac that I wrote you of. So we are now in Quebec City, and there are many opportunities here, as well as masses of people. I have already run into an acquaintance from home: Mr. Brown of Macrieff."

Sheila gave a sharp intake of breath. "Brown?"

"Who's that then, Mama?" Muirne asked. Sheila just shook her head, and flicked her hand at Neil to continue.

"It is turning out to be a simple thing to labor for a day and receive wages for my food and lodging for two days, during which I look for other lines of work. At this rate, I hope to find something substantial before the week is out. I hope to send to you then to follow. All my prayers and thoughts are with you, Gillan."

There was a pregnant silence, while each thought about what would happen if he sent for them. Muirne broke it by asking softly, "Who's Mr. Brown, Mother?"

"I think I remember," said Neil. "Isn't he the man who was hounding you to marry him after Father's disappearance? He kept coming 'round the house?"

Sheila turned to look at Neil, her eyes round in surprise. "Aye, I didna think you'd remember all that. You were only Alisdair's age."

"I was not that young, but I remember you did not like him," Neil said.

"Well, and it's a big city, so we will hope that they do not meet again, for Gillan doesnae like him either," Sheila replied. She rose and took the wooden dishes from supper to the bucket, then handed it to Sheena.

It was Sheena's turn to clean the evening dishes. She took the large wooden bucket down to the water pump next to the boarding house. She returned with the extra bucket full of fresh water for the night.

The MacLeans were quiet that night, and left off the evening routine of gathering 'round the coal brazier to tell stories. The younger children fell asleep early, while the older two listened to Sheila singing softly as she mended some knitting. They were glad to hear from Gillan, relieved he was making some headway on his journey. But they had all come to the point where they thought it best to stay put. Neil wondered if indeed they would go when sent for. He was excited, preparing in his head the steps he would take tomorrow to determine legal possession of land under the law in Nova Scotia.

* * *

When Neil headed off to the town attorney's office, Muirne was already well into her chores for the day: washing the floors of the unoccupied rooms at the top of the house. As she dipped the rag into the bucket and scrubbed at the wood, rubbing off layers of soot and dirt and other stains, her mind wandered again to the comments made by her mother about this Mr. Brown. *Do I remember anything of him?* she wondered. Neil had not told her more of what he remembered, but his tone hadn't been pleasant.

Her reverie was broken by Mrs. Conaghey bursting into the room and exclaiming over the extraordinarily hot weather.

"Well, it was quite warm while we were working to clear the road, but I didn't think it particularly hot down here in town. Maybe it was the trees on the main street giving us shade," Muirne said.

"Oh my dear, you must have been too tired to notice, for the past few days have been simply awful. I'm afraid what it'll be like later in the summer this year. How is the clearing coming along?"

"Oh, fine, fine. We hope to be back at it before the week is out, but Neil's got to find out some things to make sure we're not doing it all for nothing. That will make Father happy too; he hasn't decided on anything yet."

"I see. Well, he's gone down to Archie's office then? Everyone goes to him for land and property questions."

"Aye, Mrs. Conaghey, Archie that you recommended."

"Good girl," said the older woman. "And you're doing a fine job up here as well. I'll go see your mother and then have some of last night's roast ready for lunch, how about that?"

"That sounds wonderful, Mrs. Conaghey, thank you." Muirne's mouth had started watering at the mention of fresh cooked meat. *It is that time of year again*, she thought, taken aback at how quickly so much had happened between this year and last. As she felt the loss of their chickens for a moment, a lightning bolt struck her brain. *Chickens!* She could earn money selling eggs and meat that way, perhaps even enough to get the loom for her mother. It might take a while, but it was a start.

Feeling immensely better, she finished her washing, whistling as she went.

* * *

When Neil returned, it was past the dinner hour and late into the afternoon. He'd been sent to a number of places along the main streets of the town by the attorney. He'd talked to three business owners about their knowledge of the whereabouts of the family who had first settled the ridge, which Neil had taken to inwardly calling *Sealladh Cùil*. It meant Looking Back, and made him feel a little more connected to Dalcriadh across the water. The view of the old foundation did not make him sad, like it did Muirne. Rather, he thought of the new house they would build there, and how they could make it their home.

He sat on the floor of the hallway outside where Muirne was working in one of the upper rooms. He chewed through the slice of meat pie she had saved him from dinner. Muirne was shaking out clothes and linens at the window, preparing to wash laundry down by the pump with Sheena. "What's on your mind, Neil?"

He didn't reply immediately, but looked up and met her eyes. "Oh, this and that. A few more visits and signatures and we'll have enough evidence of abandonment to properly squat on the ridge, but there will still be a lot of work to do. There isn't a pump there, and I have no idea how difficult it would be to put one in up at the ridge. Do we need an engineer? They're sure to be expensive. We might just use the spring. But then...so yes, just this and that." He gave her a quick smile.

Muirne knew that was not what he'd been thinking about, but let it go. Another clap of thunder came from the large rug as she snapped it outside. She turned her head to avoid the dust, but still coughed. An alarmed "Hey there!" stole her attention and she looked out and down from the balcony to the walk in front of the house. Standing there was a young man, dressed in a clean brown suit, brushing himself off.

"Oh, I'm so sorry, sir! I checked before I started; you must have just come up?"

"Aye, I'm just arriving, and did not expect to be covered with dust! Och!" He was patting himself down with his hand-kerchief, but then stopped to look back up. "You wouldn't happen to be Miss MacLean, would ye?"

"Yes, that's me. What is it? Do you have a message for me?"

"Nay, I—" He stopped himself short and turned and walked quickly away. Muirne was so surprised she didn't think to call after him. It was either very bad manners or something unexpectedly urgent. Either way, she brushed him out of her thoughts. Until the next day, that is, when the same young man arrived in the morning. He was sporting a different suit, a black one this time, and was announced by Mrs. Conaghey in the house, instead of yelling up from the street.

The boarding house matron knocked on their door and invited them to the front parlor. She introduced the young man to the MacLeans as her nephew, James McLachlan. He had some information for them about the property they had their eye on. When Neil heard that, his thoughts immediately jumped to the possibility that it was not abandoned, that the family intended to return somehow. Maybe they would need to start over looking for a place to build; he might even have to follow his stepfather into the city.

But James did not tell them of any further impediments; rather, he told them what he'd found out at the law office where he worked, down in New Glasgow. When his auntie had asked him to check if there were any records on such and such a property, he'd easily found the history of the original settlers.

They were Scots, as expected, which matched up with the information from all the neighbors Neil had canvassed that day. Campbells from Applecross. They had arrived forty-two years earlier, in 1781. *Forty-two years that's been there!* thought Muirne. *And nobody coming to claim it?* There was a great part of the clan that landed together, near thirty people, and all fleeing because of a violent disagreement with a neighboring clan, which had been adjudicated by English officials from Fort Augustus.

James didn't need to explain what that meant. Judgement by an English official meant no mercy and scant justice. Sheila had heard from her own grandmother how English soldiers had pillaged towns and farms, how it was made a crime to wear the kilt or your own tartan. A man wasn't even allowed to carry a gun to hunt on his own property if he was a Scot. Sheila had told her own children some of the same stories she'd heard, enough to make them thankful the blatant violence of those times was over.

James continued. The Campbells had settled in various places around Pictou, farming land in the lowlands. The plot that the MacLeans had all been working on had come later, after they'd been established a few years. He didn't have the familiar details about why that spot, why that place, but he did have a year: 1789. There was a remark about the 'fine, new structure' planned for the property in the tax accounts.

"So how did it come to collapse and fade away? Was that more recent?" Neil asked.

"Aye, it was. They were part of the feud between the MacDonalds and the Campbells back home, see. You'll know of the Glencoe massacre."

A shiver ran down Muirne's spine as the empty glen flashed in front of her eyes, the sight of it in the gloaming before Neil had ridden up to meet them. "You're not saying it was burnt down or pulled down, because of the feud back in Scotland?"

"I am. The fine house on the hill was burnt down three years after it was built, in 1792." The date sank in. It was one hundred years after the treachery in Glencoe. "And in January," James added. *One hundred years exactly*, thought Muirne. *What a tragic waste.*

"Some of the local folk want that another family should live there now. The ones who burnt it down were never found. People say they went down to America, once the colonies had won their independence, as that was no longer British land and they could not be tried for the crime. It is uncertain."

"But why hasn't anyone tried to make a go of it before now?" Muirne asked. "That's thirty years gone by, with plenty of people coming in, no?"

"Aye, that's right." James seemed reluctant to answer. His aunt stepped in. "It's the spirits, lass. They that might be hanging about and prevent a new house from flourishing."

"Spirits? You mean the family were killed there?" asked Sheila, her voice a low rasp.

"Yes," James returned.

Sheila cleared her throat. "Were they—in the house when it...?"

"I'm afraid a good many of them were," said James. A cry from Muirne. "About a dozen of them perished in the fire; it's in the news record."

"That's awful," Muirne murmured. She was remembering the frantic dash to remove all their belongings from their house on the island. She wondered now whether any of the neighbors had not been warned as they had, merely set afire in their beds. She closed her eyes tight. *Even here*, she thought.

James cleared his throat but it was Mrs. Conaghey who spoke next. "It was an awful thing," she clucked. "I arrived more'n ten years later but they were still speaking of it. The Campbells gone from the whole area afterwards, the ruin sitting there, the rumors of the MacDonalds' whereabouts a-flying. That's most of the reason why it's empty. The rest is just people making up stories of ghosts, I s'pect, to no purpose."

There was a silence.

"Well, does all this mean there are none contesting the possession of the land legally?" Neil asked.

"It does," James replied. "So in the end it is good news I've brought." He glanced at Muirne. She wasn't looking at him, but at the floor, her eyes unfocused, deep in thought. "It's glad I am to tell you the news, since you can now move forward with your own plans for the place without worry. My thanks, Auntie, for passing on the request." He lingered for just a moment, and just as Neil was going to ask him to stay, Mrs. Conaghey did it for him.

"Oh, but Jamie, I can't let you head on back without a hot

meal in ye; your mother'd be after me with a stick for thoughtlessness. Won't ye stay and sup with us? You're not needed anywhere else at present?"

"No, Auntie, and I'd be happy to stay. Thank you."

They had a less rowdy and more constrained supper that evening as they felt out this new stranger. The MacLeans also had some things to ponder for their building plans, after this new information.

Mrs. Conaghey's lamb roast, stewed with vegetables in the heat of the summer, soon relaxed them and they were laughing and teasing with their new acquaintance. Sheila and Mrs. Conaghey exchanged significant looks, while the children entertained each other.

Chapter 33

The last week of July found them all back on the ridge. All the overgrown brush from the path to the clearing was piled high in the forest beside the path, and the remnants of the foundation were being dug out from the debris. Sheila kept them going with a ruthless practicality.

"That's tin, that is," she said, spying a blackened mug in Muirne's hand. "Aye," she said when it was handed over for closer inspection. "Put that in the save pile; it'll be one more for the party when it's cleaned up." This brought slight smiles from Muirne and Neil, a broad grin from Alisdair.

Other items had not survived the thirty year interval, rotted clothes being tossed in a pile for fire tinder, and animal droppings and other leavings being swept off the foundation to a large pile adjacent. Everyone had a job. Sheila talked constantly so they would not have one second to consider the fate of the people who had last lived here. She also didn't want to think about what it meant to be working on one home while her husband was out searching for another.

Sheila had a snatch of ribald tune humming in her head as she broke the ground at the house's edge to check whether there had been water damage underneath the foundation over the years. She leaned down to check the base of what remained of the wall and heard a sudden, angry buzzing.

With a cry, she stumbled back from the spot, landing on her behind. Alisdair was closest and turned to look at her cry of surprise. He saw his mother splayed backward on the ground, one leg kicking up in the air, her hands flailing in front of her face. Then he saw the black cloud swarming. "Neil!" he screamed.

Neil and Muirne had come around the corner of the house after the first cry went up, and Alisdair rushed to Neil's side to tug on his arm. They could now see the swarm as well.

"Stay back," Neil said, pulling Alisdair behind him. He thought wildly of how to distract wasps, but couldn't see how to avoid hurting his sister and brother as well if he drew them off his mother, who had now rolled face-down in the dirt. He ran for the pail of water, then grabbed a discarded threadbare shirt, tying it over his face. That was the best he could do. He came back to where his mother now lay motionless and chucked the water at the swarm, downing a handful of wasps and scattering some more. It was all he could do. He picked up his mother and stumbled his way away from the spot to carry her to safety as he felt a few angry stings himself.

Muirne leaned over to peer at her mother's face. "Mother, can you hear me? Mother!"

Alisdair was sent down to the creek to fetch another pail of water, and the two older children were hovering over Sheila, who sat propped up by one of the cedars, some thirty feet from the house. She was still in a faint. Muirne looked to Neil, panicky tears starting to make her breathe in a jumpy way. "What can we do? A cold cloth? We have no smelling salts to bring her 'round."

Neil took the shirt he'd tied around his face and dipped it

into the pail Alisdair set at his feet. He lay the cool cloth gently over his mother's face and neck, which had both started to pinken and swell. Muirne covered her mouth, pushing away the thought that it looked like a shroud. Neil gathered himself and spoke. "One of us should go and fetch help, someone faster than we are to bring a doctor."

Muirne rose. "I'll go down to Antigonish. It's closer and bigger, and they can send someone back on a horse. They might make it in a few hours if I run." Saying this, she stayed for neither kerchief nor farewell, but tore down the path they'd cleared. Neil turned to Alisdair, whose lip was trembling mightily against fearful emotions dammed in his face.

"Alisdair, I'll need you to be our bucket brigade, so we keep the cool water on her face, a'right?" Alisdair picked up the pail and started back down to the creek yet again. Neil glanced down at the few stings he could feel prickling his hands. He stood and gave a strangled cry.

"Of all the—" He thought they'd been careful in all their motions, measured in all their attempts to secure a new place, but now, Nature herself seemed to be rearing an ugly head to chase them away from their dream of a new home.

Neil heard Alisdair hurrying back up the path and knew he had to bring himself under control, but he was suddenly so angry at the injustice of his family's misfortunes that he let loose with his temper for a moment. He slapped his palms against a log that lay on the ground nearby. *God's blessings they were not burned in their beds*, he thought wildly, *and is it this she was saved for? God, please take the poison from her—or speed the horse of the doctor in Sherbrooke—or speed the feet of Muirne as she runs—whatever it takes to keep our mother safe.*

He gave in to his grief for a few moments, but then he heard Alisdair calling his name. "Neil, what should I do next?"

"Take the—nevermind, I'll do it." Neil grabbed up the

canteen, hoping he hadn't sloshed all the water out in his haste. But no, it was still quite heavy. He picked up Muirne's abandoned kerchief, wetted it with more cool water, and placed it on his mother's hands. "There, keep you an eye on the kerchief, and when it starts to feel hot, dip it into the cold water, like this." Neil demonstrated again. Alisdair nodded. Neil went to gather their plaids, bunching a couple of the squares of cloth under his mother's head.

* * *

Hours later, Neil glanced at the brow of the hill every few minutes. He imagined the journey Muirne must have taken, the search for a doctor, the procuring of a fast horse, the relating of details and directions to the doctor. *If I can think through all of it, it could have happened by now, no?*

His mother still lay in the shade of the tree. She'd awoken a few times at first, to find Neil by her side. He saw a sort of mute pleading in her eyes, and it cut him to feel so helpless against her suffering. If he'd known some sort of plant he could scavenge to bring down the swelling, but no. There were red bumps and scrapes all over her collar bone from when she'd fallen and flailed about at the wasps. Her ears and cheeks and neck were all distended beyond their natural smoothness, looking fit to burst. She hadn't woken for a while now, breathing raggedly through the cold wet kerchief.

As he looked up for the umpteenth time, he heard a crashing in the bracken. Off the road, through the forested part of the hill, there was a horse coming up toward them. Its rider wore no jacket, but was in his shirtsleeves: a tall, dark, mustachioed man. He pulled up the horse's reins when he caught sight of the family huddled in the shadow of the tall cedar.

"Are you the doctor?" called Neil.

"I'm the best your sister could find," came the reply, tossed in Neil's direction as he dismounted unceremoniously from the horse and dropped the reins to the ground. He carried no doctor's bag, but there was a pouch attached to the saddle, Neil noticed. The man tore it open, pulling out another wee pouch, this one with a drawstring. He drew out a small bottle from it as he strode over.

"This is a very long shot, son, but it may help."

"Aye."

"Let us hope." He knelt down and carefully applied a sweet-smelling herbal oil to her skin, replacing the cool cloths as he went. Then he bent down to listen to her breathing. "When did it happen, by your estimate?"

Neil looked at the sun, barely visible, over the low mountain across the west valley. "More'n two hour ago, sir. I'd say it was around two and a quarter."

"Well, I think she'll make it, since she's still breathing. Her throat isn't constricted, but we'll see." He rose and returned to the saddle bag. Neil marveled at the horse standing stock-still, catching its breath after the mad dash up the hill. He returned with a small glass bottle. He uncorked it and waved it under Sheila's nose. She shot up, startling Neil and Alisdair. She looked around, panting after the first gasp of recall. Her speech was slurred, but understandable.

"Alisdair... Neil, coom here to me. Oh boys..."

The man had stepped back quietly when she woke, and watched as the boys hugged their mother, carefully avoiding the exposed parts of skin that by now flared red and pouchy. She raised a hand to her face.

"I wouldn't recommend that, mistress," came the voice a few feet away. Sheila turned, emitting a painful intake of breath, to look at the stranger.

"Mam, this is the man who's just come to our aid," said

Neil. "Thank ye sir, and may we know the name of the man we must thank?"

"I'm Ed Turner, and it was no trouble. I was just in the process of buying that mare, and you've given me the perfect occasion to test her mettle. She passed with flying colors, I must say." He turned to Sheila, "So did you, I'm glad to say."

"Are ye not a doctor, then?" Alisdair still clung to his mother's skirt, but peeked his head out to observe the stranger.

"No, but I'm studying to be one, and was right near the school, where I could get that tincture of yarrow root. Have you any vinegar or alcohol near?"

"No, sir."

"Well, I suppose there's nothing for it then. We can't risk waiting any longer." He moved to the saddle bag and brought forth a small bottle with paper on the front and wax at the top.

"This was an early graduation present from my own father, some very expensive brandy," he said, musing. "And I suppose it could be put to no better use."

"Now hold still there," he said, and dropped a few drops at a time onto a corner of cloth and dabbed at certain points on her exposed skin.

"Mr. Turner," said Neil, when he had finished. "Thank ye so much, sir. Ye're helping us out of a terrible misfortune. And we've no way to pay you at present, but—"

"Well, I will be most happy to hear from you when you are back on your feet and walking, Mrs. MacLean. It's not too far from Pictou to Sherbrooke, and I hope you'll pay me a visit in future. We can talk about payment then, when you're fully recovered. For now, though," he paused, glancing around him. "I've a mare to pay for!" He laughed, and rose to dust off his breeches. His disheveled shirt he shrugged at.

"I would recommend letting those sons do most of the work around here for a few days, madam, and only moving when you feel up to it. Happy to be of some little service," he said as he threw the reins back over the mare's head and mounted.

"Goodbye!"

He left them more than a bit astonished at his exit. *What on earth kind of behavior was that?* thought Neil.

"What a queer man," Alisdair said.

"Queer or no, he's done us a good turn. Oh, Neil," she sighed, wriggling her free fingers toward him.

"I was so scared," Neil murmured to her.

"You did right," she replied. Louder, she said, "And I think we'll need some more water for our camp. And that Neil will be cooking dinner." She tried to smile without moving any of the muscles in her swollen face. "But where's Muirne? Is she the one fetched Mr. Turner?"

"Aye, Mam. She'll be walking back to us now, not as fast as the horse."

"Ah. Well, we can't do much more here, so it's back to Mrs. Conaghey. When we get back in two days' time, we'll celebrate two happy occasions: your saving my life, and Muirne finding a beau!"

Chapter 34

Before they returned to town, Sheila did indeed take the opportunity of quizzing Muirne on the subject of Ed Turner. At first Muirne only let on how desperate she'd been to find someone who could help, and how relieved she was to find two men right outside the medical college. Sheila could well imagine the state Muirne must've been in when she arrived in Sherbrooke. She probed further.

"But what was your very *first* thought when you saw Mr. Turner?"

Muirne's eyes strayed to the side. Sheila waited. "He looked like a man to rescue us," Muirne said softly. Sheila noted the 'us' instead of 'you.'

"Aye, and right well he behaved," said Sheila, omitting his abrupt departure. "What was his first reaction to ye then?"

"He was talking with another man about the mare, as he said. They were standing in the street near the school. Mr. Turner was facing me, and I'm sure saw me before I noticed him, since I was so out of breath and in such a panic. I was trying to look around but the world felt all a bit crazy by then. I felt like I'd never stop running."

She paused. "Anyway, I fairly collapsed at their feet. I had no breath to shout, so I whispered the words that came to me. *Mother—wasps—fallen ill—hurry—old Campbell steading.* They held me up and listened, I think. Then I saw Mr. Turner rush for the school, and I thought he was leaving me. But the next moment he came right back out, spoke to the other man who was holding me up, and then leapt onto the mare. He told the man to look after me, and was off."

Sheila approved of the narrative, both the behavior of the gentlemen and the conduct of her daughter. "And how long did you stay?"

"Oh, I couldn't, Mother. I had to get back here to you!" She turned tortured eyes on Sheila. "I only rested until I'd caught my wind, drank some water the man got from a pump, and then started walking again."

"Well, when we go back to Mrs. Conaghey's tomorrow, we shall send a note of thanks to Mr. Turner and friend, by way of the school. I'm sure we can find the name of it from someone in town—Mrs. Conaghey." She attempted to snicker, and Muirne's seriousness fell away. She smiled at the mention of the old gossip, now a true friend.

"Very well. We shall send a note. But don't let's tell Mrs. Conaghey all the details I've just told you, Mam."

* * *

They learned of the school: Frederick Taylor School of Medicine Practice. They sent off the note. Muirne told Neil a slightly modified version of the same tale, leaving out her remark about Mr. Turner looking like the rescuing type of man. She didn't want to bother Neil with such sentimental twaddle. They stayed in town several days to be sure Sheila's swelling would go down and not lead to complications.

There was no news from Gillan. The family thought about writing him of their near escape, but as they had no address, they let it bide.

A week went by, and the areas where Sheila had been stung—head, neck, and arms—looked to be almost normal. Sunday came, and kirk. The children attended, leaving Sheila at home with their Bible. She sat studying it, pondering their position. So precarious it had been, but they had been pulled back to safety. "Thanks be to the Lord," she whispered.

As she was sitting on the bed, she heard someone enter downstairs, and the muted sounds of two people conversing through the floor. *Who would be visiting now, during kirk?* Sheila thought. She found out soon enough. Mrs. Conaghey was off to the service as well, so it was a housemaid who knocked on her door and introduced a Mr. Turner to see her.

Sheila's heart went all a-flutter at the mention of the name —a chance for her Muirne! He entered and bowed; the maid withdrew. He held his hat in front of him, twirling the brim. Sheila asked him to sit, and indicated one of the chairs not piled with maps, dull tools, and piece-work.

"Thank you, madam," he said. She was pleased by the low timbre of his voice. Mellifluous.

"It is I who should be thanking you, of course, sir." She smiled. "Both for coming to my aid and for paying me this call, although you perhaps thought to find more people about than just me? You're rather early—"

"Yes, it's Sunday, isn't it?" This took Sheila aback. *Of course it was Sunday; who did not take notice of the bells and follow them to kirk?* "Would you have any objection to my waiting until your family returns? You are right; I intended a visit with all of you, but neglected to mark the time. Foolish of me."

A little on her guard now, Sheila inclined her head. She took up her Bible again from where she had set it on the bed and looked at him. He did not raise his gaze to meet hers, but allowed her an easy inspection of his person. The dark, curly locks remained the same. The shirt, jacket, and cravat were all spick and span, sharply pressed. Sheila wondered who did his laundry for him. His breeches, hose, and shoes were of good quality, and nothing about him looked ragged. Indeed, he had carried himself well into the room, but still she felt he was hiding something, ashamed of something. His downcast gaze seemed to be proof.

"Would you like to hear me read? I was going to reflect on the Book of Nehemiah today, and the Psalms, to thank God for my near escape."

Mr. Turner looked as if someone had poked him awake. "Ah, surely, madam, if you wish to do so, I will listen." A queer response, from someone who was otherwise the picture of manners and decorum.

She commenced to read a passage, pausing at intervals to reflect on the words herself. She heard not a peep from Mr. Turner's direction. She gave up waiting for a response and merely continued as if he were not there. After a good twenty minutes though, there was another stirring downstairs. More muted voices. Another man's. *Oh for goodness' sake*, thought Sheila. *Now what?*

The same young maid, now looking reproachfully at Sheila for having taken her away from her household duties twice, knocked and announced a Mr. MacLachlan. Sheila felt about to lose her equanimity.

"How delightful, Mr. MacLachlan. You'll excuse me if I don't get up; I've had a frightful run-in with a wasp colony out on the ridge, and I'm still recovering. To what do I owe this pleasure?" Sheila was still propped up in the low bed, but Mr. Turner rose when the second guest was introduced. They glanced at each other, coolly reading each other's stations, gauging each other's intentions.

Sheila had a moment to compare them, to size them both up as suitors for Muirne. Both men were older than her daughter, although how much older she wasn't sure. Turner looked older, more experienced, and he had a bit of an accent, which she couldn't identify other to say it sounded educated. Both men looked physically healthy, strong, and confident. MacLachlan was Mrs. Conaghey's nephew, and so she knew one of his ties to the stable community of Pictou, but Turner could be anybody, really. And he did give off such an aloof air.

Mr. Turner had been sitting on the only chair in the room, but Sheila indicated the chest to Mr. MacLachlan and he accepted with grace. "Mrs. MacLean, I had indeed heard of your accident, and was coming to pay you a visit to see if there was anything I could do. I realize that you'll want work to continue on the property, and maybe I could help with the possession paperwork. But first things first, are you feeling well enough for a visit?"

"Well enough, Mr. MacLachlan. But let me introduce one of my rescuers. Mr. MacLachlan, Mr. Turner, from Sherbrooke. Mr. Turner, this is Mr. MacLachlan, our landlady's nephew."

They nodded politely to each other. *So they haven't met before*, Sheila thought. *But there is definitely tension there.* "I was just reading from the Bible since I can't yet make it to kirk, Mr. MacLachlan. Do you go to a different one from your aunt?"

"Er, yes, missus. My mother, Auntie Ann's sister, married a Seceder—an anti-Burgher—and so converted. Theirs is an earlier service, and I have already attended."

Sheila's mind drew back a bit, although she tried not to let it show on her face. "I see. Are you a Seceder as well, Mr. Turner, to pay such an early call a-Sunday?"

"Ah, no, madam. It's just that I am not very religious in any particular sect. I attend no church since—for a long time." Sheila noticed the sudden flush of red creep up from his collar, and wondered again at his very odd behavior.

"I see." She paused. She was not feeling up to this complicated double interview all of a sudden. "Well, gentlemen, I thank you for your pains in coming here this morning, but I must say I am feeling rather tired and the need for a rest—"

"Of course, missus," MacLachlan said, springing up.

"Of course, madam," Turner said, raising himself up more slowly.

MacLachlan looked like he was going to speak, but hesitated. "Yes, sir?" Sheila prodded.

"Might I return this afternoon, after you're more rested and the family is here? I had hoped to talk with you all."

"Yes, I think that'd be all right." She inclined her head to each of them as they exited, and her mind was whirling. She pulled up the thick bedclothes and fell fast asleep.

* * *

When the family returned, they found her still asleep. They crept quietly 'round so as not to wake her. Muirne made up the dough for bread and Sheena heated the congealed chicken fat over the brazier to start a broth. Neil and Alisdair came home with meat scraps from the butcher and a bag of charcoal from a neighbor.

"It's a miracle, the people in that kirk," Neil whispered to Muirne. "Who helped them when they arrived, I wonder?"

Soon enough, the smells of cooking permeated the whole room and down the hall. Sheila stirred in the bed. She woke and rolled over, a smile on her face. "That smells like meat, if I didn't know better," she said.

"It is meat, Mam!" said Alisdair, skipping over to her side. "We got scraps from the butcher, and he said to wish ye well."

"That's Mr. Robinson, is it?" Her eyes sought Neil's. "Well, then, we will have to send a hearty thank you tomorrow when his shop is open. He didn't bring that there meat into the kirk session, did he now?"

"Noooo," giggled Alisdair. "We walked with him back the way, and he stopped to get the bag from his shop."

"I see. Much easier that way, I s'pose." The gentle ribbing continued as chores were done and the meal was cooked. Over their tea, Sheila brought up the subject of her visits that morning.

"And Mr. MacLahlan is likely to return," she finished. She eyed her daughter for her reaction to this news. Muirne shrugged.

"Very well, Mother. And they were both good company, then?"

"Well, I'd not say they were bad, but there is something queer about that man Turner." She looked at Muirne again. "You said ye found him in front of the medical school talking about that horse o' his?"

Muirne nodded.

"And ye did think to send him a note of thanks at the school for his help?"

Muirne nodded again. "Hmph," was all Sheila's reply. *Then he must indeed go to the school as he says, or the headmaster would've written back saying there's no such man there under his instruction.*

Neil observed all this back and forth with some interest. He did not know either of the men, but if they were both there to try to sway his mother and dance attendance on his sister, then he would damned well find out more about them. Mrs. Conaghey was not an objective source, after all.

He was juggling the times for when he would need to be

in town and when he would need to be back on the ridge, figuring whom he could question on the subject, when his mother asked him a question.

"I was just trying to figure that out myself, Mam. As soon as you're up and about, I'll go on back to the ridge to finish up sorting those piles, and see what can be done about the foundation still there. Don't worry," he said. "I'll keep a long stick and a careful watch."

"Very funny, boy. You just be careful, a'right? We'll soon catch ye up."

Chapter 35

That afternoon, as members of the family rested, or read the Bible, Muirne went out on an errand. She took Sheena with her. She was going to see about chickens.

Mrs. Conaghey kept four of them, but did not have any more space in the coop for more. Besides, Muirne was hoping she could keep the earnings a surprise until she had enough money for the loom. *Well, that would take a verra long time*, she reflected. *Maybe I'll have to ask Neil's help to have enough before we move out of town. I wonder how long that will be.*

Sheena trailed her quietly, but her eyes were looking everywhere. Muirne had told her they were going to a farmer's wife who lived on the west edge of town. She had new-hatched chicks to give away, not having solicited the services of the rooster. And Muirne had heard this at kirk that morning, or more accurately, during the little knots of conversation that sprang up upon leaving.

It was a fine day, and a Sunday; everyone was disposed to chat. And so Muirne had found her opportunity. They stopped at Mrs. Thompson's for tea, fetched the chicks, and a few boards with which to construct the roost, Mrs. Thompson being charmed by the idea of a secret coop to earn a present for their mother. "But where will you keep it?" she asked.

"I think the next yard over would work fine," Muirne said. "The man there is a typist or a pressman, and buys all his food. Not married. He may well end up a good customer." Muirne grinned.

"Aye, well, you just be sensible, girl. You'll be marrying yourself soon, I s'pect. Have ye yer sights set on anyone?"

Muirne blushed and ducked her head, which made Mrs. Thompson laugh, but made Sheena wide-eyed with curiosity. They both thanked Mrs. Thompson, and left to return home. Sheena broached the subject right away.

"*Have* you set your cap at someone, Muirne? Is it one o' those two as visited today?"

"Wheesht, never you mind, Sheena."

"I dinna even see Mr. Turner yet. D'ye like him?"

"He's a fine sort of man, and he did us a very good turn, but no, I'm with Mam, there's something queer about him."

Sheena thought about that. "It's odd, no? We know so little about the people here, but they're so kind."

"P'raps. Now," Muirne prepared to change the subject. "Do you think we can build this roost on our own, or will we have to let Neil in on our secret?"

Chapter 36

The next week found the children back at the ridge, all except Sheena, who'd volunteered to stay to help their mother, as well as secretly feed and water the chickens. The five little chicks were shooting up and popping out quickly on the seed and grubs in the yard, and Sheena was gleeful to have a duty that would result in a secret present.

Neil led the rest of them back with borrowed tools and the packed food they'd managed to get from the butcher and the grocer. They had drawn up a line of credit with both men, and were careful to take only what they needed for the trips to the Sherbrooke plot, since otherwise they could barter with Mrs. Conaghey with their labor. No new word had come from Gillan, and no money either.

Neil reflected on this as he hammered together long poles. A part of him was glad Gillan had not yet found success because he had been so dead set against staying near Pictou. Neil had felt that working on finding a farm as soon as possible was the best way, and his family had been right there with him. His confrontation with Gillan before he left had been awkward, but Neil still thought he'd been right to stand firm.

When he came back, he resolved to stand his ground. How could Gillan not agree that they had a good situation here now? Earlier in the summer it had been precarious, sure, but now, it was there, within their grasp. Just like the ship's passage, he trusted Gillan would eventually come around, with his mother's help.

While Neil was hammering, Muirne and Alisdair were collecting stones of the same size and shape from down by the creek. Muirne was taking no chances with disturbed wild creatures, whether wasp, spider or snake. She carried a long stick to poke under each rock before they dislodged it from the sandy riverbank dirt. It was slow going because they were being so careful and so picky, but Muirne was taking the opportunity to quiz her little brother about geography and multiplication tables, and was content.

Onto this scene of quiet industry there suddenly came a crashing noise from the trees. Muirne stopped to listen at the creek at the bottom of the hill, while Neil did the same from the top, so loud it was. It swept past Muirne and Alisdair through the forested part of the hill, on the other side of the crest so they could not see it. Neil scanned the horizon, then saw the lines of a man on a dark horse just before they emerged from the shade of the trees.

"Hullo, the house!" Turner cried, smiling under his hat. It was the same mare, Neil saw, but different saddle and bags atop. Decorative metal winked brightly from the back of the saddle, newly polished. The man swung down easily.

"Not much of a house, ye ken," Neil returned, shaking his hand vigorously. "What brings you up here again, sir?"

"Well," and here his eyes darted around the ridge site. "I had hoped to catch a glimpse of your sister, young man—"

"Don't try that on with me, now!" Neil cried in mock outrage. "You're not so much older than me yerself, man."

"You're what—nineteen? Twenty?"

"Seventeen."

"I'm twenty-one."

"See? A few years. 'Young man,' indeed." Neil saw his eyes go round the place again. "Is it truly Muirne you're looking for, unchaperoned and—"

"Oh rot, man. I've come to help as well. What d'ye think of me?" He went to the saddle packs and took out more tools, the same ones Neil had borrowed, and more: hammer, saw, clamp, level.

"Is that a magic saddle pack, then?" Neil teased. If the man had truly come to help, and had intentions after meeting Muirne, he was certainly acting right smart about it. Maybe even moving a bit too fast and loose. But it was tempting to respond to the man's friendly advances.

"Nay, I just figured you'd take kindly to some help, and borrowed these myself."

As he was unloading the tools and looking more closely at what Neil was working on, the trudging steps of Muirne and Alisdair could be heard coming up the path. They both held cloths full of stones. As they crested the hill, they let go the edges and released them with a clatter and a giggle and an exclamation. Neil saw Muirne ruffle Alisdair's hair from a dozen yards away. He glanced at Turner, who was likewise following their approach with his eyes.

"Mr. Turner!" Muirne sounded surprised. "What a pleasure. Have you come to check on us, that we haven't had any more accidents?"

"No, Miss MacLean, actually I've come to help with the men's work. I've even brought tools, since I thought an extra pair of hands might need an extra pair of tools. Was I right?" He turned to Neil.

"You were," Neil said gruffly. *All this levity.* "Now if you'd

like to help me securing these poles and skinning some more
—"

"Surely. Let me just take off my coat and we shall dive in."
Neil himself wore no coat. Turner took his off and set it aside
on a stump. He sported a clean shirt and loose cravat, along
with a plain grey waistcoat. Neil noticed Muirne looking at
him and tried to glare at her. She didn't notice.

"Doing well with the stones then, Muirne?" he asked.

"Oh, aye." She turned toward Neil, correctly reading his
face. "We'll do another go before dinner, right, Alisdair?" They
started off down the path again. Neil snuck a look at Turner,
and sure enough, he was watching Muirne go, a sort of hunger
on his face. Neil resolved to talk to his sister bluntly about this
after the man left and Alisdair was asleep. If she did like him,
they had better make it formal and announced, before he took
advantage, which he looked like he could easily do.

* * *

Neil got his chance later that night, as the fire crackled low
and the stars shone above them. Alisdair was snoring very
lightly, and Muirne was sitting propped up against a tree,
thinking with her eyes closed. It was pleasantly warm for the
evening, after the hot, sticky day.

"Muirne," Neil said softly to catch her attention. He was
laying down on his plaid, his head supported by his hands
crossed behind. She opened her eyes and looked over.

"Do ye like Mr. Turner, then? It's obvious he wants you."

Muirne looked down quickly. "Is it?" she said.

"Aye. And if there's to be something between you, it
should be honorable and formally expressed so there isn't any
deceit or secrecy. Since Father's not here—"

"You'll stand in as watchdog, is that it?" Neil was surprised at the bitterness he heard in her tone, and watched her body hunch forward in the firelight and moonlight. "We're stuck, Neil. We've been wandering for almost a year now, and we're split up. We've no money. No jobs. If it weren't for the kindness of the people in this parish, we'd have died on the way here." She let that ugly statement sink in before continuing.

"Father's left to seek a job with pay. You've stayed to try to build a home. Mother is trying to keep us together, but—can't you feel it? We've no *place!*"

Neil got up to move toward her and sat so their sides touched, both propped up against the tree. "That's what this is, our place." He paused. "And that was a very long way about not answering my question, missy."

A puff of air escaped Muirne's lips in a short laugh. "Well," she said languidly, "I think Mr. Turner is an opportunity. I do like him. And I think he'd be able to provide a good home. Student he may be, but he was as able here this afternoon as he was with Mam and her wasp attack."

"Hmph," Neil replied. He'd been all right with the saw—because it was also a surgical tool?—but hopeless with the ties to secure the rafters together. Neil had had to do all of them while Turner held them in place. He still wondered about the man's background, and knew his mother had as well. He'd have to find time to make inquiries, now that he knew Muirne's mind.

"All right then," said Neil. "I'll see what I can find out about him, since we know so little. Ye ken that's necessary, newcomers as we are? Ye willna find it an interferin', brotherin' thing to do?"

Muirne chuckled and lay her head on his shoulder. "No, brother, I'd like that." After a few moments' silence, he felt her sigh. She said, "But what will Father think when he comes back?"

"We'll cross that bridge when we come to it," said Neil. The stars gradually winked down on them in the balmy night, and there was nothing preventing them from dreaming easy dreams of what life could be like, here in their own place.

Chapter 37

When the three MacLeans returned to town, they were met in the yard by Sheena, grinning ear to ear.

"You'll never guess how much I've done with the chicks," she stage-whispered as they walked to the door together. Alisdair looked up at the mention of chicks.

"Have you made the roost all homey for them then?" Neil asked. He'd been let into their secret.

"I have, and more," replied Sheena.

"Have you plumped them up in the past five days, then?" Muirne asked.

"I have, and more," Sheena replied with a barely suppressed squeal of delight. "You'll never guess!"

Older brother and older sister looked at each other, now on the threshold. "What is it, Sheena?" he asked in a whisper. "Tell us before we go in."

"I've already got three customers lined up for when they start laying!" She grinned, evidently pleased at her own business sense and initiative.

"Well, and that's very well done, Sheena," Muirne said, putting her arm round her sister. "But that won't be for a while yet, so be sure not to make rash promises." Sheena nodded, her smile dimmed only a shade.

Their hands were empty, since they left the tools on the ridge, hidden from sight. They meant only to check on the family, and stock up on oatmeal and potatoes and beans, before returning to their camp.

It was a weekday, and Mrs. Conaghey was at home. Her immediate commencement of patter upon their arrival reminded Neil of his need to find out about Mr. Turner. He wondered when he might steal away to the tavern or the grocer's to ask around. Thankfully, his mother was up and about and wore only a simple cold cloth draped over her collarbone and her head to stave off the infection. She said she'd be going back with them when they left in a day or two.

"All right then, do we still have credit at the grocer's?" Neil asked his mother.

"Yes, Neil. Will ye go down this day or wait till tomorrow?"

"Well," said Neil, ducking his head to glance out the window and assure himself of the time. "There's plenty of time left in the day; I'll go now, and be back in time to provide you with supper." He smiled a secret smile, proud of his subterfuge.

Sheila didn't notice. "All right, then awa' with ye. The others might prefer a bit of a scrubbing before launching into more chores, am I right?"

Muirne gave an exaggerated nod of her head while Alisdair did a fast shake of his. Sheila laughed. "Muirne, you're first. The fire's hot, you just need to fetch the water." She handed her two buckets from the hallway, and Muirne took them down to the pump. Meanwhile, Sheena asked Alisdair about the progress they'd made on the ridge.

"Is there a house yet?"

"No, but there's a floor," Alisdair replied.

"Are there any walls?"

"Not a full wall, but Neil's got frames up for two of them. And we collected all the right size rocks to fill in the wall frames to make it nice and warm, that's what Muirne said," he recited.

"Fill in the——" Sheena started, but stopped. "Is that really how you do it?"

Alisdair shrugged. "Maybe it's how they do it here. It might've been Mr. Turner's idea. He came several times to help."

Sheila's ears perked up at this, and she listened more closely to the children's conversation.

"He did? Does he know how to build houses, then?"

Alisdair laughed. "Nor any better than our Neil! But he was helping all the same. He's pretty strong, ye ken."

Now it was Sheena's turn to shrug. Sheila was wondering how Muirne had received him, whether he had stayed the night—heavens, she hoped not—when her thoughts were interrupted by the clomp of boots on the wood of the porch outside.

She heard the muted tones of Mrs. Conaghey's greeting. *Could it be Mr. McLachlan then?* she wondered. *It seems he has been o'erleaped in the game,* she thought with a stab of pity, for she thought him a decent young man.

The clomping stopped, as did Sheena and Alisdair's chattering, as they all looked to the door to their room. Its knob turned and the door swung in slowly. Through it stepped a grisly, mangy-looking mountain man. He wore ragged canvas trousers, a linen shirt so dirty as to be actually brown in spots, and a stained leather traveling coat reaching to his knees.

His eyes traveled the length of the room, settling on Sheila's. A cry broke from her lips, followed by his name. "Oh!

Gillan!"

He fell to his knees, one hand out to grasp the support of a stool, just as Sandy Wilson came thundering up the steps to the upper hall. Sheila started forward, but he held his other hand low with fingers spread out in a stopping motion. She stopped. "What is it, Gillan? Can ye talk? Are ye only weary, or is it something—"

Sheena and Alisdair had by now recognized him, but were still rooted to the spot in their amazement. The open doorway then showed Sandy, followed by the astonished Mrs. Conaghey. The lanky Sandy had tears in his eyes and a greenish bruise on the side of his face. He was wrangling a cap in his hands something terrible. All eyes turned back to Gillan as he emitted a low strangled sound, something between a cough and a shout. Sheila tried again, kneeling in front of him and looking up into his face. "Gillan, can ye talk? Are you hurt?"

She was cut off by the roar from his person, which was itself cut short as Gillan crumpled forward in pain. Sheila turned toward her younger daughter. "Sheena, go run and fetch the doctor who lives by the kirk. And if you see your brother or sister, hie them hence, for God's sake. Where is Muirne with that water?"

Sheena bolted toward the door, but stepped gingerly around the space Gillan took up near its entrance. Alisdair edged toward his mother, his gaze locked on the crumpled figure all the while.

"Da?" he whispered. The great shaggy head came up, but not far enough to look out at his son's eyes. The hand on the ground reached forward to grasp something. Alisdair moved forward and caught the wandering hand in his own. He put it to his cheek and soothed his father. "Don't worry, Da, you're home. We'll take care of ye now."

Sheila looked with mute distress at Sandy, who couldn't

yet put two words together in the face of such a homecoming. Muirne returned then, nearly losing her hold on the buckets as she careened to a halt behind her father in the doorway. "I nearly ran into Sheena—" Her eyes sought her mother's.

"It's your father come back, and in a bad state." Sheila took the buckets and dumped their contents into the tub heating on the brazier. She tossed in a few cloths in preparation. *But how to lay him out?* she wondered.

"Gillan," Sheila said. "Can you make it to the bed, man?" He gave no sign of hearing at first, but when Sandy lined up on one side and Muirne on the other, he pushed himself up from the floor into a position between them. They barely managed to get under his arms before his full weight pulled downward again, but they did. They pulled and dragged him over to the far wall where the bedding was, and laid him down as carefully as they could. He fell the last few inches with a gasp.

Alisdair moved to sit next to his father where he could make sure to observe his chest rising and falling with breath. Sheila stirred the barely-warm water with a wooden spoon, her eyes staring determinedly down into the pot, not allowing her shock at yet another strange entrance into their lives to engulf her in despair. Muirne asked about a doctor and was informed that's what Sheena was about. She grabbed the buckets back and went for more water, returning rather more quickly.

"I'm to the grocer's now to fetch Neil." The mention of the name caused Gillan's head to turn and a groan to escape his lips. "And I hope Sheena is back before me with the doctor," Muirne added.

She was. As Muirne vanished out of sight past the corner, Sheena hove into view from their one window from the other direction. She was accompanied by Mr. Coldwell, Pictou's resident doctor, carrying his black bag.

Mrs. Conaghey ushered the doctor into the room, and finally sought Sheila's eye. "Is there aught I can do for ye, missus? Is your boy coming in? Do you need any cloths or smelling salts?"

"Yes, I think we will need more clean cloths, thank you, Mrs. Conaghey. And Muirne is out seeking Neil. We should all be together soon, and—" her voice had caught, and she steadied herself, resuming her determined stare. "We shall see what the doctor says," she said simply.

Mr. Coldwell was already examining Gillan, shucking off his stained coat and shirt to examine him. They saw the large bruises then: yellowing around his right shoulder, a purple one below his left ribs, a yellow-green mass on his upper left arm. And the wide cuts on his neck and hands that had been stuffed with a paste of herbs and bound with strips of his former shirt. Sheila was appalled, and could not help but show it. What had happened to her optimistic, strong man? Why on earth had he been assaulted in such a fashion, since a methodical assault it most certainly resembled. Or maybe a very bad tumble down a hill? The speculative questions flew around and around in her head, and soon she felt dizzy enough to sit down herself.

She looked to Gillan, seeing only his boots hanging off the bed since the doctor obscured her view of him. Those boots— she shivered. They weren't his.

As the doctor was cataloguing Gillan's ills, Sandy started talking in a low murmur.

"There weren't nothing we could do, missus, they just set upon us! They worked us both over, but seemed to concentrate on Mr. MacLean here."

Sheila interrupted. "Who did it, Sandy?"

"We couldn't see them, missus. They came upon us just at

sundown on the road back. We had news of a new sawmill to start and so were setting back, when these two big men fell into attack, without saying a word! So strange I couldn't believe it, until the second one hit me across the shoulder."

Sheila saw how he was standing, with one shoulder higher than the other, the weight on one foot. "Ye're nae hurt too then, Sandy?" The doctor glanced over his spectacles at this.

"Not as badly as this. But do sit down, boy. I'll see to you next."

Sheila wanted to ask Sandy more questions, but then Neil rushed in, followed by Muirne. Sheila saw her son's eyes wild with something; was it fear? Anger? More like the desperation of an animal cornered. He approached Gillan's body and gazed at his face.

On hearing Muirne's hurried message, he had bolted out of the shop without so much as an excuse hurled in the direction of the shopkeeper. Muirne had run in his wake, shouting for him not to be mad, to slow down, to wait for her. But he'd had to make it back to Gillan's side in time—Muirne had said he looked bad enough to die. Neil needed to see him, tell him about their situation here, their prospects. That might give him will to live, if his failures in the city had cast him down.

What he was confronted with here was not merely failures, however. His stepfather had indeed been badly beaten. Dr. Coldwell's cleaning out of the cuts with alcohol had made even the semi-conscious Gillan cry out in a pitiful, gurgling way. He applied another solution and put on clean bandages. When he had cleaned him up as best he could, he gave the family his prognosis: three broken ribs, multiple inflammations of the internal organs, most worriedly the spleen, and a dangerous fever. They heard his orders with solemn attention: rest, broth and hot milk, and keep him warm.

"I'll be back to check on him this evening, and bring my

bloodletting implements. We'll worry about those ribs once he's past the fever."

They all turned to Sandy once Mr. Coldwell left. He couldn't give them much more information other than how the trip had gone up until the attack: they'd met that old Mr. Brown near Tadoussac, as had been written, and there'd been no love lost between them. They'd seen the new sawmill near Quebec City, and Sandy had been impressed. They'd started back full of optimism. Then those mysterious blackguards had fallen on them, and it had been a miserable struggle the next twelve days to make their way eastward through the wilderness to Pictou.

"We did get a lift the last thirty miles with a Pictou farmer, though," he said.

None of it comforted them, not even the lift. There was no reason for two men to attack them so fiercely on the road, as they had no money to steal. And for Sandy, who was lanky as a beanpole and about as solid, to have suffered less damage? They must have had it in for Gillan. But why?

The MacLeans settled in for a long night and an uncertain morning.

Chapter 38

The doctor came back in the evening, and let several pints of blood into the specially cut china bowl. Neil stayed at Gillan's side to make sure he didn't move and upset the process, while Sheila watched, her skin ashen and her gaze empty. Dr. Coldwell left a number of bottles with her, the contents of some of which were to be drunk, while others were to be spread across the places where the skin had been sliced open to prevent infection. They had all dropped into deep sleep following the astonishment of Gillan's dread appearance and the despair following the doctor's diagnosis.

Sheena was the first to wake the next morning. She rolled over to look at where her stepfather lay to make sure it hadn't been a dream. His large body was still visible under the blankets, unmoving. Her mother lay curled up on the floor beside, her head resting on the side of the wrapped mattress, an arm outflung toward her charge. Sheena sniffed.

She rose and crept over to them. There was as yet little light from the day, but the coals in the brazier cast a reddish glow over things and made their outlines visible. She looked down on her stepfather, willing him to open his eyes, but he made no move. Sheena felt her breath coming fast, and felt she was about to panic with the sadness that hung over the whole scene, their whole life. She grabbed her thick shawl and quickly retreated to the outside hallway, where she took a few steadying breaths, then descended the stairs.

She collected the refuse that could feed her chicks from the back dooryard, and went to tend them, taking comfort in their simple-minded gratitude. She waited in the cool dawn, breathing in the foggy air. When she saw movement in the upstairs window, she was reluctant to start back to their rooms. It was a cooler morning than they had been used to during their summer trips to the ridge.

Sheila was up and bustling around to rouse everyone for the day's work. When she came to Sheena's place and found it empty, she looked sharply round. When she saw her younger daughter creeping back in a few minutes later, she expelled her breath slowly, and called to her with a look and a hand.

"Where've you gone, Sheena?"

"I—I was just out for some fresh air, Mother. It's nice and cool out today, it is."

Sheena had not thought her mother would notice or worry. She wriggled under her mother's continuing stern gaze. "I have a small project, Mother, that I'm working on. It needs tending every morning and night, but other than that, it's a surprise." She spoke softly, hesitantly.

Sheila grabbed her in a hug. "Oh, my girl, I'm not doubting. Of course it's fine, my good girl. You'll let me know when it's no longer a surprise?" Sheena nodded, relieved.

The others had woken, taken a cup from the water pitcher, and gone out for their own, not-so-secret chores. Sheila remained with her husband to doctor him, accepting that they would not be going back to the ridge for some time.

The family was back together for the noon meal, Gillan

still unconscious, but emitting a groan from time to time. They held a family conference over what might have happened.

"Don't you think that Macrieff man may have had summat to do with it?" Neil asked. "He's mentioned in Da's last letter, and we know he was a fair rascal last time they met."

The younger children looked questioningly at Sheila at this remark, for they did not remember any Mr. Brown of Macrieff. Sheila sighed.

"Aye, well, that Mr. Brown deserved more'n he got, let me tell you. He was certainly a rascal, and it's no wonder he's here, as no one on the island would want him. The wonder is that your father would have run into him. It may well be Brown, Neil, taking it out on your father here where there is little law and order."

Muirne looked at the sleeping form, and whispered, "Could it have been about unions? I know there was talk about them at home, causing mischief when there was a strike on. Do they do that here too, where Father might have been going to get work?"

"Oh, I doubt it," said Sheila. "Too many people wanting to work, I'd wager."

They fell silent again.

"What are we to do about him then?" Neil asked. "Are we to stop work on the ridge while the weather is so fine, and find ourselves homeless still at the end of the summer? It's already close on September, and it gets colder here than at home, and quicker, they say."

"Or we split up again," Muirne said. The sadness now fell around them thicker than before. It seemed to fill the air like so much thick cotton, but then there came an insistent knocking from down below to dispel it. Evidently Mrs. Conaghey was out on her rounds again, and someone wanted to be let in. Alisdair jumped up to perform the duty.

He came back trailing a slack-jawed Mr. Turner in his wake. Apparently he had been apprised. As he stood in the doorway, he attempted to make excuses for his appearance. "I am so very sorry to drop in on you without invitation, ma'am. I had thought to accompany you back up the mountain, and so came to seek you in town. I had no idea—"

"My husband's only just arrived yesterday, Mr. Turner. Although he did encounter Mrs. Conaghey and pass a few words, so the whole town may already know," said Sheila.

A brief grimace came and went on the man's face. "Had I known—" his voice ended abruptly. "I'm sorry," he said. "I'm sure you don't need me here. I shall go. I wish him a rapid recovery." Without a glance at Muirne, he turned and left the doorway he had occupied. She felt some urge to go after him, but decided it could wait, if it happened at all. Would Mr. Turner still want her with yet another burden into the bargain?

When there was a change in Gillan's symptoms later that day, the doctor was called back, and his violent shivering was deemed to be a result of an infection settling into fever. Sheila stayed close to him, mopping his brow, listening for any words from the mouth of her husband, sensing the end was near.

The others came and went, dozed and woke later in the night, and constantly wondered what had happened to bring their father so low. What would happen to them now? During one vigil, Muirne hovered close by her mother's side. Sheila had remained grim and quiet but Muirne noticed when she started making a small noise. She was trying not to awaken anyone, but she was sobbing. Muirne put her arm around her mother's waist as they knelt by the bed, and her mother clutched at her head. Muirne could feel the heaving of her chest, but felt only bleakness herself.

"Muirne?" her mother whispered.

"What is it?"

"I've been such a bad wife, these past months." Her eyes were bleak and staring at the unconscious Gillan as she whispered her guilt to Muirne. "I haven't loved him as I should have done."

Another grimace of pain on Sheila's face.

"But, Mother, I'm sure you—"

"*No.*" It came out grating and low. "I took back my trust from him. And he knew it. It was the last thing he needed." She turned to her daughter. "When you marry, Muirne, ye mun work through it for yerself, but never desert a man who's done his best by ye." Her last syllable curled up into a high-pitched sob, ripped from the mouth of the woman who was trying so hard to keep it in.

* * *

Past two o'clock it was when Sheila closed his eyes for the last time. Neil was up, saw what she'd done, and came over to put his arm around her. She wept, but quietly. Now, in the dark, she could weep for all the harsh blows Fate had dealt them in the space of a year.

"We'll pay for his burial on credit," she choked out. "And go back to the ridge." Neil smoothed the cloth over her shoulder blades, wondering what would be done about Muirne's two suitors, but electing not to bring it up until after the burial. He would talk with Muirne when the time came and see what she wanted. For now, it was mourning time. The mourning of more than just a husband and a father, but of their hopes of a new start for the family. It would be a new start, but for rather a broken family.

Chapter 39

They held the wake the next night. Mrs. Conaghey's large front room was pressed into service, and many people crowded in to pay their respects to the newcomer's family, now left without a protector. Sheila oversaw things in a borrowed black gown, while her children settled for their darkest clothes.

Mr. McLachlan came and presented his formal regrets to Sheila. He paused and pulled an envelope from his coat pocket. He continued in a different vein.

"Mrs. MacLean, I have procured the final document releasing claims for the prior owners of the ridge property. I meant to give it to you yesterday, but thought it best not to interrupt at such a moment. However, now I think it best that you have all the information at your disposal, so you may decide how to proceed."

Sheila, although somewhat numb from shock and the long parade of visitors, blinked at his speech.

"Thank you, Mr. McLachlan. We know very well you could have held onto this longer for your own advantage, so I do thank you indeed for coming forward with it now. We will certainly need to discuss this in our family to decide what—

where to go and how—well, it affects everything," she finished.

Mr. McLachlan had the good grace to bow slightly and return a compliment to the family before moving away discreetly. Flustered, Sheila's eyes sought Neil's; he was talking with one of the shopkeepers from the village. Muirne was sitting alone at the table where Gillan was laid out. Neither of her children looked up to meet her gaze. She yearned for a quiet moment in which to break down.

Some of the visitors had just gotten out their fiddles and a guitar however, so she realized she would not have her moment for at least another hour. As she tamped down the emotion welling up, she felt a surge of gratitude for these near-strangers who made them feel so at home, so welcome. The next moment she wished again that they would all retire, as a wave of panic hit her concerning their future. She decided to go sit by Muirne as the music caught the attention of the crowd.

The musicians started with a dirge, a slow, keening song sung by two of the ladies from down the street. Everyone was quiet and respectful. Then the musicians launched into historical songs, marching songs, hymns of the glorious dead, songs to relieve the hurt of a thousand years of battles. The MacLeans listened, and received the energy of the people of Pictou.

There was some furious dancing, legs pounding the wooden boards enough to jostle the table and send a few more sober folks toward the body to make sure it did not topple. It was nigh on midnight when the instruments were put away. People shuffled out, throwing well wishes out behind them; wearily, the MacLeans lay down for bed. Several of the same folks would be back to carry the body to the kirkyard the next morning.

For the first time Neil could remember, he woke late. He felt groggy, but saw that the sun was well advanced and that his mother was up, mixing porridge on the brazier and toasting bannocks in the coals. His siblings lay scattered about. After a somber breakfast, they went down to Mrs. Conaghey's sitting room in the same funeral clothes.

Their landlady didn't join them, out of respect. Sheila had already gotten word from her that the gravediggers would extend her credit, on Mrs. Conaghey's word that she would pay the bill within the year, which was a blessing.

They sat all on different seats at first, until Sheena broke the stillness by leaving her caned chair and coming to sit by her mother's knee. Alisdair soon did the same, curling up over her lap on the settee. Sheila put her hands on their two heads, looking over at Neil and Muirne, sitting by the fire. Her jaw was tight but a quiver in her throat showed she felt the despair sharing the room with them.

When the mourners arrived, they all made their way to the graveyard behind the rough Presbyterian kirk. The gravediggers were there as promised, propped up against a tree with their shovels. At the MacLeans' approach, both men straightened with respect. The Reverend Maurice Brown spoke the prayers softly, and the family watched Gillan in his freshly sawn box being laid to rest. They returned to the boarding house to find that Mrs. Conaghey had laid out a spread of cold roast beef and hot floury potatoes and mashed neeps, sparkling with salt. They sat together eating, a bit of spirit back in them with such food, and talked of *Sealladh Cùil*, the home on the ridge.

* * *

The next morning, Neil woke first. He started gathering his

things together in the quiet. He shook Alisdair and Sheena awake, then Muirne and his mother. The common things were packed next: the blankets, the rugs, the few dishes and pots, the small scraps of soap and the last few pages of writing paper. It was quiet in the dim light that filtered into the room. Muirne tore a piece of paper in two, sharpening a pencil with their cooking knife, and scribbling a few lines. Her activity gave off a fervent energy, where Neil's was business-like, closed. Sheila swept from place to place, back bent, while the younger two children mainly huddled in the corner.

Muirne finished writing and pinned the scrap of paper under one of the legs of the brazier. Neil remembered their finding of the note at the Currans' house, all that time ago. He looked around. *All our worldly possessions*, he thought. *On the move again.*

They filed out in the early darkness, finding it again cool for the summertime. Hoisting their creels, they all followed Neil to the main road, turning east and sighting a soft glow of blue over the hills; they would soon have light enough to guide them through the rougher parts of terrain.

More silence, except for the tramping of feet. Their walking was rhythmic and almost musical, the sound of ten feet shushing and crashing and thumping their way through the bracken and ferns. They camped for the night, exhausted with their burdens and lacking the energy to speak.

When they reached the bottom of the ridge the next day, they stopped to fill up their bottles and pots with water from the stream before continuing. They crested the top of the ridge well after dawn had turned the sky pink, then a hazy white. Alisdair, obedient but sleepy to that point, now looked around as if he hadn't known this was their destination. "Mam?"

"Yes, Alisdair." The first words to pass Sheila's lips for hours came out rough.

"Is this where we live now?"

"Aye. This is where we live."

"Soon there'll be a house, lad, don't you worry," said Neil.

They looked over at the piles of refuse and salvaged timber. It was August yet, but there was much work to be done for the frame to be up and filled in by the start of the cold season, in just a month's time. But they would do it; it had to be done.

Muirne got started on the fire for cooking the breakfast porridge, while Sheila took care to place all the important documents from Mr. McLachlan together in one place and carefully weight them down with stones and a marker. Neil directed Sheena where to go to find the ready kindling for her sister's fire, while he busied himself unrolling the bedclothes.

They broke their fast with porridge and water. Sheila seemed hesitant to begin a morose conversation, just when their camp activity had shaken off the oppressive yoke of somber gravity.

"With Gillan gone, I think we all agree that staying here is best. Does anyone have any other ideas?"

All eyes were downcast, except Muirne's, who met her gaze evenly. She shook her head slightly. Sheila continued.

"We will all have to work very hard to make this house safe for the cold season. We will have to make do with however much we can get done before the snows start. If we come upon problems, we may have to send for help, but as this could cause a delay, I prefer we solved whatever comes ourselves. Improvements can always be made later, but for now, we need thick sturdy walls and a pitched roof for snow—" She glanced at Neil for confirmation.

He nodded. The list continued.

"—Door and window openings that are as square as we can make them. That's for the house. We will also have to clear room for planting what autumn crops we can. Potatoes and turnips and onions. That will do us for a few months. Without a gun, we can't hunt, but we can trap, with string and nail."

Here again, Neil nodded. He had talked to those shop-keepers during the wake about survival skills for these woods, and hoped to see those skills honed quickly enough to ensure his family's food supply over winter.

Sheila looked to each of her children in turn. She put an arm around Alisdair. "You are my wealth, children. I have faith we will survive this winter, that this house will become a happy home, in time." She gave a watery smile and kissed the top of Alisdair's dark blond head, then turned toward the pile of rags to start.

A house, and a garden: these were their goals, and the work of them would consume their attention for most of the day, every day, from now until Michaelmas.

They set to work.

Chapter 40

They had no visitors. Sheila worried that their abrupt departure may have been too unconventional for the townsfolk, that it might have seemed irretrievably rude. But her spirit gloried in the work, putting aside the mystery that had ended Gillan's life, the last time she had seen his eyes on her face, whatever he had been unable to tell her.

Any pause from the work of cutting, sawing, tying, or packing in stones found them facing each other around the fire, munching on the rotating oat biscuits and tattie scones. By evening, rest was enforced by the darkness, but one or another of them would be by the fire, knitting, writing on the chalk slate that had been the last gift of Mrs. Conaghey, or otherwise using its flickering light.

Sheena and Muirne had bequeathed the chicks to Mrs. Conaghey for safekeeping and whatever profit she could have by them, good hens as they would be. It would be a paltry start to all they owed for her kindnesses to them, they knew. Their dream of selling eggs to save up money for a loom had joined the many other hopes they'd had for this new world, drowned in the waves of sorrow with which Providence had plied them.

Neil tried the methods of trapping he'd learnt, and referenced the notes he had from a taxidermist's pamphlet, showing where and how to set a loop trap, how to skin the animals, and more. Another new set of skills, beyond the dock work he'd tried, the mill work his stepfather had done, the boat-tending he'd known at home. Neil often looked at Muirne when she was at work on the house and wondered what she thought of the situation, whether she was not thinking to marry up and move to town.

But there was no time or place to talk privately up here. It strained the quiet sometimes, but also made them feel more completely a unit, acting as one. Everything they did was done in hearing of each other. It did not mean that there were no secrets; indeed, it may have created more.

The days went by quickly. The taxidermist's pamphlet, along with a picture manual on edible and medicinal plants lent by Mr. Turner, proved vitally helpful in securing additional sources of food for the family: not only rabbit but also berries, nuts, and mushrooms. Neil looked with distaste at the lichen promised to be edible, for it reminded him of the seaweed from home, that cursed substance that started them on this whole journey.

They scraped by until one day, Neil stepped out from under the steeply-pitched roof, from out the solid, filled-in, stone-and-wood walls, to find the land shrouded in a white mist. A dozen feet could he see only, and he watched as his breath issued forth in a steamy cloud. Had summer turned to fall so abruptly?

He looked down and saw a different kind of white mist: tiny ice crystals, lodged in the red masses of dead bracken around the house. Flakes of snow that evaporated upon a touch of his hand. It was beautiful, and he was overwhelmed with the feelings of wonder and gratitude, mixed with desperation and delirium, that coursed through him.

Had they done enough? Only time would tell. He hitched his plaid over his shoulders and hunkered down on the edge of the hill, watching the white curtain float away and reveal the forest, *their* forest. He was joined soon by his mother, and she took his hand as they watched the remnants of snowy clouds scuttle away from view.

Acknowledgements

Thank you to the many people who have encouraged me and championed my work throughout the writing process. To those on social media who have retweeted, commented, liked, and followed: you have provided many a pick-me-up. Those little measures of attention can mean a lot when you're struggling to get through a tough spot in your work.

Thank you to those who agreed to be beta readers and gave me the benefit of their input, impressions, and thoughtful expertise: Cathy, Gill, Tonya, Sarah, Rooske, and Kindra. And to the first reader, who gave even more, thank *you*.

Thank you to Claire Rudy Foster, my editor, whose grounding input and incisive commentary made editing *almost* a joy this time around.

Thank you to literary community rockstars Laura Stanfill of Forest Avenue Press and Elisa Saphier of Another Read Through Bookstore, whose faith, energy, and love for books shines through in all their enthusiastic efforts.

Thank you to the Masterminds, the writing dates, the Monday GSD club, the Gaelic hangers-on, and all those unique, wonderful people I play with, both in Portland and around the world. Whenever I need a kick in the pants to readjust my mindset, I head for a Portland coffee shop to be reinvigorated. My favorite haunts are The Clearing Cafe and Tabor Bread.

A Note from the Author

Did you enjoy this book?

Please consider posting a review.

Reviews like yours help the book find its way to the hands of new readers! This helps self-published authors like me gain readers online and through word-of-mouth networks. You are cordially invited to visit my author website at www.margaretpinard.com for blog posts, events, news, and giveaways. I will be posting helpful Bonus Content for the *Remnants* series there as well!
Reviews are much appreciated at any (or all!) of the following sites:

www.amazon.com
www.goodreads.com
www.powells.com

Or spread the news through your own networks by recommending the book to your friends on Facebook and Twitter.

My eternal thanks for your time, attention, and encouragement.

About the Author

Margaret Pinard has spent her first few decades traveling the globe in search of adventures to incorporate into her writing, including living in the lands of the Celts, the cities of European fashion, and several dolce far niente Mediterranean cultures.

Her favorite genre is historical fiction, and she especially delights in fiction that makes you feel like you've been transported to a different time and place. Her first novel is *Memory's Hostage*. Her second, *Dulci's Legacy*, grew out of her first NaNoWriMo attempt in 2012. *The Keening* is the first in a new series called *Remnants*. She resides in Portland, OR.